JADE'S PHOTOS

Also by Randy Rawls

Beth Bowman Series
Hot Rocks
Best Defense

Tom Jeffries Series
Thorns on Roses
The Runaway

Ace Edwards Series
Jake's Burn
Joseph's Kidnapping
Jade's Photos
Jingle's Christmas
Jasmine's Fate
Jeb's Deception

JADE'S PHOTOS

By

Randy Rawls

JADE'S PHOTOS

Copyright 2003 by Randy Rawls

Cover art and design by Victoria Landis
www.victorialandis.com, victoria@landisdesignresource.com

Rawls, Randy
Jade's Photos / Mystery / Randy Rawls

ISBN: 978-0-9899904-1-7

DEDICATION

Especially for Tracy and David, my children, with my love. And for Ronnie, always My Honey. For those who tolerate me and critique my writing: Sylvia, Earl, Ann, Gregg, Richard, Stephanie, and Vicki. For the Texas writers' group who were so helpful in the writing of the Ace Edwards Series: Bob, Pepper, Dorothy, Carolyn, and especially for Alberta who is no longer with us
For Joanne at *Murder on the Beach Mystery Bookstore*, a friend to every author.

JADE'S PHOTOS

BOOK ONE—ACE'S STORY

CHAPTER ONE

I don't know where you are or what you're doing at three in the morning, but ninety-nine percent of the time, Arthur Conan Edwards, Ace to my friends, is home alone, wrapped in my Dallas Cowboys blanket, dreaming sweet dreams of beautiful women. The other one percent, Jake Adams exacts his unique form of revenge by waking me. Why? Beats me.

Terri Hart, the woman I met in an earlier case, had the leading role in that night's dream. My waking process began with Terri lightly raking a fingertip across my cheek. I rolled to my right, toward the center of the bed and whispered, "Terri." Maybe it was the sound of my voice that finally drove me from sleep, I don't know, but suddenly consciousness was there. Two amber eyes were inches from my nose, and a claw gleamed in the moonlight as it reached for my face.

"What the hell—" My question disappeared under the buzzing of the telephone. I glared at Sweeper, one of my cats, who now groomed himself. I swear he had a self-satisfied grin on his face. Could he have known the phone would ring? Nah, no way.

I rolled to my left, untangling from the sheets and Striker, my other cat, who had attached himself. Not a simple task. One of those facts of life I'll never understand is how a twelve-pound cat anchored to a coverlet draped over your body weighs two-hundred-fourteen pounds and has the consistency of a balloon filled with water.

As I wrestled myself free, the accursed phone committed its noise again, and my answering machine kicked in:

Hey, you've got Ace Edwards here. Give me a name, give me a number and *enough to make me want to call you back. When time allows, I'll be in your ear.*

Okay, so my ego might have swelled a little after my back-to-back successes in Cisco and Canton. But I had a few bucks in the bank, a couple of working cases in my files, and enough pocket change to buy premium cat food. I didn't have to grovel before prospective clients.

I finally found the phone and cut in on a man who was busy using my microchip to record a tale of woe. Just as he said, "She had pictures," I interrupted.

"Hey, enough, enough. It's me—Ace Edwards. I'm live on the phone. Slow it down a bit."

"Arty, is that really you? I'm so glad I caught you at home. Jake said—"

"Hold on. Slow down, identify yourself, and then tell me why you're calling at three in the morning," I managed to say in what I thought passed for a civil tone.

"It's Johnny, Johnny Nichols. Jake told me to call you. He said you'd get me out of this mess. He said—"

Since it was my phone and my three in the morning, I cut in again. "Hold it right there, Nichols. Leave Jake out of this and tell me why you're calling." Nichols. The name faintly dinged in the deep dark recesses of my memory.

"Damn, Arty. That's amazing. Jake said you'd get pissed if I used his name. Man, he really knows you."

"Look, either produce a story or hang up. I don't really give a damn which and don't call me Arty."

"Okay, okay, don't hang up. I need your help. I'm in a bind and need the best PI I can get. Jake—uh—I heard you're good."

"You're getting the idea. Now, what exactly is your problem?"

"I'm being blackmailed."

That got my attention. Blackmailers are the slugs of society, leaving their slimy trail wherever they go.

"By whom?" I asked.

"I'd rather not say over the phone. In fact, I don't want to say anything else. They took stills, a video, and recorded everything. They might be listening to everything I say."

He sounded like he might weep at any moment. That was close to the last thing I wanted to hear in the middle of the night. "Stop where you are. Here's what I want you to do. Do you have a cell phone?"

"Of course. Doesn't everyone?"

"Good. Hang up and call me back on your cell. Not much chance anyone will be bugging that."

"Well . . . okay. I can do it, but . . ."

"But what? What's the problem?"

"This is the only cell phone I have. Should I call you back on this one?"

"You mean you're already on a cell?"

"Well, yeah. I couldn't call you from home—not with this kind of news. If my mother-in-law finds out—"

"Hold it." The conversation seemed to be going nowhere. "If you're on a cell, it's probably safe. Does that sound reasonable?"

"I guess so," he said. "You're the expert. Do you have one of those things that can tell if someone is listening? Jake said . . . oh, I shouldn't have used his name, should I?"

"That's okay. I'll let it ride this time, but watch it." If I didn't do something, I'd never get back to sleep and to my dreams of, oh well, you know. "Tell—me—why—you—called." I hoped he'd move along with his story.

"I'm being blackmailed, and if I don't pay, she'll tell my, uh, I just have to pay. But I don't want to. I want the pictures, the negatives, the video, the sound recording—everything. I want you to get them. Jake said Arty Edwards is the best. That's why I called."

Using Jake's nickname for me again definitely cemented my attention. "Stop right there. First, don't ever call me Arty again. Nobody calls me that. Especially some guy who wakes me at three in the morning with a story which makes no sense at all. So you have no more than thirty seconds to say something that'll convince me to stay on the line. Otherwise, it's bye-bye-birdie. Talk."

Twenty minutes later, I had agreed to head east in the morning to meet him for lunch. His story impressed me so much I'd have left immediately, but I needed someone to cover my other cases. Unfortunately, not all the PI's in Dallas are as understanding as I am when awakened at oh-dark-thirty—especially "Kit" Carsen Levitt.

CHAPTER TWO

Sleep wouldn't come so I grabbed an overnight bag. My standard is clothes for three days when I'm within a hundred miles of Dallas. Striker and Sweeper, my cats, immediately volunteered to assist by jumping into the bag and rearranging my jeans and shirts until they were perfect. Of course, my part in the exercise was to take them out of the bag—several times and refold everything.

"Boys, I'm headed to Grand Saline in the morning." I often talk to my cats, and almost as often, they ignore me. This time they chose to listen, or acted that way. "The guy who called is being blackmailed. Said his name is Johnny Nichols. He's been stepping out on his wife, and somebody got the goods on him. Don't know anything else, but he hit the magic word—blackmail. You know how I hate that. I'll fill you in when I get back."

"Meow," Striker said.

Striker has very high morals, so I took this as disapproval of Nichols' behavior. On the other hand, Sweeper's view of life is more earthy. He stared at me, undoubtedly waiting for juicy details. I couldn't supply any because Nichols had been so hyper, he hadn't told me anymore.

At six, I dialed Kit's number and heard her growl a hello, her normal demeanor when awakened. She's also a PI, and we share cases when we have an overflow. At one time, we talked about forming a partnership. Of course, we couldn't agree on the name of the agency. I opted for Edwards and Levitt, but she argued for Levitt and Edwards. A few years ago, before I met Terri, we even talked about forming another type of partnership where she would have converted to a hyphenated last name: Levitt-Edwards.

However, common sense prevailed and we decided a friendship as close as ours should never be ruined with marriage vows.

"Kit, it's Ace."

"Yeah, so what? What time is it?"

As I inferred, Kit wakes up grumpy. A picture flashed through my mind—a picture processed before Terri. Most people wake up looking their worst. With Kit, sleep relaxes her facial features into a mask of contentment while her hair frames her face into a portrait of loveliness. She is a fine looking woman, grumpy or not.

"It's six a.m., time for you to be up and about." I forced a smile into my voice.

"Why? I have no reason to jump out of bed. I'd rather get my beauty sleep." Her tone changed. "What gets you up so early?"

"First, my dear, your need for beauty sleep is equal to my need for another double-chocolate malt. I'm up because I'm heading out of town and need your help. Can you pick up the Barnes and the Lattimore cases for me?"

"Barnes, the roaming husband and Lattimore, the philandering wife? Hell, I told you what to do with them weeks ago." She sighed. "Yeah, I suppose so. Maybe I can solve both by putting them together. That might clip their horns. What's up with you?"

"Another Jake referral. Guy from Grand Saline called last night and needs help."

"Jake? Another three a.m. call?"

"Yep. Jake's M.O. never changes."

"Is this another old college chum?"

"Not sure. His name is Nichols, and that rings a bell somewhere. Since Jake told him to call, he may be. I'll know when I get there."

"That's my Ace. Charging off into the unknown to meet the unknown. Why don't you hire a secretary? At least, he could fill out a form."

I ignored the masculine pronoun. If Kit had her way, men would perform all the jobs traditionally identified with women.

She chuckled. "When are you going to tell me the true story about you and Jake? I know you guys grew up together, but what's the rest of it? Why do you resent his help?"

"It's not that I resent him, it's just that—well . . ." I searched for the right words. "Oh hell. Okay. I resent him. He's always been so damn rich it's tough not to. Maybe some night over a six-pack of Killian's, you can psychoanalyze my feelings about Jake."

"Sure, just as soon as you get over Terri Hart. The last time I bought the six-pack, it turned into a case, and you moaned about her all night."

She had me there. "Okay, I'll wait. What about Lattimore and Barnes?"

"Yeah, I'll cover. Do I get full fees? I gather you're going to get paid well by Jake's friend. You did before."

"Not sure yet," I said, wondering why I hadn't brought it up. "We'll work it out when we meet, but I expect he'll live up to Jake's standards."

"Okay, go and do good. I'll drop by your place and pick up the files." She hesitated, then laughed a throaty laugh. "Make sure your nosy neighbor is looking out his window. I'll make his day."

* * *

After my conversation with Kit, I put out enough cat food and water to last the boys a month. That would insure they'd eat well for three days. From the storage room, I dragged out the extra litter pans. The boys are very particular about the freshness of their litter, and they have their own distinctive ways of letting me know when it is too stale.

They must have approved because when I set the last litter pan in place, they rubbed between my ankles and purred loudly. I picked them up, one under each arm, and Striker rewarded me with a sandpaper caress.

Sweeper's response was equally demonstrative. He said, "Meow" and wiggled his way out of my grasp. Without so much as a thank you, he rushed off to test the food supply.

"Okay, if that's how you feel, I'm off on another great adventure," I said, setting Striker on his feet. "You two take care of the house. I might return." My sarcasm went unappreciated as crunching drowned out my words.

I grabbed my overnight bag and walked outside. The weather was Texas-perfect, which means as good as it can get, and my red Chrysler Sebring convertible begged to let its top down.

I waved to Mr. Harbinger who lives across the street, and watches my place when I'm gone. Actually, he watches it when I'm there also. He's a nice guy, a seasoned-senior, and I'm fortunate to have him for a neighbor. Besides, any time I need to know what's going on in North Dallas, I simply walk across the street with a six-pack of Killian's. He and I share a fascination for the Irish brew.

I made sure he saw my overnight bag, and he rewarded me with, "Looks like you're heading out again. Another big case?"

"Yeah," I replied. "I'll be gone a few days."

"Well, don't worry about a thing. I'll keep a watch, like I always do."

I grinned because he spoke the truth. I looked around, and saw Kit's mini-convertible coming down the street. Actually, it looked more like an overgrown, four-wheeled, low-top roller skate than a car, but she loved it. Every time I advised her to get a grown-up car, she told me it would someday be a collector's item. That could be true. After all, I don't understand people who collect stamps, so there might be people who'll collect early Geo Metro convertibles.

I waited by the curb as she pulled to a stop, all three cylinders in perfect sync. When she climbed out, my heart did at ratty-tat-tat. She looked great in jeans and a tight T-shirt with her short blond hair. I even noticed the running shoes with no socks adorning her feet.

"Hi, Ace. Is this a special reception or are you simply trying to give Mr. H a new lease on life?" She walked up and planted a wet kiss squarely on my lips, slipping her tongue into my mouth. When she pulled back, she grinned at my breathlessness. "That ought to hold him for a while."

Her eyes narrowed. "You're doing better. Terri's still there, but I think I see a weakening of the leash. Maybe someday—" She walked toward my front door and switched the subject. "Okay, give me what you've got on Barnes and Lattimore. You do have a file, don't you?"

We talked and drank coffee for the next two hours. We even managed to fit in the Barnes and Lattimore cases. The boys both vied for Kit's lap from the moment she sat down. I'd have been jealous except they've always loved her. It's tough being a single father.

Finally, I had to say, "Sorry. While I'd love to spend the day with you, hell, the rest of my life with you, I need to get on the road. Excitement and riches await me."

Kit laughed. "The rest of your life—ha. More like a half-hour or so. Although I admit, the idea has merit."

And indeed it did, but we both knew that was a door that should remain closed.

* * *

Thirty minutes later I was headed east on Interstate 20 at my discreet seventy-four miles per hour, top down of course. Seventy-four is my top speed with the Chrysler in its decapitated state. Above that, it's breezy.

For any of you who haven't driven through the country east of Dallas, you must put it high on your list of things to do before the big sleep grabs you. The beautiful ever-changing countryside raced by me, as did most of the pickup trucks, SUVs, MMVs, RVs, SPUTs, and sedans. Seventy-four is not fast enough on a Texas interstate.

Nichols had agreed to meet me at a restaurant alongside the interstate at the Texas Route 64 exit. He picked it, so I assumed we wouldn't be overheard there. His paranoia lay heavily on my mind. I once heard a wise man say, "Just because you're paranoid don't mean the bastards ain't out to get you."

CHAPTER THREE

Walking into the restaurant, I heard, "Arty, over here."

That miserable nickname again. It was tempting to turn and leave, but I'd given Kit my only active cases. That made this one important to my bank account.

It was a balding, overweight man who'd called out. "Johnny Nichols?" I asked, as if there could be another person in the restaurant calling me Arty.

"Yeah, I'm glad you're here. I was worried if I'd recognize you, but you haven't changed a bit."

That caused me to look more closely. Johnny Nichols? Yes, he did look slightly familiar, but who, where?

"I didn't expect you to recognize me," he said to my quizzical look. "The last time you saw me I was thirty pounds lighter with shoulder-length hair. Jake and I were drinking buddies in college and occasionally, when we could get your nose out of the books or the broads, you'd go for a beer with us. Remember O'Malley's Bar and Grill?"

You bet I remembered. That's where I discovered Killian's, beginning a love affair I'll take to my grave. In fact, if I change my mind about cremation, I'll request a case of Killian's to go.

"Yeah, I remember O'Malley's." My right-brain kicked in. "Johnny, no J-O. You're J-O Nichols. Whyn't you tell me this morning?"

"J-O." He chuckled. "There's a nickname I haven't heard in a long time except from Jake. He hung it on me, just like he hung Arty on you."

I let that pass. I couldn't tell him it was my own mother who did it. "Okay, truce," I said. "No more J-O and no more Arty."

"Yes, I can definitely live with that," he replied, vigorously shaking my hand.

I noticed the softness. Physical labor hadn't recently crossed his path. "Before you tell me what's going on, we need to discuss my fees."

"No problem," he interrupted. "Jake told me you get twelve hundred a day plus expenses. I set up a separate account and transferred seventeen thousand into it. That'll cover fourteen days. Jake said you always wrap things up in two weeks."

I stared, probably open-mouthed. I was thrilled at his figures and his preparation. Looked like I owed Jake another one. Johnny must have misinterpreted my silence.

"If that's not enough, I can squeeze out a little more. It'll be a strain, but I need you." His face demanded a response.

I recovered. "No, that'll do. We'll work within those boundaries although I can't guarantee it'll be wrapped up in two weeks. I don't know the whole problem yet. If it runs longer, we'll re-negotiate."

During the above conversation, we'd ordered drinks. Coffee and water for both of us. When the waitress delivered them, she took lunch orders, then moved away, leaving us in privacy.

Johnny pulled out a flask and added a healthy shot of an amber liquid to his water. "Want some? It's mighty fine scotch."

"No, I'll pass. It's a little early in the day for me."

"Oh yeah. Jake said you still drink Killian's. Must be tough when you're in a dry county like Van Zandt."

The waitress rescued me by delivering my potato soup, BLT, and fries. When she set Johnny's lunch down, I saw why he was overweight. It was a sixteen-ounce porterhouse and a Texas-sized baked potato oozing with butter and sour cream. For bread, there was Texas toast. He told her to hold the vegetables.

He attacked the steak with an enthusiasm my cats reserve for special treats. Finally, when there was nothing left but a clean bone, I said, "Okay, fill me in, just an overview now. We'll go into details later."

"She's young and beautiful," he said. "She offered what I can't get at home, and I partook. Her husband captured it all in photographs and on videotape. She wants money. I don't want to pay. That's the overview."

"An old story, my friend," I said in my most sympathetic voice. "Why not go to the police?"

"No, no way. That's all I'd need—something like this getting into the public view. My mother-in-law would bounce me out on my ass so fast I'd skip like a stone on a smooth lake."

Mother-in-law? That was the second time he referred to her, the first during our three a.m. conversation. My right-brain screamed for me to pursue it, but I chose instead to ask, "What about your wife? Does she know?"

He shrugged. "She knows there are lots of women. She closed her bedroom door years ago and doesn't care as long as I don't bother her."

"Why do I get the impression you're more afraid of your mother-in-law than your wife?"

"This might be tough for you to understand. I was not my mother-in-law's first choice." He chuckled. "Probably not her second, third or fourth, either. When Louise and I were dating, the old lady did everything she could to break us up. Then Louise told her she was pregnant, and I became number one in the groom parade. From that point on, neither Louise nor I seemed to have a voice in anything. The old biddy swung into action, and we were quickly married." He scowled. "No taint of scandal could be allowed to touch the great Evans name."

I looked into his eyes, and he turned from my gaze. "C'mon, Johnny. I've been in this business long enough to recognize crap when I hear it. What's the rest?"

"Dammit, Ace. Not going to leave me much, are you?"

"Nope."

"When Mrs. Evans told me I would marry Louise, she laid down certain rules, but she also sweetened the pot. Now, I never liked work very much, and her rules were perfectly acceptable at the time. Especially since I thought Louise helped draft them. I was in love with Louise and, I admit, with the Evans money. In a nutshell, the rules were: I would finish college, and Louise and I would produce a male heir. If not the first born, we'd try again. Furthermore, I'd do nothing to bring disgrace to the family. In return, she'd finance our marriage and our lives." He sipped at his empty water glass before waving the waitress over and asking for more. His coffee cooled, untouched.

The second water arrived, and he blended it. "When we returned from the honeymoon, Louise's mother called me to the big house and added the consequences for breaking the rules."

"Such as?"

"She'd throw me out on my ass. If Louise wanted to go, she could, but the kid would stay. She'd cut Louise out of her life and her will. She'd also make damn sure I never got a decent job."

"You bought into that?"

He responded through his water glass. "Yeah, I did, and until now, I've lived up to my end of the bargain. Oh, there's been a lot of bimbos, but no scandal."

"What about your wife and your child?"

"Five months after the marriage, Louise had a son, our son. We named him Matthew Thomas Adams-Evans-Nichols, hyphenated last name and all, after Louise's father and Mrs. Evans maiden name. You can guess who picked it." He sighed deeply and drained the glass. "When Louise came home from the hospital, she moved into a separate bedroom. I'll never forget her exact words. 'Mother has the heir she bought, but it's the last one from me.'" He stopped and looked longingly at his glass, where even an ant couldn't have found moisture. Nevertheless, he picked it up and tried again. "I haven't been behind that door since."

I stared at Johnny. Gradually, college memories seeped into my mind. He was two years ahead of Jake and me, but partied with the younger crowd at O'Malley's. Stories I'd heard from Jake and others filtered in. J-O was the butt of the jokes, the hanger-on, the one who never led, who never had an original idea. I guess it carried over into his post-college life, even his marriage. The other thing I remembered was he always had money and talked constantly about his women.

"Ace, I'm not proud I sold my soul, and I'm not proud of where I am today." He hesitated, then his voice rose in volume and confidence. "Dammit, I've put up with enough crap in my life. I'm not going to let that old woman throw me out." He suddenly lost his defiance. "I have nowhere to go. I need her money."

Feeling sorry for him was difficult, but lack of compassion is a poor reason to reject a case. "Okay, Johnny, I'll do what I can." I wondered what my choice would have been if I'd had to choose. "Now, cut to the problem. I need everything you know about this woman and her husband. I assume you want me to negotiate a total buy-out."

"Is that the best way to handle it?" He appeared to think for a moment. "If you can buy everything they've got—pictures, negatives, video—okay. I'll pay, if I have to. Really though, I don't give a damn how it's done." He played with his glass. "Wouldn't stealing the stuff be better?" His voice hardened. "Best yet would be to grab everything and dump their bodies in the Sabine River."

"Slow down, Johnny," I said with a grin. "If anything happens to those two, you're dead. Not only will everything come out, but you'll be the number one suspect." I turned serious. "So, watch your mouth." I paused. "And, if revenge is your game, forget it. I don't play that way."

"What?" He stared at me. "You're a damn PI. Since when do people like you have religion? What the hell am I paying for?"

"At the risk of repeating myself," I said firmly, "that's not my game. If you need someone to set them up, you've got the wrong guy."

"Bullshit," he countered. "If I'm paying twelve hundred a day, you'll do what I say."

"Wrong again, my friend. Looks like you just keep losing." I stood, reaching for my wallet. "I'm not about to be a party to what you're suggesting." I threw a twenty on the table. "If the bill's more than that, cover it, and don't forget a nice tip."

I left the table feeling good. I walked through the parking lot, my mind concentrating on the trip to Dallas—and what I'd tell Kit.

"Ace, wait up."

I hesitated, then moved on. As I opened the car door, a hand touched my arm.

"Don't leave," Johnny said, breathing hard. "Jake tried to tell me how honest you are. Guess I didn't listen."

I faced him. "Understand me. I spent ten years on the force in Dallas. I'm straight, have always been straight, and will die straight. You'd better get yourself another guy."

"No, you're still my choice. I'll toe the line."

I stopped, numerous thoughts racing through my mind. First, I wanted to bring down the scum who were blackmailing him. If they'd go after him, they'd go after someone else, perhaps someone more honorable than Johnny. And apparently, they had foolproof bait to entrap a man. If I were still on the force, Johnny would deserve police support. Second, if I dumped him, my caseload would be down to zero. Third, I was back to the blackmailers. I just hate people like that. My closest brush with death came when one began to shoot.

"Go inside and wait for me. If I don't show in the next ten minutes, hit the yellow pages, but don't give me as a reference." I put my hand on his shoulder and twisted him toward the restaurant. "I'll think it over."

I sat in the car and fiddled with the radio, trying to find some real music to help me think. No luck—just the usual noises. I had a hard conversation with myself.

CHAPTER FOUR

"I decided to stay on the case." I had Kit on the phone and had brought her up to date on the day's happenings.

"Another example of your ability to pick clients," she said.

"Yeah? Do I sense envy?"

"Try this. After I left your place, I drove by the Lattimore house. I arrived in time to see Lady Lattimore pulling out of the driveway. She looked like she was in a hurry so I followed. She drove straight to a bar."

"At what, eleven o'clock?"

"Let me see. Close. She hit the bar at eleven-oh-seven. Unlike you, I keep detailed notes."

"Yeah, yeah, yeah. Get on with the story." She was right though. Her case files look like a detailed biography. Mine resemble a skimpy diary.

"She was in the bar for fifteen minutes, then came out—"

"Excuse me," I heard through the handset.

"Who's that?" Kit asked.

"Beat's me. Must be on your end."

"No sir, it's me, Denny, the desk clerk. I'm sorry to interrupt, but you have a *very* important call. I figured you'd want me to break in."

"Who? Denny?" I questioned. "Oh, you mean here in the motel. So, who's calling?"

"It's Mrs. Evans, sir."

"Who's Ms. Evans?" Kit asked. "You already got somebody lined up out there? I know you're smooth, but that's really fast, especially for an old guy."

I chose to ignore the not-so-hidden insult. "No, I don't know any woman named Evans, except Dale, I mean. Take a number, Denny, and tell her I'll get back to her."

"Uh, no sir, I can't do that," Denny replied quickly. "It's Mrs. Evans, and she don't take no for an answer."

My brain finally engaged. "You mean the rich Ms. Evans from Grand Saline."

"Yessir, that's the one. Can I put her through? Please—and soon? She's already been on hold for three minutes."

I made a note to check the front desk to see what kind of timer he used. "Okay. Kit, I'll call you later."

"Don't bother, I'm going to wash my hair." Kit did not sound thrilled. Who can understand women?

"Denny, patch her through."

I heard clicks on the line, and when they cleared, I said, "Hello, Ace Edwards here."

"Young man, I am not accustomed to waiting. Do not let it occur again. I assume this is Arthur Conan Edwards."

The voice showed age, but it was strong and demanding, a voice accustomed to having its way. Also, buried under a lot of Texas was another accent.

"Excuse me, Ms. Evans. Just who are you, and why are you interrupting my calls?" I countered.

"Mr. Edwards. You know precisely who I am, even as I know you are a barely successful private investigator from Dallas who met with my son-in-law at lunch." Her words were clipped and precise. "It is my money with which he will pay you—if I allow it. I have not *yet* made that decision. The number one question to be answered is, can you protect the Evans name?"

That set me back for a moment. I stalled. "Ms. Evans, I'm not sure this is something I can discuss with you."

"Mr. Edwards. First, I am not a Ms., one of the younger so-called liberated females who are ashamed of their sex. I leave that title to women who have something to prove. I was happily married for fifty-two years and am quite satisfied with my life. You will call me Mrs. Evans. Second, I suggest you reconsider your last remarks. There are other private investigators that my son-in-law can hire and will hire if I so instruct him, and I might add, for less money."

"Ms., uh, Mrs. Evans," I replied as my mind whirled furiously, looking for a way to cope. "Please understand. When I agree to represent someone, I treat that representation seriously. What transpired between Johnny and me is private and will remain that way until he chooses to tell you."

"Private? My son-in-law has no privacy. I bought that when I bought everything else in his pathetic life. Now, will you extricate him from this disgusting episode thereby saving the Evans name?"

Her voice had the charm of a coiled rattlesnake and sounded as deadly. It made me more sympathetic toward Johnny. "Mrs. Evans, let me say again, I'm not at liberty to discuss our conversation. If he chooses to tell you—"

"Mr. Edwards, you are either a fool or a man with integrity, probably the former. Even though I detect a touch of education in your voice, I hear you using contractions—marks of the lazy and uneducated." She paused. "I shall decide your fate at dinner tonight. You will be here promptly at six-thirty for cocktails. You may dress casually. There will only be the two of us."

"Mrs. Evans—" She was no longer there.

I set the handset in its cradle and stared at it. "Wow, what was that?" I asked aloud. The phone ignored my question, so I continued. "She sounds formidable. Guess I'd better unpack some clean jeans for dinner."

My overnight bag was on the bed, still zipped as the boys and I had packed it. I shuddered as I considered the condition of the jeans and polo shirts I'd rolled and stuck in it. I remembered Johnny had worn a tie at lunch and wondered if Ms., excuse me, Mrs. Evans had a dress code. If so, I might be back in Dallas sooner than I expected.

Then I had an inspiration. As terrified as Denny had sounded, I guessed he'd help. I called the front desk, and as soon as I mentioned having dinner with Ms. Evans, Denny was anxious to assist. He even offered a tie.

* * *

At six twenty-eight, I rang the bell of Ms. Evans house,
although calling it a house is like calling the Grand Canyon a ditch.
I wondered where she'd gotten her money and who managed it. If I
could ever get a few dollars ahead, I might want to consult him.

A middle-aged man in black tie and tails opened the door. "May
I help you, sir?" He went over six feet and clearly looked down his
nose at me.

I stared, then glanced at my jeans. Silently, I thanked Denny for
taking my dilemma seriously. He'd picked up my shirt and jeans in
their rolled up, wrinkled condition and returned them one hour
later. The shirt was wrinkle-free, and the jeans pressed and
starched so stiffly they could stand on their own. He'd even found
someone to put a shine on my Dan Post boots.

When I'd checked myself in the mirror, I thought I looked
pretty spiffy. I even brought my best black Stetson on this trip and
wore it proudly. Then I faced a butler who dressed better than I
have ever dressed. I have to confess I've never worn tails. Black tie
and standard Tux, yes. Tails, no, and I hope I never will.

I must have waited too long to answer because he said, "The
delivery entrance is at the rear. Please move quickly. Madam is
entertaining this evening."

"I'm Ace Edwards," I said in a small voice. "I think I'm the
guest of honor."

Without hesitating or blinking an eye, he stepped aside. "Of
course, Mr. Edwards. Please come in. Madam instructed that I take
you to the den where you may wait. I will take your hat."

The way he said it, I was afraid he'd actually take it so I
whipped my Stetson off and handed it to him. He accepted it
between thumb and forefinger like a used tissue and placed it in a
coat closet.

Before I could register a complaint, he looked down his rather
long nose again. "The bartender has not yet arrived. However,
Madam says you are probably a beer person."

Now I ask, what would you have said? I drew myself up to my
full five feet, eight inches height and said, "Yes, but only Killian's

Red and, if you don't have it, I suggest you send for some right away." Ha, score one for me.

"I assume you're speaking of George Killian's Irish Red Premium Lager first brewed in Enniscorthy, Ireland in the mid-eighteen hundreds."

Ha, indeed. Not only had he taken away my point, but had scored two against me. "Yes, that's my beer," I replied. "Do you have any?"

"Of course, sir," he said as he walked away.

I had little choice, but to follow. He led me into a room off the main hallway.

"You may be seated," he said, leaving the area.

I spent a moment looking around. I admit I was impressed. The bar shone with a luster that only comes from expensive wood, properly treated. The windows were floor-to-ceiling with drapes of some rich looking material resembling velvet. I smiled, remembering the scene from *Gone with the Wind* when Scarlet wore a gown made from the green velvet drapes of Tara.

As I walked around, breathing in the luxury of the room and its richness, I heard footsteps behind me. A man with a scraggly beard came bounding into the room.

"Oh, sorry, sir. I didn't know anyone was here." He pulled up short and quickly straightened his jacket, which I noticed, was smartly tailored and identified him as the lost bartender. "I'll be with you in a moment." He hurried behind the bar.

He appeared to be about forty years old with a salt and pepper beard, scraggly as I said earlier, and sparse hair, certainly not as much as I have.

He busied himself for a few moments, then turned toward the backside of the bar. "Madam says you drink Killian's Red," he said over his shoulder. From a refrigerator, he took a Killian's and from a freezer, a frozen mug.

When he'd poured the beer and passed it to me, I silently congratulated him. No head. He might show up late, but he knew how to serve beer.

"You're Ace Edwards, aren't you?" He moved quickly, polishing the bar, cutting lemons and limes, setting out maraschino cherries and all the other things that bartenders do. At the same time, he kept up a line of patter. "I saw you in the Robin Hood BYOB Night Club. You were with the Jamison woman. Oh man, ain't she a looker—I mean, ain't she an attractive lady? Mrs. Evans says I need to improve my grammar if I'm going to work here." He chuckled. "Course she's been saying that for fifteen years."

"Yes, I'm Ace Edwards," I replied. "What's your name?"

"Billy, Billy Lapscott."

"Well Billy, it's nice to meet you." I stuck out my hand. "And your grammar's just fine with me."

He carefully wiped his hands, then shook mine. "I heard you brought Melon Sampson in. You must be good cause he wuz a bad'un. I once seen him whup three guys in a bar fight."

I noticed his grammar had slipped, probably down to its normal level.

"Let's just say I was lucky," I said modestly, giving thanks I hadn't had to face Melon in fisticuffs. "Do you work here often?"

"The bar? Only when she's entertaining—or having somebody special in, like you," he replied, instantly making me feel good, but suspicious of the evening facing me. "She doesn't do it as much as she used to, but Matthew Thomas lets me bartend when he entertains."

"Matthew Thomas?" I asked.

"Yeah, Matthew Thomas, her grandson. You know, Mr and Ms. Nichols' kid. You had lunch with him today, didn't you?"

I wondered if everyone in Van Zandt County knew my business, but all I said was, "Yeah, he's an old college buddy."

He gave me a look that clearly said, "Yeah, right." then went back to polishing the bar.

"How old is Matthew Thomas?" I hadn't considered he was old enough to be entertaining.

"Hmmmm," he said, stroking his beard. "Must be twenty-two, twenty-three. Let me see, he was born the year—"

"That's close enough," I said.

"You ain't met him yet, have you? Hellava nice guy, in spite of how he wuz raised. He'll be home this week. Sure hope you get to meet him."

"Oh, and how was he raised?" I smelled a story.

"By his grandma, that's how. Hell, she took him in and treated him like her own. His ma and pa wuz just too busy—" He froze in the middle of his speech. "Ah, sorry. You're Mr. Nichols' friend, ain't you?"

"It's okay. It's been a long time since we were close."

"Well, don't matter, don't change nothing. They wuz lousy parents. If it hadn't been for Mrs. Evans, Matthew Thomas woulda been all alone." He clammed up and went back to vigorously polishing the bar.

I sat and sipped my beer, letting random thoughts skitter around in my head. Just as I had formed the perfect comment, I heard a rustling sound behind me and a voice said, "Mr. Lapscott, you were late. We will talk about that. Is my martini ready?"

"Yes, ma'am, Mrs. Evans. It has been in the freezer for exactly twenty minutes, just as you like it. Beefeaters with a wave of vermouth." As he spoke, he opened the freezer and produced a martini glass filled with a colorless liquid. I recognized it as one he'd filled just prior to serving my beer. The glass instantly misted in the humidity of the room, and he added two olives on a red plastic sword. "Here it is, ma'am. I hope it meets your standards."

Ms. Evans accepted the glass and sipped the liquid. "Superb as usual, Mr. Lapscott. You are forgiven for your tardiness—this time. However, do not allow it to occur again." She took a second sip. "My taste buds tell me this martini, as superb as it is, has been in the freezer no more than twelve minutes. Is that correct, Mr. Lapscott?"

He ducked his head, looked at his watch, then grinned. "Actually, more like eleven minutes, ma'am."

They both laughed. Obviously, this was a private joke, and I wasn't invited.

"Mr. Edwards, I presume," she said. "I can see from your attire that you and Jonathan were friends in college. You dress as he did when he first arrived here, similar to what Mr. Lapscott would wear if I did not insist otherwise. Fortunately, I am able to encourage a degree of civility in both their wardrobes."

That explained the tie Johnny wore at lunch. I wanted to comment, but discretion overcame my normal sarcasm.

"Surely, not all private investigators in Dallas dress as poorly as you. When I said casual attire, I had no clue you would arrive in jeans and boots. If I check the closet, I will find a western hat, correct?"

"Yes, ma'am, you will." I took a moment to look her over. She was thin, blond and wore a royal blue outfit that swirled around her. It was a formal affair with layers of loose silky-looking material that billowed as she moved. Her face placed her in the fifty to sixty age group, perfectly made-up and almost wrinkle free. However, her neck said she was probably older than my initial impression. The slight swell of breast peeking from the top of the gown was young looking and provocative. Overall, she was an attractive older lady who'd taken care of herself, perhaps with the assistance of a highly skilled plastic surgeon. She wasn't a native Texan. There was enough accent to say east coast, maybe northeast.

"Well, Mr. Edwards, do you approve?"

"Excuse me, ma'am. Approve of what?"

"Mr. Edwards, if we are to have a successful relationship, you must not act as if I am one of your barroom ladies, especially one with limited mental capacity. Many men have studied me, for more years than I like to admit. I know when a man is giving me the once-over. So, do I meet your approval?"

"Yes, ma'am, you certainly do."

"At least you have the decency to blush. You are aware that I am old enough to be your mother—seventy-two by calendar count. Now, enjoy your beer. You surprise me with your choice. Killian's is not one of the more popular beers in East Texas. I am told that it is a full-bodied lager that is too bitter for most Americans. Is it possible that you are deeper than you appear?"

I wasn't sure what response was appropriate so I simply tilted my glass for another swallow.

She added, "You need not rush, you have time for another while I have my second martini." She spoke to the bartender. "It is ready, correct, Mr. Lapscott?" With a flourish that caused her sleeve to float, she tossed down the remnants of the first one.

Billy laughed aloud. "Yes, ma'am, you know it is. I wouldn't be standing here if I hadn't fixed a second one." He opened the freezer and produced a second martini.

"You must have had a provocative conversation with Mr. Edwards. Your grammar and enunciation have slipped again. You know misuse of the language labels you as lower class."

I pondered her comments before deciding I'd had worse insults hurled my way. You might wonder why I stayed. Simple. She fascinated me. I'd never met anyone like her, and the evening had just begun.

Billy smiled.

"Speaking of proper grammar, Mr. Edwards, where did you achieve that name, Ace? Surely, your parents did not bestow that at birth."

I stared at her, recognizing again this might be a tough evening. "Not exactly, ma'am. It's not on my birth certificate, but my dad gave it to me, and I'm proud of it."

"Really? Why?"

"My father was an ardent Sherlock Holmes fan. He vowed when he had a son, he'd name him after the famous sleuth. My mother did not agree, however, he was adamant. As Mom told the story, during her eighth month of pregnancy, she sat writing names she liked and initials—things like that. She wrote Sherlock Holmes Edwards. She says she jumped to her feet in triumph. As soon as my dad walked through the door that evening, she presented him with this fact. If he insisted on naming me as planned, I'd go through life with the initials S-H-E. Dad was aghast and quickly changed his choice to Arthur Conan Edwards. While Mom still was not thrilled, she acquiesced, and that's the name on my birth certificate. Very quickly after my arrival, Dad shortened it to Ace."

I stopped and gave her one of my famous grins. "That's how it happened, and I'm proud of it."

"Completely believable. Typical of the middle class." She sipped her drink.

If she had any clue of the insult, she didn't show it so I moved on. "Mrs. Evans, I'd really like to know why you invited me here tonight."

"Mr. Edwards, your question is another indication of your lacking in the social graces. It is gauche to discuss business before dinner. Please do not bring it up again."

CHAPTER FIVE

I'd walked into a buzz saw, and Ms. Evans had flipped the switch. For the next hour or so, life would be easier if I behaved as a proper guest—and nothing more. Fortunately, the beer was Killian's.

Ms. Evans finished her martini and signaled she was ready for dinner. I left half a Killian's on the bar. One look from her told me the dining room was off-limits to beer.

She led me into a room capable of grazing a few cattle, or feeding fifty or so humans. The table in the precise center of the area, rested on an Oriental carpet as big as a two-car garage. I quit counting chairs when she informed me we would sit together at the north end. She, of course, took the end position, the position of power. A smartly dressed servant set salads in front of us as we settled into our chairs, then stood by with a multitude of dressings, toppings, and other delights, some of which I'd never associated with a salad.

The dinner was excellent and properly upper crust; some kind of steak with tasty stuff scattered over and around it and steamed vegetables. As Ms. Evans drained her wineglass, the butler appeared and assisted with her chair. "Mr. Edwards," she said. "The time has arrived for us to adjourn to the library. We have business to discuss."

I pushed backward from the table, figuring the butler would never help me and replied, "Good. I'm intrigued by your summons and by your knowledge of my business here."

She led me into another room that matched the size of the dining room. However, instead of being outfitted to feed a crowd, it was floor-to-ceiling bookshelves and windows. The windows and window coverings matched the ones in the bar, while each shelf was crammed with books.

"You may sit here, Mr. Edwards," Ms. Evans said as she pointed to an overstuffed chair that could sleep three homeless people. "Mr. Lapscott will be here momentarily with your Killian's."

Even as my brain considered her comment, Billy walked in, balancing a tray with drinks.

I accepted my Killian's gratefully and said, "Suppose I preferred something different after dinner?"

Billy handed Ms. Evans a crystal snifter with a finger of a dark liquid. "Your Grand Marnier, ma'am." Then he turned to me. "Mrs. Evans said her research shows you always drink Killian's when it's available."

"Humph," was my best reply. "I once drank scotch and enjoyed it."

"That would have been at that BYOB place outside Canton," Ms. Evans said.

I gave up. It was too spooky. It seemed I knew less than anyone in the room, and I was the subject.

"Mr. Edwards, you're not sitting."

That was Ms. Evans, and her tone said she was accustomed to people jumping when she spoke. However, I quickly decided to leave rebellion for another evening and settled into the chosen chair. I found I had a choice. I could have my feet on the floor by sitting on the front edge of the seat, or I could have back support with my feet well elevated. I spent the next moment shuttling between the two, trying to decide which was more comfortable, or at least, more dignified.

"Cigar, Mr. Edwards?"

I looked at Ms. Evans, no easy task at that moment because I was in the rear support position and saw a huge cigar in her hand. Her other hand hovered over a humidor.

"Uh, no thanks," I managed to mumble. The cigar she held was big enough to make a tobacco farmer deliriously happy.

"Do you object to my smoking?" she asked.

"No, ma'am, you do just as you please."

"I see what you truly think, Mr. Edwards. First, you disapprove of smoking. Second, you disapprove of cigars, and third, you disapprove of my smoking this cigar. Am I correct?"

"Uh, yes—um, no—um—ah." I fell quiet. That was one of those lose-lose situations.

Ms. Evans chuckled. "You seem ill-at-ease. Am I unnerving you?"

"No, I'm just wondering when we'll get down to business."

"Patience, young man. Let an old lady enjoy her after-dinner cigar." With that she put flame to it, and, after a moment of controlled puffing, the cigar tip glowed red. I winced when I inhaled the smoke. It stunk.

"You probably find it strange that I smoke these. A legacy from my husband." Her features softened, and her voice changed timbre; softer, more intimate. "When we first married, Matty smoked cigars. They were the most foul-smelling things I had ever encountered. Finally, I told him if he did not stop, I would start. As you can see, he won that battle of wills, and now I am addicted."

I guessed it was one of his few victories over this formidable woman.

She sat in a smaller chair across from me, and I noticed that her feet touched the floor while her back was supported. "Jonathan contracted with you to find his blackmailers, yes?"

I looked at her, wondering where she got her information. "Mrs. Evans, as I told you on the phone, I'm not at liberty to discuss my conversation with Johnny."

"I will tolerate your loyalty to Jonathan—at least for now. I will tell you what transpired." She pointed the cigar at me. "Jonathan undoubtedly told you that he and my daughter have a rotten marriage. He may have used the word frigid when he referred to Louise. It is one of his favorite terms." A frown crossed her face, causing her majestic forehead to wrinkle. "Indeed, their sex life is dead and has been for the past twenty-two years. Did he tell you why? When Louise was pregnant with Matthew Thomas, your friend had affairs with three different women and, when none of them were available, visited the men's clubs in Dallas. There, he partook of the back rooms. I suspect you are aware of his escapades since you were one of his college chums."

"Mrs. Evans, I'm not sure you should tell me this—"

"I am the judge of that, and my judgment is you need to know. Louise wanted a quiet divorce immediately after the birth of her son. I would not allow it. There has never been a divorce in the Adams lineage. Louise demonstrated her common sense and stayed with him, but there have been no intimacies since. I forbade them."

She stopped talking and during the quiet, I digested what she'd said. If the opportunity arose, I'd grill Johnny on his side of the story. At this point, my opinion of him had slipped another notch. Based on what I remembered from college, her story sounded credible.

I slid forward in my chair. "What do you know about the people who're blackmailing him?"

"Attempting to blackmail, Mr. Edwards. No money has changed hands yet. They are a low-life couple named Jade and Hugo who moved into this area six months ago. Jonathan is not the first man who sampled her charms. She appears to share them with almost anyone, and, rumor has it she and Hugo have used blackmail before. It is my opinion they should be dealt with fiercely and permanently. For that reason, I was disappointed when I learned Jonathan had contacted you."

"Excuse me," I said, sliding to the rear of my chair. She'd caught me off-balance with that remark. "Why?"

"Oh, I know your reputation. I have reason to believe the stories are exaggerated. However, even if they are true, this performance calls for a different type of person."

"And what kind would that be?" I asked with an edge in my voice.

"Calm down, Mr. Edwards. I need someone with less scruples, someone who will take whatever action is required to insure the Evans name stays unsullied. Preferably, someone a lot larger than you, with muscles where you have a beer gut, or do you wear a money belt?" She smiled while I shifted uncomfortably. "The young man you will face is much larger and can probably lift you with one hand. Do you understand now, or are your feelings still smarting?"

"Mrs. Evans, don't let my appearance fool you. I'm not quite the pushover you seem to think. I can—"

"Yes, but can you make those two disappear, never to bother us again?"

"Disappear? Exactly how do you mean that?"

"Surely you are intelligent enough to decipher my words. My interest is the Evans name. Those two present a threat. As long as I never see or hear from them again, I shall be happy."

"And Johnny?" I asked.

"Jonathan is immaterial. Matthew Thomas, my grandson, has a brilliant political career in his future. I have reared him to become Governor, Senator, perhaps President. I will not allow Jonathan to be a distraction to that progression."

My stomach rolled over, and it had nothing to do with dinner. "Since you apparently know all about me, you must know I would never act unlawfully," I said, my voice rising. "And *that* includes making someone disappear."

"Yes, I believe you. However, it simply reinforces my opinion that you are unsuited to the job which must be done. Now, have you decided to return to Dallas? Or, are you foolish enough to accept this assignment even though we both know it is too much for your meager experience?"

"Ms. Evans," I said, not caring what she thought of my use of Ms., "I accepted this case from Johnny. I will pursue it until Johnny says otherwise. But I will do so in a lawful way, and he knows that." I crossed my arms over my chest and waited for her next comments.

She sat quietly, staring at me. I kept my mouth shut, determined that she make the next move.

"Mr. Edwards, Matthew Thomas will be home this weekend. Since you appear determined, it will be an excellent opportunity for the two of you to meet. Be here at seven o'clock, Sunday evening for cocktails." A smile played around the edge of her mouth. "Dinner will be served promptly at seven-thirty. Again, the dress will be casual, however jeans are not acceptable. Surely, you will have time over the next few days to shop for more appropriate attire. If you need assistance, I shall have Mr. Coker, my manservant, accompany you. Mr. Lapscott will restock the Killian's."

She smiled, then sipped her drink as I sat, dumbfounded. When she looked at me again, the smile was gone, and she snapped her fingers toward the door. The butler instantly appeared. "Mr. Coker, present Mr. Edwards with the license number."

The butler handed me a folded paper.

"That, Mr. Edwards," she said, "is the license number of the car the young man and woman drive. They use the last name of Noble, Jade and Hugo Noble. He prefers the nickname, Killer. You may well find they have other names in other places. You do have a way of checking this, do you not?"

"Thank you," I said, rather than give her the response that had risen to my tongue. "I have ample resources to trace this number and to backtrack the Nobles, or whatever the real name is."

I would have said more, but she cut me off. "I suggest you begin the investigation—the sooner the better." She stood and walked from the room.

Simultaneously, the butler stepped to my side. The evening had ended.

CHAPTER SIX

The butler—Ms. Evans called him Coker—showed me the door after retrieving my Stetson. Again, he handled it as if touching it was an act of gallantry. I walked toward the car, the events of the evening swirling in my mind. I hoped they'd settle into some sort of pattern.

"So, you met the Bitch-Who-Ate-Boston."

I started, my concentration broken, and saw Johnny moving toward me. "What did you say?" I asked.

"I said, you met the Bitch-Who-Ate-Boston, my mother-in-law," he answered.

"I met your mother-in-law, but the name doesn't quite fit. Why do you call her that?"

"She must have been on her best behavior. Wait 'til she gets to know you better, or you fail to do what she wants. Then you'll understand."

"Boston, you said. So that's her accent. How'd she get here?" Ms. Evans intrigued me. An old adage says, know your enemy. Having her as an adversary would be unnerving, but if it were inevitable, knowledge would come in handy.

"You mean she didn't tell you about how Matt, or Matty as she called him, came east and swept her off her feet. You'll probably get that version next visit."

I wondered how much Johnny had drunk before he ambushed me. "Why don't you tell me, then I can compare versions when she decides to talk."

Johnny laughed. "Okay, but let's find a place to sit. This might take awhile." He led me down a paved drive to a large cottage about a quarter mile from the big house. "This is where I live—at the old bitch's convenience, of course. Have a seat."

I looked him over again and decided he'd seen the bottom of a scotch bottle—from the inside. We sat in rockers on the verandah. The house angled away from the big house. "Okay, tell me her story," I said.

Johnny laughed again. "I'll give you her story, but not until we have something to drink. Killian's?"

There's only one answer to that so I nodded as he walked into the house. I marveled that I was so important that everyone stocked Killian's.

A few moments later, I was comfortably rocking with a cold beer in hand.

"Here's the way she tells it," he began. "Matt's family had a stake in the salt mines here in Grand Saline as well as oil wells in Van and a large ranch near Wills Point. Of course, being the gentleman that his dad was, he had others doing the work while he lived here enjoying the profits. When Matt was twenty, he was sent to Boston on family business. Lottie's father was a wheel in the brokerage firm that handled the Evans investments, and that's who Matt saw."

"Lottie?" I interrupted. "Her name is Lottie?"

"Okay, Loticia Adams Evans. She'll tell you she's a direct descendant of John Adams, signer of the Declaration of Independence, first Vice President, and second President of the United States." He frowned. "I could also give you dates and assorted other facts about the Adams' lineage. Lord knows, I've heard them often enough. Yes, Matt called her Lottie, but everyone else calls her Mrs. Evans."

"Okay," I said, grinning. "Continue."

"As I said, Matt had business with her father. He invited Matt for dinner. When Lottie and Matt met, she was twenty-three at the time, Matt fell madly in love with her and pursued her without pause. He even postponed his departure and wouldn't leave until she agreed to marry him." Johnny smirked. "She says it was a quick wedding because Matt couldn't stay in Boston indefinitely.

Her father didn't mind because he approved of Matt, however her mother was upset. There was only enough time to pull together a hundred or so guests, a dozen bridal showers, and a ceremony in the most beautiful cathedral in Boston." Again, he smirked. "Remember, this is her story, not mine. To continue, she left all the memorabilia from the wedding in Boston when they came west. It was destroyed in a fire."

"I take it you don't believe her story. What did her husband say?"

"Slow down, Ace, I'm getting to it. But to answer your question, whenever she told her story, Matt's eyes threatened to roll right out of his head."

I chuckled. "Okay, how does the other version differ, and whose version is it?"

"Her husband, Matt. One night when he'd had a few drinks, and Lottie had told him to sleep in the garage, we had a long talk. According to him, her father was a low-level clerk at the brokerage firm and insisted Matt come to dinner. Lottie threw herself at him with the concurrence of her parents. Her father kept coming up with delays that forced Matt to stay in Boston. Lottie was at his elbow constantly. Finally, after he'd been there for about three months, she proposed. He figured, what the heck, he could do worse so he agreed to marry her. He admitted she had really gotten under his skin, and he loved her. Besides," Johnny laughed, "he said she was a wildcat in the sack. They had a quickie wedding before a Justice of the Peace with her parents and the JP's wife as witnesses." Johnny concluded his story with an even bigger laugh. "The funniest part is he said it was the best move he ever made."

"Yeah, those are definitely different versions," I said as I wondered where the truth lay. "Did they come here right after the wedding?"

"Yeah, and it's good they did. It was March 1941. Matt's father died during the summer, and Matt took over the business. Then, the Japs hit Pearl Harbor in December, and Matt enlisted in April '42, or I should say, volunteered to be an officer. Matt went off to war, and Lottie cleaned house—the business house, that is. The old timers around here say she was hell-on-wheels. She canned everyone who might challenge her as head of the Evans Empire. Then she went to work on the community to establish herself as the local queen. She even became a Southern Baptist."

"How'd Matt take all this?"

"He was in Europe during most of it so his input was minimal. She played successfully in the weapons business, putting money where it would do the most good, and told him she helped the war effort. Of course, it didn't hurt that she tripled every dollar she invested. When the war ended, Matt came home to considerably more wealth than he'd left. When Matt saw that, she was golden."

I pondered that comment a moment. "Do you mean she played in the black market?"

Johnny shrugged. "Depends. Some say no, some don't say anything. It's not smart to say bad things about Mrs. Evans."

"What'd she do after Matt returned? Did he take over the business?"

Johnny laughed and slapped his knee. "No, my friend. She informed him she didn't intend to return to the kitchen, as if she'd ever been in the kitchen—his words, not mine. He retired and spent the rest of his life as one of the idle rich. Matt was a realist and knew how to best butter his bread."

"Much like you," I said.

"Ouch," he replied. "I see you two talked about me. But one thing I bet she left out. I loved Louise when we married, but as soon as our son was born, she became a replica of her mother. After awhile, I gave up. Yeah, I've led a wild life, but not until after Louise locked her bedroom."

Another enigma. Which Johnny was the real one? This case had a distinctive cast of characters, each with more than one story. I wondered if Louise would add a third version.

I shoved those thoughts aside and said, "You tell a good yarn, but you leave out a lot. Why didn't you tell me Ms. Evans knows about Jade, Hugo, and the blackmail scheme?"

"She does?" he asked, a huge question mark in his voice. "Oh shit, I'm in for it now. Did she tell you that?"

"Yep. In fact, she gave me a more detailed version than you did." I felt no urge to make him feel safer—quite the contrary.

He sat quietly for a moment. "So, what now? Will she pay them? Are you headed to Dallas?"

"She says no, and what I do depends on you. I took this case for you, and that's where it stands until you decide otherwise. If you want to play the blackmailers' game, I'll bill you for time spent, and move out of the way."

"Ace, I don't think you understand. If we have to buy the stuff, she'll take it out of my monthly allowance. If we don't, and it goes public, she'll bounce me out on my ass. My only hope is for you to get me out of this mess." His head dropped into his hands.

"Johnny, you're a pathetic specimen for a human being." I stood and looked down on him in his chair. He appeared very small. "How in the hell did you get this way?"

His head lifted, and he met my eyes. "I don't know, Ace. I suppose you're right. I don't like myself very much, but this is what I am. I can't let her throw me out. I have no place to go. You gotta help me."

His voice carried a sad, pleading tone that made me want to grab him and slap some manhood into his sorry life. Of course, I didn't. I simply continued to look at him, thankful my parents gave me confidence while teaching me the value of work. They also taught me to finish any job I started, which locked me into this case unless Johnny fired me.

"Good night, Johnny. It's been a long day." I checked my watch. "I'm beat. Some SOB woke me at three a.m., almost seventeen hours ago. We'll talk in the morning. Nine o'clock, same place we had lunch. You're buying." I left him sitting in his pool of self-serving misery.

CHAPTER SEVEN

A ringing phone woke me, and when I picked up, a perky young voice said, "It's seven a.m., your wake up call. The sun is up, it's beautiful outside, and it's my pleasure to be the first to wish you a nice day."

I mumbled something, hoping it was intelligible, then hung up the phone and rolled out of bed. One hour later I had showered, dressed and was sipping my third cup of coffee while munching a doughnut in the continental breakfast area of the motel. One doughnut seemed sufficient since Johnny would buy breakfast in an hour.

The thought of calling Kit crossed my mind, but that wouldn't be smart. She'd undoubtedly ask me questions for which there were no answers—like my progress on the case. When she found out there was none, she'd make snide remarks about Killian's. Yes, we've had that conversation before.

I flipped on CNN instead and caught up on the latest scandals involving our elected officials. Of course, the coverage had its usual anti-conservative bias so Republicans took the brunt of the scandal reports. The same acts by liberals went unreported.

At nine, I entered the restaurant and saw Johnny in deep conversation with a young waitress. She giggled and said, "Ooh, that'd be nice. I'll see you tonight."

I could only shake my head. Obviously, he had learned nothing.

"Ace," he said. "Good morning. Have you met Jeannie? She's new to the area. I'm going to show her around tonight. She'll be back in a few minutes with our breakfasts. I ordered pancakes, eggs, bacon, sausage, ham, and grits for you. I told her you were on the way. She's excited about meeting a big city private eye."

"Good morning, Johnny. I'm glad to see you're in such a good mood." I wondered how much of his cheerfulness was the result of what appeared to be a successful rendezvous for tonight. "But next time, leave me out of your conquests."

His eyes never came near me. They watched Jeannie's derrière swishing among the tables. Now, chauvinist is not in my vocabulary, but even a brief glimpse warmed my heart. Apparently, Johnny and I shared one personality trait, an appreciation for the softer sex.

"Johnny, remember why we're here. Aren't you in enough trouble?"

"Oh. Ah. Yes, maybe. But she's such a delicate young thing and has no friends here. You don't think I should disappoint her, do you?"

"You should do whatever you think is right. But keep in mind your last tryst brought me here."

"Yeah, okay." He frowned. "Oh well, there'll be other nights." He looked sad for a moment, then brightened. "Here she comes, with our food. That's one hell of a sacrifice I'm making for you."

"For me?" I sputtered. Platters of arriving food interrupted my thoughts. There was enough to feed the Dallas homeless.

"Oh, Mr. Edwards," Jeannie said. "Johnny says you're a famous private investigator from Dallas. May I have your autograph? I collect autographs. I even have one from that famous author." She hesitated, obviously lost in what passed for thought in her cranial space. "You know, Randy. Ah, Randy somebody. He's such a nice old man."

It took a moment, but I extricated myself, shooting daggers at Johnny all the while.

After Jeannie finished cooing and swished away from us, I turned to Johnny, breaking his concentration on her backside. "Let's talk. I need everything you have on the blackmailers. Where'd you meet her, where'd you take her, any, and everything you can tell me." He opened his mouth, but I cut in, "Skip the sex stuff. I have no interest in how good she was and especially in how good you think you were."

Johnny must have appreciated my humor because he let out a hardy laugh. "Spoken like a true gentleman, but you'll miss the most exciting parts."

"Excitement—I can live without it. Just the facts, sir, just the facts," I said in my best Jack Webb imitation.

Johnny rewarded me with another smile, this one filled with pancakes and began to answer my query.

"I met her in Dallas. Louise and I had a fight that morning so I took off and spent the day shopping."

"Shopping?"

"Yeah, shopping. You know, shopping for beer, shopping for scotch, shopping for vodka, and any other booze I could find. There's some fine shopping spots once you leave Van Zandt County."

"Okay, you went bar hopping. Now, on to how you met Jade."

"I was leaning on a bar somewhere, I'm not sure where, when I felt a tap on my shoulder. Someone said, 'Don't you think you've had enough for one day?' I guess I squinted, because she continued, 'I've been there. You can't even focus, can you?'

"I tried, only to discover the voice was right. She took my arm. 'Let's get out of here and get some food before you fall flat on your face. I don't think these cowboys would bother to step over you.'

"She took me to a restaurant and forced me to eat a burger and drink coffee. I have no clue how long we were there, but by the time I could focus on my watch, it was nine o'clock. Also, I discovered I sat across from a beautiful blond with all the equipment in the right places."

"I'd have been disappointed if you hadn't told me that," I said in my most sarcastic manner. "I suppose she invited you to her place to finish sobering up."

"That's it exactly. I was in no condition to argue, even if I'd wanted to. So off we went in her car."

"Where was your car?"

"At that point, I didn't know and didn't care—someplace in Dallas, I suppose. My head still spun, but the rotations had slowed enough to allow a glimpse of the future if I played my cards right."

"You willingly piled into her car and headed for points unknown?"

"Sure, wouldn't you? Anyway, when we got to her place, well, this is where I have to leave out the most exciting parts—per your instructions."

"Did you stay the night?"

"Yeah. Sometime after all the sex, I fell asleep or passed out or whatever. When I awoke the next morning, she was dressed and waving a cup of hot, steaming coffee under my nose. One look at her brought back a flood of memories that would cause a hooker to blush. She was the hottest—"

"Sure, sure," I cut in. "Not interested. Move on."

"That's about it. I got up, dressed, grabbed the car, and drove home." He grimaced. "Not exactly home as we grew up to know it. Louise never missed me."

"Stop. Hold it right there. You said you *drove* home. How did your car get to her place?"

A look of puzzlement crossed his face. "I—I don't know. I hadn't thought of it before. She must have had it brought over."

"How did she know what you drove, where you'd parked, how'd she get the keys, and who moved it?"

"Hell, I don't know. What are you—" A look of comprehension landed on his face. "Damn. She bird-dogged me."

"Bingo. My guess is she picked you up early in the day and trailed you from bar to bar until you were appropriately blotto. Then she moved in for the kill. Her partner was probably close in case you raised a ruckus. He'd have rushed in to defend the delicate young flower from the belligerent drunk. Later, she gave him your car keys, and he brought the vehicle around."

"Dammit, Ace. You make me sound like an idiot, like she set a trap, and I walked right in."

Shrugging, I said, "If you step in a pile of brown stuff, and it smells . . ." I purposefully let my voice trail away.

He sat quietly for a moment, then let out a long sigh. "Yeah, there's a stench there. Especially when I consider what happened next."

During his story, Jeannie had returned to the table several times with coffee and to make sure we enjoyed ourselves. Each time, Johnny interrupted himself to stare at her, and she matched him, leer for leer. I could only wonder what a beautiful young woman could see in this overweight, older man. Who can understand women—of any age? Johnny, I understood.

I had tired of sitting and had drunk enough coffee to keep me awake for a week. "Look, let's get out of here and drive around the countryside. It's a nice day to drop the top, and you can tell me the rest of the story."

After we lowered the top, and headed down route 64, I said, "Okay, pick up where you left off. When did you next see her?"

"About a week later. She called on my cell phone. Said she didn't want to call me at home. Oh, Ace, she laid it on thick. Talked about how much that night meant to her, about how she'd never had a man like me. Without embarrassing you, I'll just say when the conversation was over, I'd have gone through hell to get to her." He paused, frowned, then continued. "Guess I was thinking below the belt."

I swerved to miss the remains of an armadillo in my lane. "Oh? What about Jeannie? She's got you pegged as a pigeon. What's it take, a smile, two boobs, and a skirt?"

"Easy, Ace. That might be true, but I don't like to hear it."

"Then wake up. If you walk around with your dick hanging out, there'll always be a Jade. How do you know Jeannie's not another Jade?" I glared at him. "When in the hell are you going to grow up?" I swerved back into my lane. My irritation showed in my driving.

"Get me out of this crap, and I'll be more careful. That's all I promise. So get off my case."

I caved. He was hopeless. His attitude had driven my speedometer to ninety. I decided to slow down, and I owed Johnny nothing beyond stopping the blackmail scheme. I would take his money with a clear conscience. Well, Ms. Evans' money.

"Did Jade give you a payment schedule?"

"No, she said she'd be in touch. Hey, it's only been three days. Do you want me to call her?"

"No, I'll take care of that. Give me her phone number and address. There's a pad and pencil in the glove box."

* * *

During the afternoon, I made contact with Jade to set up a meeting. It took some finagling, but we finally arrived at an agreement. I picked the location, but was disappointed she wouldn't meet until Saturday, three days away. The up side was it gave me time to set things up to my liking. The down side was it gave Jade and Killer the same opportunity. She assured me it was because she had to visit her sick mother in Ft. Worth. I believed that so much, I offered to rent her Big Tex when he's not in use at the Texas State Fair.

CHAPTER EIGHT

"Will you do it, Kit?" I was back in Dallas on the phone. Since there were three days before my appointment with Jade, I had decided to visit the boys.

"Dammit, Ace. Of course. Have I ever failed you?" She chuckled. "You must be getting weak in your old age. You can't handle one woman? No, forget that. You have no clue about females."

I let that one lay. No way would I risk a comment.

I'd arrived home about two hours earlier, and the boys were thrilled to see me. Of course they were. Their food dishes were low, and their litter boxes the opposite. After I refilled and cleaned, they wandered off to do whatever cats do when they're ignoring their human servants. Then I called Kit.

"Great, Kit. To celebrate our alliance, let's have dinner tonight."

"Oh Ace, what a sweet idea. But I'll have to take a rain check. You already told me about Terri. Anyway, my hair looks like a fright wig, and this is my night to do it. Don't worry, though. I'll be in Grand Saline when you need me."

She hung up with a chuckle, leaving me to wonder how long it took her to do her hair. She wore it very short—and straight.

The boys were on my bed pretending to sleep so I sat down to brief them on Johnny's night with Jade. The alleged snoozing continued. Finally, Striker stood, gave me a disgusted look, jumped off the bed, and left the room. Sweeper hadn't moved except for one eyelid that crept open before slowly closing again.

"Okay, Sweeper, it's you and me. If your morals were higher, I wouldn't have anyone to talk to."

He stretched and purred. Both eyes were open now, and he looked at me expectantly.

I finished Johnny's story, then told Sweeper the deal with Jade. "So, that's it. I meet her Saturday, and we'll see what happens."

Sweeper bounced to his feet, rushed at me and feinted with his left front paw. I say feinted because while I watched his left, he drove the nails on his right through my jeans into my thigh.

"Hey, what's that for?" I yelped.

My question went ignored as he deftly withdrew and leaped to the floor. Once there, he ran in circles a couple of times, then flopped onto his side and lay still.

"Huh, have you flipped? Too much catnip?" He ignored me.

I reached over to check him, but when my hand was almost to his body, he stood, glared at me, flipped his tail in the air, and ran from the room. That left me with no clue what his exhibition was about.

Both of my boys appeared disappointed in me—Striker, because Johnny was my client and Sweeper, because he considered me stupid, or so it seemed.

The phone buzzed. I picked up and did my usual. "Ace Edwards."

"I told you not to answer the phone with your name. Suppose I was an irate husband. I'd know I had the right person and from there—"

"Okay, Kit. You've said it all before. Are you calling to tell me your hair is clean, dry and properly straightened, and you want me to come over?"

"No, you idiot. I'm reminding you to call Tom Roberts and check out Jade and Hugo."

"My dear Kit, of course Tom is checking them out." Actually, I hadn't thought of it, but it was a great idea. "Now, if you finish your hair, we'll still have time for dinner."

"Call Tom, I gotta run." Click.

I had the impression she did not intend to have dinner with me—ever again. But back to business. I punched Tom's number into the phone.

Tom Roberts was an ex-cop like me, but unlike me, he invested his retirement fund in education. He took enough courses to become a computer nerd and now made a large and steady income solving other people's problems. Not bad for an ex-cop. Of course, being such, he kept his ear to the curbstone. If you needed to nail a rumor, Tom Roberts had heard it. Since we were partners on the force, and I pulled him out of a few tight spots, he did research for me on the cuff. I assured him I'd pay when my first oil well came in.

"Tom Roberts, your window to Windows," I heard.

"Need some minor assistance from the best in the business," I said. "It'll only take a couple of minutes."

"Edwards, I assume," he replied. "Anyone else would identify themselves and not try to butter me up. What do you need that'll eat up my day?"

I chuckled. "Tom, you malign me. Have I ever led you astray?"

"Humph, how about the time you told me to take the shortcut through the dark alley while you stayed on the well-lighted street?"

"Hey, I came to your rescue and pulled two of those punks off. When I did that, the other two quit beating on you and took off."

"Selective memory is a sign of old age, Ace. My memory says I got jumped by four punks who put me in the hospital for a week. You received a citation and two days off for valor. Now, what's on your mind?"

"Yeah, but I offered to hang my citation in your cubicle," I countered. "I even sent you roses."

"I remember—red. The nurse who was hitting on me suddenly lost interest. Now, enough BS. What do you need?"

I told him about Jade and Hugo and their blackmail scheme, then gave him the plate number Ms. Evans had supplied. "I need anything you can get on them, especially any bargaining chips I can use to change their minds."

I heard a long sigh hum through the phone. "I'll do what I can. Give me a few days. Maybe by Sunday."

"I have a meet set for Saturday and need planning time. How about this afternoon?"

"Ace, dammit, I am not an extension of your under-financed agency. I have other work to do—for *paying* customers."

His emphasis on the word paying caused me to remind him I'd pay as soon as I struck oil.

"Okay, this afternoon." Click.

None of my friends wanted to talk to me today.

I wandered around the house for a while, doing manly chores like laundry. If my hands were busy enough, right-brain might kick in with some revelation that would help me resolve the blackmail scheme without sullying the Evans name. I'd reached the point where it wasn't important what happened to Johnny, although technically he was my client. Ms. Evans was my real employer. It was her money.

Late in the afternoon, as another load of wet laundry entered the dryer, the phone rang. My first impulse was to ignore it. What is it about a ringing telephone that causes us to drop whatever we're doing and rush to do its bidding? I did just that, telling myself it might be Tom with my information.

"Hello, Ace Edwards here."

"I keep telling you not to identify yourself when you pick up the phone. It makes you a sitting duck for every telemarketer in the country."

"Hi, Kit. Did you change your mind?"

"Sure, and you've quit mooning about Terri. No, I need to talk to you about Barnes and Lattimore. You do remember them, don't you?"

"How're my horny friends doing?"

"Now that you've got me doing the chasing, they're your friends?"

"Just fun-loving people out to enjoy life," I said through a chuckle.

"Yeah, right. Your fun-loving friends are about to run my buns off. After Saturday, you can have these cases back. They both have the morals of alley cats."

"Easy. The boys might hear you, and they have very high morals. Well, Striker does."

"Oh, excuse me. Tell the boys I didn't mean to impugn their character, but these are two sex machines. How much am I getting an hour?"

"Ah, my dear, we don't do this for the money, we do it for the good of mankind," I said. "And womankind," I added as an afterthought.

"Whatever," Kit said with a sigh. "How much do you want on these characters? I have him with three different women in two days and her with two guys. Is that enough?"

"Maybe. Maybe not. We can talk over dinner tonight. Both spouses are out to bleed them in divorce court. They made it very clear I'd better bring in stuff that'll make the judge blush. Are we there yet?"

"You want videos?" she asked.

"Yeah, that'd be great."

"This is really going to cost you."

"Make sure they're close-ups for the judge." I chuckled. "Real close."

"You'll take what I shoot, and I'm not getting near either of them. They're headed for STD-ville." This time, she laughed.

"Seriously, just a couple of more days. If they stay on the prowl, we should have enough."

"Okay, I'll tail them a while longer. But, as far as I'm concerned, they're just two dogs in heat, willing to screw anything with the right equipment."

"Great. How about dinner tonight?"

"Sorry, but I hear my hair dryer calling." The phone clicked in my ear.

So here I was again, turned down by Kit. Of course, on the bright side, I was no worse off than I was before she called. I pulled out my notes on Barnes and Lattimore and reviewed them. With what I had and what Kit had just told me, I decided to put together a report on Sunday and wrap up the cases. We must have enough to pad the divorces.

* * *

At six, I was on the phone with Tom. He grumbles a lot, but he's efficient. "Hugo and Jade Noble are a nasty pair. From their track record, they're anything, but."

"But what?" I asked.

"But Noble," he said, chuckling. "Hey, you need to get out more often. Your sense of humor has definitely slipped."

"Just the facts, sir, just the facts."

"Okay. I picked them up in El Paso. Hugo's last name, and the name on the marriage license is Noble. Her maiden name was Luden. The plate number you gave me, along with the car it's registered to, was stolen, and used in a robbery. The cops were all over Hugo, but Jade supplied him with an airtight alibi, and they skipped town. You gave me a Chevy. The plate is registered to a Beamer?"

"That's the info I had, an old Chevy," I answered.

"Sounds like they grabbed a second car, one that wouldn't stand out, and switched the plates. It works. It's tougher to spot a plate than to spot a car and a plate."

I could only sigh with the realization that these guys weren't rank amateurs. "What's their record?"

He paused, and I heard the crinkle of papers. "Hugo's done time. The normal things you'd expect. He cracked a guy's skull in a bar fight and did six months. Another time, he put a buddy in the hospital for a month when they disagreed about who was the best running back, Jim Brown or Walter Payton. There were a few other arrests without convictions. All in all, a pretty nasty guy."

"Sounds like the kind of characters I attract," I said, a chill surfing up my spine. "What about Jade? Anything on her?"

"Nothing much. She has a couple of arrests: alleged prostitution and purse snatching—no convictions. The witnesses changed their minds."

"I don't understand."

"Just what I said," Tom replied. "The witnesses decided they'd fingered the wrong woman." He paused. "Oh, Hugo was free at the time. The investigator thought Hugo had something to do with it— like maybe threatening to rearrange the witnesses' faces."

"So she's clean?"

"Unconvicted. Not clean. You best be careful with this couple. They're mean as alley cats."

I thanked him and hung up, thinking he was the second person that day to malign cats. I was glad the boys hadn't heard.

CHAPTER NINE

I arrived at the meeting site an hour early. The previous night, I'd called Jade and reminded her of our appointment and the rules. She wasn't thrilled to hear from me, especially when I asked about her sick mother in Ft Worth.

We'd agreed on the rest stop on the west side of Interstate 20 at Texas Farm-to-Market-Road 16. I slowly cruised the parking area looking for a trap. Mostly, there were cars with out of state plates: Louisiana, Florida, Oklahoma, New Mexico, Arizona, and one from Maine. That last one caused a second look. Lost tourist. Nothing that fit the description of Jade's car caught my eye.

The best observation spot was a parallel space past the restrooms. After positioning my car so the rear was toward the meeting site, I scooted down in my seat and adjusted the mirrors. The picnic table where we were to meet was in full reflection. Now it was time to check the facilities.

I'd warned Jade to leave Killer home, telling her all deals were off if he showed. But just in case, I wanted to know what was available in the travel center. I might need it as a refuge. It consisted of bathrooms, a reception area, and a souvenir shop, each open to the public. I watched people go in and out, enough to give me a sense of safety if Killer came after me. Of course, he might not be shy about performing in front of an audience. If so, my chances of escaping a severe beating or worse were slim.

Walking back to the car, I surmised that meeting at high noon in a public area was my built-in safety factor. After settling down in my seat, I checked the mirrors. The picnic table was still empty. It was the first one after the rest rooms, a standard concrete table with benches. A trio of trees, pin oaks maybe, shaded it. That was a bonus since the Texas sun pounded down.

I settled in to wait, put on a Frank Sinatra CD, and opened my latest Bob Gaston novel. Over the top of the pages, my eyes scanned the mirrors, watching for anyone meeting Jade's description. She'd told me she would wear a white blouse and red skirt with black flats, no stockings. Nice working girl attire.

At eleven-thirty, a car grabbed my attention by pulling into the last diagonal space, closest to the picnic table. The driver was blond, alone, and simply sat in her car, an old Chevy. She leafed through a magazine, or pretended to as her eyes scanned the parking lot.

At eleven-forty-five, she got out of the car, and I caught my breath. She wore a cut-off white T-shirt that was all but sheer. Even from my distance, I was sure only nature supported her. Her shorts left little to the imagination, although mine worked overtime. She stretched, extending her arms over her head. You picture the results. She walked to the front of the car, lifted herself onto the hood, and crossed her legs. It was a perfect photo-op for an auto tools calendar. If that was Jade, I understood and envied Johnny. Of course, if it was Jade she'd forgotten the proper dress.

After a few moments on the hood, she jumped down and walked around the area, continuing her stretching. I struggled to maintain my surveillance on the rest of the parking lot.

At two minutes before twelve, she walked to the picnic table and sat with her back to the parking area. She produced a mirror from her handbag and began to repair her makeup.

I grinned. She obviously watched too many movies.

Her eyes followed me in her compact mirror as I walked up. "Jade Noble?" Maybe using her last name would shake her.

"Who—who are you?" she said in a little girl voice. "I don't know you. Please leave me alone."

So much for shaking her. Apparently she'd done this before. "While your act is admirable, I know you're Jade Noble, and we have business to discuss. I'm Ace Edwards. Johnny sent me to pick up the pictures, videos, and negatives. Also, the floppy disks if you saved them on the computer. I'll check your hard drive later. Did you bring everything?"

"Why, Mr. Edwards," she said, batting lovely blue eyes. "You know we can't do business that way. What would my friends think?"

It may have been my imagination, but I swear her eyes flashed an invitation at me. "I think they'd say you're smart and saving yourself a lot of trouble." I cranked up my best Bogart. "Save the act for the next drunk you follow into a bar. The only way you'll show a profit on Johnny is play it my way. Here's the deal. One payoff and one only. Ten thousand, and you deliver all the negatives, tapes, etc. If you double-deal me, you'll discover I have some very nasty friends."

"Is that any offer to make to a lady? Ten thousand? I don't think so. I hope this is when you make me a real offer, a very nice financial figure. Make sure it starts above fifty thou."

I grinned, admiring her chutzpah. Obviously, she didn't know my reputation. "No Jade, that's not the game. I make the rules, and here they are. You give me what I ask for, at the offered price, and I don't tell Sheriff Galoway to pick you up, and charge you with prostitution, extortion, theft, and a few other felonies that we'll work out. You are aware that the Sheriff and I are best friends, aren't you?" Okay, the last was a bit of a stretch, but we had worked together in the past.

She stood and looked me in the eye. I hadn't realized how tall she was. "Mr. Edwards, or whatever your name might be, I have never stolen anything in my life." She stopped and grinned. "Edwards, what a stupid alias. Who the hell do you expect to buy that? Shit, I've spent more nights with Smiths and Edwards than you can find in the Dallas phone book, and, like you, they were all phonies and bullshit artists." Her face hardened. "Now listen, you four-flushing sonnavabitch. You ain't getting shit until I get cash, and I mean a whole lot more than ten thousand. So how much is Johnny willing to pay? Don't bother with the fairy tale—cut straight to the bottom figure."

"Excuse me, Jade, but you probably need to sit back down and cool off. You'll scare the tourists."

"To hell with the tourists. What's the word? I've got things to do, like drop a package in the mail if you don't talk fast." Her face took on a cunning look, her eyes slanting upward in the corners like the boys when they think they have the upper hand.

I walked around the table from where she stood, taking my time. Her eyes bored into me, but I played it cool. "Sorry dear. I told you what you're going to do—turn over what you've got and walk away, far away, with ten thou. So, produce before I lose patience." I flipped my business card onto the table. "Call me when you come to your senses." With a last glare, I headed toward the Sebring.

"Not a chance, you jerk."

I looked back and saw another transformation. It was like a different woman had magically appeared. Her face was ugly with veins standing out on her forehead.

"Take your shit and shove it. Tell Johnny the price just went up. I want two hundred thousand, and he has one week to put it together. When I return to this picnic table at twelve noon next Saturday, I expect to find a brown paper bag with used bills. After I've counted it, I'll leave everything in," she spun, looking around, "in that trash can."

I followed her gaze and saw a container that looked like it hadn't been cleaned for a few days—or a few years. The flies loved it though. My attention snapped back to her.

"That's the best deal he'll get," she continued, stamping her foot. "If he doesn't deliver, one copy goes to his mother-in-law, a copy to the *Dallas Morning News*, and copies to the Dallas TV stations." She crossed her arms. "Take that message back to *Jonathan* and his mother-in-law."

I put on my best ugly face. "No deal, dearie. She already knows and won't pay a dime more. She hired me to meet you. Reconsider what I said. It's your best bet for staying out of jail."

I saw a question mark flit through her eyes before she said, "Nope. Won't work. You're bluffing. I'm not."

"Miss, you obviously don't know Ms. Evans very well. She knows how to play this game. Hell, she probably invented it, and she has about a forty-year head start on you. When she gets mad, someone else pays. In this case, you're elected." I turned again to walk away, but decided to give her one more shot. "This time, you're the loser. I hope you enjoyed that night because the sex is the biggest payoff you're gonna get unless you change your mind in a hurry."

I headed toward the car.

"Damn you, Edwards. You're not going to queer this for us."

It clicked that for the first time, she said us, but I was so busy playing my game the implication didn't sink home immediately. I wished it had because someone grabbed me from behind. A hand as big as a wheel on my car clamped over my mouth, and I found myself lifted off the ground in a rib-crushing bear hug. A grunt in my ear said, "You gonna do what she says."

He stepped off, carrying me as if I weighed nothing. A couple of quick responses popped into my mind, but a lack of oxygen kept me from voicing them. Several other thoughts flowed through like, *This must be Killer. Where the hell did he come from?* I struggled, but to no avail. I looked to where we were headed and wasn't thrilled. The trees and bushes along the back of the rest stop were thick enough to hide us from the world. I tried to bite his hand, but he had my face in such a grasp that breathing was a problem that overcame my urge to bite. If the tourists noticed, they must have thought it normal Texas entertainment.

We crossed a small gully and passed into the bushes. He took his hand away, and I managed to squeak out, "Put me down, and I'll whip your ass."

The ground rushed up and smacked me on the butt. He'd taken my advice, slamming me to the ground in the process. I rolled to my left, just in time to miss a nice western boot swinging by my ribs in a vicious kick. My tailbone screamed in pain, but I continued my scramble, hoping to gain my feet before the boot returned.

"Settle down, big boy, or I'll blow a hole in your spine that'll leave you in a wheelchair for the rest of your miserable life—if you live."

I interrupted my roll and looked toward the voice.

"Thank you, Mr. Noble. It's always nice to meet a man who follows orders."

I knew that voice and was glad I did. Kit had ridden to my rescue as we planned. She stood behind Killer with her hand in her jacket pocket. I hoped it wasn't her finger forming a point.

I rose to my knees and saw Jade begin a move so I scrambled to my feet. Since Kit had taken on Killer, I felt obligated to neutralize Jade. "Hold it right there, lady. Please don't do anything stupid that might get Killer hurt. That's one mean woman holding that gun."

Jade relaxed without saying a word. My attention returned to Killer and Kit. "Hugo, if you're smart, you'll get the hell out of here and take your slut with you. The next time I see y'all, you'd better have all the stuff you've got on Johnny. Jade knows the deal, now beat it." I concentrated on Killer, giving him my best intimidating glare. As my speech to Killer echoed through the trees, lights flashed in my head. Even as I fell, Killer spun on Kit.

* * *

The next thing I remember, my head hurt like hell, and it was raining. At least, it seemed like rain with all the splashes on my cheeks. The droplets came from a beautiful apparition above me.

"Wake up, you stupid son-of-a-bitch. If you die on me, I'll—I'll kill you. You're the worst, dumbest, stupidest—"

I managed a groan before consciousness left again.

* * *

I awoke a second time and found myself on the grass with my head in an angel's lap. That created a conundrum since I have no expectation of seeing angels after I die. My eyes continued to clear, and I realized it was Kit.

I'm not sure which felt better, the wet compress she held on my forehead or the touch of her other hand on my cheek. "Hi. Come here often?" I said in my best standup comedy voice.

"Shut up, you lout. You'd better rest while you can."

"Okay, so what happened?" I lifted my head a millimeter, and dozens of baseball players banged two-run doubles off the walls of my brain. "Ouch, think I'll rest a moment. You aren't going anywhere, are you? I am a little fuzzy though. Last I remember, we had the upper hand."

Kit explained while I danced in front of Killer in my tough guy mode, Jade slipped a sap from her purse and used it to caress the back of my head. I fingered the lump as she confessed she'd taken her eyes off Killer to watch me tumble like a wet dishrag. He took the opportunity to bash her in the mouth.

Kit's lips were not pretty, and my head felt like the 82d Airborne Division was conducting maneuvers inside—with full artillery support.

"I guess you really showed them," she said. "Now, *you're* in the driver's seat."

"Kit, do I detect a wee bit of sarcasm?"

"Who me? Your number one fan? The little woman who got clobbered by a Neanderthal while covering your ass? The little woman who waits by the hearth each night, dinner warm in the oven, waiting for her man to call, and he seldom does? You stupid son-of-a-bitch, the only reason we're not dead is because, because— Hell, I have no clue why they didn't finish the job."

"Uh, Kit, other than the fact you don't cook, is there a problem here?"

"No, there's no problem. I'm just hauling my aching face back to Dallas where I'm going to bed for a week. By then, maybe, just maybe, my lips will have returned to normal, and I might, but probably not, have forgotten I'm in love with a stupid jerk that screws up every case he touches. Does that answer your question?"

I hesitated, filtering her words through the booming noises in my head. Love? Had she used the word love? By the time I scripted a reply, she was in her Geo, pulling out of the parking area.

I stood and waved as confusion flooded through my head and heart. Love? No. Too strange a word. I must have misunderstood her. To her retreating bumper, I said, "But I always solve the case."

CHAPTER TEN

Morning came and my eyelids creaked open. Even that was too much movement. My head exploded into a black cloudburst of pain as light seeped through throbbing eyelids. Slowly, ever so slowly, my legs struggled with the sheets, attempting to untangle themselves without involving the upper body. Left-brain whispered, *Coffee. I need coffee.* Right-brain just hurt.

After enough pain to win me redemption for all my sins, I sat on the edge of the bed, both feet firmly pressed against the floor. *Aspirin. Where are the aspirin?* That prompted memories from the previous evening when I ate aspirin and tried in vain to reach Kit. Either she wasn't answering the phone or was out until the wee hours. At one a.m., my body refused to cooperate any longer, and I gently put myself to bed.

In the shower, I remembered the other call I made among the calls to Kit—Jade, several times. There was no answer, I mean no human answer. Her electronic chip invited me to leave a message so I did. As best I could remember, I'd said, "Jade, Killer, this is Ace Edwards. You won yesterday, but you can't escape me, so you may as well cave in. If you don't, I won't be responsible for the consequences."

Thirty minutes in the shower forced life into my body and put a big dent in the motel's hot water supply. I remembered the miniature coffeemaker in the room. After setting it to brew, I slipped on a pair of jeans and T-shirt and padded barefoot to the continental breakfast area. I smiled and said, "Good morning," especially to those who stared at my bare feet. After filling two cups with coffee, stirring in artificial sweetener, and grabbing two doughnuts, I returned to my room.

I flipped open my binder and made notes about yesterday's debacle. No matter what I wrote, it still read like a major screw up, and the lump on the back of my head reaffirmed it with every breath.

The room coffeemaker finished its magic allowing me to drink my coffee level up to where I could face the day. Thoughts of breakfast crowded in on top of the two doughnuts, however, I stalled hoping Jade or Kit would return my calls. Of course, that also gave Ms. Evans time to call. With her spy system, she probably knew about yesterday.

At ten, I gave up and pulled on my boots. Might as well catch breakfast before the local fast food joints switched to burgers. As I stepped through the doorway, the phone rang so I doubled back and grabbed the handset.

"Mrs. Evans wishes to speak with you."

Before I could identify the voice, another voice came on, one I preferred not to hear. "Mr. Edwards, I trust you now understand why you are the wrong person for this case. I warned you Hugo and Jade are beyond your meager talents."

"Good Morning, Mrs. Evans," I said. "It's so good to hear from you. Are you having a nice day?"

"No, my day is not progressing well, especially after hearing about your despicable performance yesterday. Even with your lady-friend from Dallas, you failed. Are you ready to drop the case? If not, should I hire a professional to assist you?"

Enough, right-brain screamed, and the left side agreed. "Mrs. Evans, I contracted with Johnny. I intend to fulfill that obligation. Now call off your spies and quit bothering me." I consciously forced myself to calm down. "Yesterday was only the first chapter in this episode. Things will be different next time."

"Perhaps, Mr. Edwards, perhaps. Next time they might kill you. I look forward to chatting with you tonight."

She hung up so I replaced the handset, my anger surging to the surface again. "Dammit—" The phone rang, and I grabbed it. "Ms. Evans."

Another voice intruded. "Edwards, yesterday was just a sample. Next time, I won't stop Killer. Get out of town before he really gets mad. You know that asshole Nichols is getting just what he deserves. He's been double-dealing his wife for years, and now, he's going to pay."

"Jade, so good to hear from you. Sorry, but I don't see you as an avenging angel. What you're doing is called blackmail, and it's not only illegal, but it's one of my favorite things to hate. So, you're in my sights, and you and your husband are going down."

"Edwards, this is your last warning—"

"By the way," I interrupted, "the El Paso police still have a bolo out on you guys. Should I call them?"

"You bastard—," she screamed as the phone clanged in my ear.

* * *

After a quick breakfast, I drove to Dallas to go through my closet in preparation for dinner with Ms. Evans and Matthew Thomas. She'd strongly said jeans and a polo shirt were unacceptable.

The boys met me at the door, displayed minimal affection, then rushed to their food dishes to show they'd made progress emptying them. As usual, my first order of business was to feed and water, then take care of the litter.

The pain still banged around inside my cranium so I took more aspirin and climbed into the shower to drown it. The hot water felt so good I stood and let it beat down on me. Also, it postponed the necessary scavenger hunt in my closet to find something that might pass Ms. Evans' scrutiny.

As I dried myself, the phone rang, and I answered with my usual, "Ace Edwards."

"Damn, I hoped to get your machine. What are doing home?"

"Kit, I'm so glad you called. Are you okay?"

"Sure, I'm fine. Of course, it takes a whole tube of lipstick to cover the swelling in my lips, but I'm okay."

Ouch. The sarcasm flowed through the phone line, abrading my face. "I'm so sorry, Kit. I didn't think you'd get hurt."

"Think, you think? That's only one of your problems. You don't think. If you did, you'd have never set up a meet in such a stupid place. All the advantages belonged to that brute and his honey."

"Okay," I countered. "Guilty as charged. But I'm still sorry you were hurt. You know I never wanted that."

"You, you—damn you, Ace Edwards. You're the most pathetic little boy-man ever." She paused. "Okay, you didn't plan it. You thought you had full control of the situation, but when that woman caved your head in, it scared the hell out of me."

Right-brain screamed, *Keep your mouth shut, this is a special moment.*

After what seemed like an hour of silence, she continued, "I didn't call to scream at you. I hoped to get your machine. I knew I'd get emotional, and I never want to do that with you again—at least, not until . . ."

Her voice trailed away leaving a warm glow in the center of my being. Words jumped to my lips, but right-brain prevailed again. I stayed quiet.

"I simply wanted to tell your machine you should call if you need help. I know it's not too smart, but call me if you need me." The little click sounded that told me she'd ended the call.

I stared at the phone with emotions racing like thoroughbreds through my body. Kit was a special woman, and I knew we could have a wonderful relationship. But I couldn't take the next obvious step, not until Terri faded farther into the background.

Reluctantly, I laid the phone down, pulled on a pair of jeans, and turned to my closet. Ms. Evans' dinner party was still on my schedule.

CHAPTER ELEVEN

I stopped in Ms. Evans' driveway, and a young man greeted me, insisting on parking my car. He looked old enough to shave so I handed him the keys. I brushed wrinkles out of my clothing, knowing it looked good. After popping the cuffs of the dress shirt out of my jacket, I straightened my tie. Ms. Evans could have no complaints about my appearance tonight.

I rang the doorbell precisely at seven, the time Ms. Evans had instructed me to appear. The butler—I'd learned his name was Marston Coker or just Coker in the vernacular of butlers—swung the door inward even before the echo of the bell died away.

"Good evening, Mr. Edwards. May I take your hat?"

The final touches to my ensemble were my Stetson and my Dan Post boots. I removed the hat and handed it to him. He handled it as before, two fingers.

"Follow me to the billiards room. You are the last to arrive."

Walking down the long hallway behind Coker, I debated whether his comment was a put down. According to my Timex, I was on time. When he opened a door on the left, I decided it wasn't worth the effort and concentrated on the room.

"Mr. Arthur Conan Edwards, private investigator from Dallas, Texas, unaccompanied," Coker announced.

Five heads swung my way, and I quickly took inventory. Ms. Evans was present, of course, wearing a royal blue gown that was simple, yet elegant. My gaze shifted to the second female. One look convinced me this must be Louise. She was a younger version of Ms. Evans. The two of them stood together, apparently chatting before Coker's announcement. She wore a pantsuit in the same color as her mother's outfit, and while it wasn't as elegant, it looked great on her. She was stunning, a gorgeous woman at the peak of her beauty. I estimated her to be in her mid to late thirties, no older than early forties, and immediately decided Johnny was an even bigger fool than I'd previously thought. If this was the woman he'd double-dealt, he deserved his fate.

My gaze drifted around the room to Johnny leaning against the mantle, a cocktail glass in his hand. In front of him was a young man who appeared to be in his early twenties. He too resembled Ms. Evans so I assumed this was Matthew Thomas. As Johnny moved toward me, I noticed the room was quiet, all conversation stopped, and all eyes were on me. Even Billy Lapscott had quit polishing the bar and looked my way.

"Evening, Ace," Johnny said as he stuck out his hand. "Hope you don't mind, but we started without you. Billy, get Mr. Edwards a Killian's."

"I anticipated his arrival," Billy said, handing me a beer. "I have a case on ice just for you, sir."

"Thank you," I said, then leaned closer to him. "I notice your grammar has improved."

He grinned, winked, and returned to the bar.

"Glad you could make it," Johnny said. "Of course, when Ms. Evans told me she invited you, I knew you'd be here. No one refuses *her* invitations."

Johnny's breath struck me full in the face. I wondered when his party began.

"Come over and meet Matthew Thomas," Johnny added. "He knows you're here to help us with a sticky problem so you don't have to be coy. Of course, I haven't told him the nature of the problem."

Johnny wore a dark blue suit with a tiny red pinstripe making me feel dowdy, and I saw that Matthew Thomas dressed similarly. Now, I don't know much about the cost of fancy clothing, but I figured I could feed and house the cats and me for three or four months on what Ms. Evans and Louise spent on their outfits. The men's suits matched them in quality, if not in price. Even Coker's and Billy's clothing put me down.

"Well, Mr. Edwards, I see your taste in clothing has improved, but not much. That tie should only be worn to the Texas State Fair, and then only during the week, and that jacket? Leather patches?"

"Good evening, Mrs. Evans," I said, ignoring her cattiness. I held up my yellow Texas roadmap tie. "You know what they say, Texas is a State of Mind. However, if you'd told me this evening was semi-formal, I'd have worn my tux." I made up my mind before leaving the motel I would set the mood for the evening, and that would be one of equals, not mistress and servant.

She raised one eyebrow and her mouth began to form words, but seemed to change direction in mid-stream. "You need not be embarrassed, Mr. Edwards. Some people are not born to dress properly. However, I did inform you that tonight would be casual. I only changed my mind this morning so your casual attire is understandable—but not those boots. Louise and I do enjoy the opportunity to dress up. At my age, there are not many such occasions." She changed gears without hesitation. "You must meet my grandson, Matthew Thomas. You will discover he inherits his brilliance from my ancestor, John Adams."

Damn, I thought as I tried to sort out whether she apologized or not, *even when I win, I lose.*

"Mr. Edwards, I am Matthew Thomas Adams-Evans-Nichols," a voice from behind my right shoulder said. "It's a pleasure to meet you. *Grand-mère* gave me a full briefing on your résumé. Your credentials are adequate. Welcome to our humble abode."

I turned to see who had rescued and insulted me simultaneously and saw that the young man had joined Ms. Evans, Johnny, and me. Johnny stood where he'd been when Ms. Evans interrupted us. He had a glazed look in his eyes as they darted between Ms. Evans and me. You know, like a cat caught between two dogs. I supposed he was unaccustomed to seeing anyone stand up to his mother-in-law, even in a minor way.

Matthew Thomas had his hand extended so I took it and gave a hearty shake with a bit of a squeeze. "Yes, I've heard of you, too. It's a pleasure to meet you. How many years before you're qualified by age to become President?" His hand was firm and countered my squeeze with one of its own.

There was a flash in his eyes very similar to what I saw in his grandmother's that first night. Then, the flash was gone, and they seemed to laugh along with his words. "Twelve, Mr. Edwards, however, I do not intend to be President until I'm at least forty. I have no illusions. Experience will benefit me when I become leader of the Free World."

That stopped me. I'm fully accustomed to playing word games with egocentric, semantic bullies, but his words weren't a game. His eyes said he believed them. I glanced at Johnny and saw him studying his glass, which somehow had become empty. Even as I looked, Billy appeared at his elbow with a refill.

I turned back to Matthew Thomas. "Interesting. How's school?"

After that, we spent the evening in what passes for social chatter, and, surprisingly enough, I enjoyed it. I learned Matthew Thomas loved himself, played tennis daily, worked out three times a week, and believed he was destined to be President.

Louise, on the other hand, did not fit either of the two descriptions I'd received, neither the frigid prude Johnny had described, nor the victimized young woman Ms. Evans had intimated. She appeared to be a woman whom, under different circumstances, I'd want to get to know.

She was beautiful with coal black hair, hazel eyes, lovely pale skin, and a figure that fit the total package. Her voice carried a soft East Texas accent that made each word sing. Talking with her was a delight, but I noticed her eyes seldom lingered on me for long. Instead, they danced around the room, alighting on her mother, Matthew Thomas, and, especially, Johnny. When they locked onto her mother, there was an initial defiance that soon faded into a look of servility. However, what really caught my attention was the mellowness that reflected when she looked at her son and her husband. From what I saw, her eyes absorbed both men the same way, loving pride and question marks.

At dinner, I sat beside Louise, across from Johnny. Ms. Evans, of course, took the end position with Louise and Matt on her left and right, respectively. As it had been previously, the dinner was excellent and consisted of foreign looking things that aren't served in the restaurants I frequent.

After dinner, we returned to the Billiards Room where Ms. Evans lambasted me for mishandling Jade and Hugo. About all I could do was acknowledge my shortcomings and attempt to change the subject. In the former, I was successful, and she was quick to agree, but in the latter, no such luck. Her last remark was a zinger. "Fail again, Mr. Edwards, and I will not be as forgiving. That is the least of your worries. Hugo may not be as forgiving either."

As she walked away, I cringed at the thought of facing an unforgiving Hugo.

"May I have a few words with you—privately—Mr. Edwards?"

I turned to find Matthew Thomas at my side.

"Maybe we could step outside," he said, glancing over his shoulder. "I do not wish to upset *Grand-mère*."

"Sure. Fresh air is good." I signaled Billy for another Killian's, then turned back to Matthew Thomas. "After you, my friend."

We left the Billiards Room and turned toward the rear of the house. We stepped through French doors onto a large verandah facing the empty countryside.

"You must see this view during the day," Matthew Thomas said. "It is quite beautiful and will be relaxing after a day on the campaign trail."

"The campaign trail?" I gulped. "Aren't you jumping the gun a little? You're still in college."

"No, *Grand-mère* is laying the groundwork for a run for office as soon as I complete my law degree next year. She has not yet told me the office. Who knows, I may be the next Dog Catcher for Van Zandt County." He chuckled, however his eyes said he would never run for such a low-level office.

"Does that mean you'll start at the county level?"

"No, I do not believe so. *Grand-mère* has friends throughout the state who owe her many favors, both financial and otherwise. She will pick the office based on what is available and the certainty of election. She says I must set the tone as a big winner in my first campaign. She really is quite brilliant, you know."

I wasn't as sure as he, but decided to ignore the commercial. "So, what do you want to talk about?"

"My father likes to believe that his *affaires d'amour* go unnoticed by *Grand-mère*. As I am sure he has told you, he does not care if Mother knows. I cannot tell you how many times she has hidden her head in shame at his philandering. However, my father has no privacy. *Grand-mère* has friends who delight in advising her of his activities."

"Whoa," I interjected. "Maybe your friends at Harvard talk funny all the time, but I make my living in Dallas. Correct me if I'm wrong. Your grandmother knows all about your father's sexual escapades and so do you. Is that it?"

"Correct."

"So, you probably know all about the latest that has resulted in a blackmail scheme?"

"Correct."

"And, you probably know I was hired by your father to bail him out?"

"Correct."

"And, just a guess, mind you, but you probably know I met with the blackmailers yesterday?"

"Correct. I also know you and a Kit Levitt, another PI from Dallas, met defeat at the hands of the Nobles. In fact, they left both of you on the ground and walked away laughing at your incompetency."

"Then you already know everything," I intruded, "so why am I out here?" My irritation grew considerably upon learning that Jade and Hugo had laughed at Kit. Me, not important, but they shouldn't have laughed at her.

"I want this situation resolved, and it must happen quietly, discreetly, and quickly. There can be no whisper of scandal—my campaign begins next year. *Grand-mère* says you rejected the obvious solution."

"That being?"

He smiled. "Do not be obtuse, Mr. Edwards. Jade and Hugo should simply *never* bother us again."

"Never is a long time. Perhaps you'd care to elaborate." I decided he should be specific about what he was intimating.

"Mr. Edwards, it is my impression that you are attempting to lead me into saying something. Perhaps you could enlighten me with what you wish to hear."

So much for my game. He obviously chose to say nothing I could quote. Excellent legal training. Politics would be a waste of his time. He had a great future as a trial lawyer. Even so, I pushed on. "I just wonder how you expect me to arrange never. An accident, maybe? What kind? Car crash? Drowning? Russian roulette?"

Another smile. "I have no idea what might happen, but they apparently live a rather risky lifestyle, and I believe they both have unsavory reputations. I would not be surprised if one of their friends hurt them. Of course, I am only speculating. Actually, I suspect they will live to ripe old ages and harass innocent citizens during all their years. You may rest assured that after I am elected to office, I shall pass laws that deal with such scofflaws. In the meantime, I cannot stand idly by and let my career be hampered. *Grand-mère* has sacrificed too much—and the world needs me too badly."

I looked for a smile, but his expression said he was serious. No wonder his parents had given him over to his grandmother to raise. His ego would intimidate any normal person.

"However," he continued, "if something should happen to them, I trust you will obtain the information that incriminates my father. Give it to me or *Grand-mère*."

"As I told your grandmother, your father hired me. When I have something to report, it will be to him. That also includes any blackmail material."

"Excellent, my good man. You do just that," he said. "Now we really should rejoin the party. I trust I have answered whatever questions you had when you invited me here." With that, he entered the house.

I mulled over his comments while right-brain reminded me the invitation had been his, not mine. That left me wondering if I'd stumbled through that famous looking glass.

* * *

I drove to the motel slowly, re-running the conversations of the evening through my mind. Several things rose to the surface: 1) Johnny became a wallflower in the presence of his mother-in-law. 2) Ms. Evans had no respect for me and probably for no one except her grandson. 3) Matthew Thomas was her clone. 4) I couldn't tell where Louise fit into this mess. 5) I seemed to be the only person in the group who thought it wrong for Jade and Killer to meet an untimely ending. 6) Billy knew the right temperature to serve Killian's.

CHAPTER TWELVE

The phone rang awakening me from a peaceful sleep. I checked the clock radio and read the dial—seven o'clock. The phone rang again eliciting a curse.

"Hello, Ace Edwards here," I mumbled.

"Ace, she called."

"Huh, who called? Who is this?"

"Johnny. She called. Jade called. She wants to meet."

Although his words had slapped much of the sleep from my head, I still said, "Call me back in thirty minutes. A shower is more important right now." I wasn't really drowsy anymore, but Johnny slid a notch lower after I met Louise.

After ten minutes under the hot water, I was adjusting my perspective over a cup of coffee when Johnny called again.

"Okay, give me the details," I said in a more sociable voice.

I heard him take a breath. "Jade called. She wants to meet."

"Good, now we're getting there. What else?"

"She wants ten thousand as a first payment."

"Okay, that's a good opening," I said, forcing excitement from my voice.

"But Ace, I don't have ten thousand unless I pull it from the account I set up for you."

That got my attention. Even though I knew Ms. Evans probably controlled that account, I wasn't inclined to let Johnny dip into it for Jade. "Give me a moment." It was time to be serious. "Can you scrape up a thousand?"

"Yeah, I can do that, but she said ten."

"I heard you, but she'll take what she can get. What's the big deal now? Ms. Evans probably knows more about your night with Jade than you remember."

"Yeah, you told me. But we still have to keep it out of the papers. We must consider Matthew Thomas' career."

Now that was something we agreed on. No one in the Evans family seemed to think of anything else.

"When and where does Jade want to meet?"

A small chuckle wrapped around his next words. "The same place you met her—the rest stop alongside Interstate 20."

"I remember where it is. When?"

"Same time—high noon."

That made me wonder how much imagination Jade had. Of course, since they were successful before, they probably figured they could do it again. Not this time though. She wouldn't get a chance to sucker punch me nor would I allow her displayed assets to divert my attention. I'd stay alert—like a cougar on the prowl. No more Killer sneaking up on me.

"I don't think she likes you," Johnny said. "She said some pretty nasty things and warned me not to call you." He hesitated. "I guess I have to meet her, don't I?"

"We'll both be there. This time it'll be different. You'll be the staked lamb drawing the lion into the trap. I'll be the mighty white hunter waiting for the kill." I allowed myself a chuckle.

"That's a terrible analogy, Ace. Don't you have anything better? Go without me. That's why I hired you."

"No, Johnny. You hired me to get you out of this mess. That, I'll do. But you have to play, too. Now shut up a moment."

I pulled out a fresh piece of paper. Doodling and writing key words sometimes helps me pull a plan together. After a couple of moments in which I thought, doodled and listened to Johnny breathe, I gave him instructions.

"So, where are you going to be?" he said. "What will you do?"

"Based on how you resisted her charms the last time you two met, it's best for my health that you don't know. Just know I'll cover your ass. Now, get busy. You have a lot to do by noon."

I hung up the phone and checked my watch. Eight-fifteen. Grabbing the handset, I punched in Kit's number.

A sleepy voice answered, "Hello."

"Kit, it's Ace. I need your help."

"It's too early. I was out half the night following Barnes around. She didn't score until one o'clock, then they didn't leave the bar until two. By the time I put them to bed, got home, and put myself to bed it was three-thirty. So, what's so important you'd call this early?"

"Ouch," I said, my conscience shouting at me. "Sorry, but I couldn't wait. I need you this morning. Can you get here by ten-thirty?"

"I suppose so if I skip my manicure. But why? What's going down?"

I quickly told her what I needed, then hung up to work on my preparations.

* * *

Kit let me out at eleven-fifteen, and I ducked into the woods alongside Interstate 20. When I was about ten feet in, I stopped and checked behind me. Kit was supposed to return to Dallas. But who knows what a woman will do?

She dropped me about a half-mile from the rest stop, and I struck out in that direction. A few minutes later, I had stretched out on the ground watching the meeting place. Killer's bulk gave him enough of an advantage without adding surprise to it. I was determined to know his whereabouts before making my move.

I carefully studied the area, hoping no one decided to take a quiet walk in the woods, or to walk their dog this way. There was a buzzing around my ear, and I swatted as quietly as I could. That made me wonder about ants, especially fire ants. The last thing I wanted was a swarm of those nasty buggers coming after me.

At eleven forty-five, Jade's car pulled in. She got out and perched on the hood, same as our first meeting. No Killer. Her outfit was also identical, short shorts with the emphasis on short and a T-shirt that didn't protect her belly button. From where I lay, I couldn't tell if it was as sheer as the one she wore previously.

At five before twelve, she jumped down and went through her stretching routine. Even from my distance, there was no doubt she was braless. Pirouetting with her arms high over her head, she looked straight at me, or so it seemed. I hunkered down, then realized her eyes stared to my left.

Slowly, I turned in that direction and the noise of someone moving through the brush rewarded me. I held my breath. A form took shape about fifteen yards away—a very large form.

Killer. He stopped and casually leaned against a tree. He must have trusted Jade to distract anyone in the area. Looking back toward her, I had to agree with him. She had bent over and grabbed her ankles pointing her beautiful derriere in the air. That position and the shorts left few secrets.

Scanning the area, I saw every man within view and most of the women, stared at her. The women's expressions were quite different from the men's—Venus and Mars, but this time the planets were reversed.

At that moment, Johnny entered the scene in a Mercedes convertible. Several of the women shifted their gaze toward him. None of the men's heads turned.

He parked and called out, "Jade, hope I'm not late. Sorry it took me so long to get our lunch together." He held up a metal lunch box, the old fashioned type that are practically indestructible.

Jade released her ankles and stood with hands on hips. A frown furrowed her brow.

Johnny continued in a loud voice. "Come on over and let's have lunch." He walked to the designated picnic table, put the lunch box on the table, and sat facing me.

So far, so good. Johnny had followed instructions perfectly.

Jade glared at him, then glanced toward Killer, followed by a brisk walk to the table. She stopped with her back to me, clearly saying something in an agitated way, her hands flailing the air. Johnny stood and reached out his hand. She promptly slapped it.

I let out a quiet sigh of relief. Now if Killer would just follow my script.

Johnny pushed the lunch box across the table. Jade took it and turned it around. I heard an explosion, "You sonnavabitch." Her voice dropped, but her jaw continued working.

I knew she stared at a padlock I'd told Johnny to put on the latch. She picked up the box and turned in my direction. "Killer, get in here and see what this idiot has done," she yelled toward the woods.

Some of the tourists stared at her, but most continued about their business. They probably thought all Texans yell at trees.

I scooted down a little deeper and waited, hoping Killer would join her. My wait was brief. Killer thrashed about and moved from the woods. When he reached the table, Jade handed him the lunch box. He turned it in his hands, then gripped the lock and ripped it off.

I hadn't expected that. I wanted them to argue with Johnny about the key allowing me time to make my move. He didn't open the lid, but placed it on the table. He dropped on the bench beside Jade.

Jade pulled the box to her and lifted the lid. That was my cue to move. I stood, brushed off leaves and dirt and started toward the bench quickly and quietly. I depended on their curiosity to protect me as I closed from behind.

Jade peered into the lunch box, and I was close enough to hear, "Are you sure there's ten thousand in here?"

I took two more quick steps and answered for Johnny, "No, there's only one thousand. Say thank you."

Jade and Killer turned as one. Killer began to rise. I shoved the barrel of my Baretta so it formed a point in my jacket pocket. "Try me, Killer, just try me."

He settled onto the bench, but didn't relax. His eyes tracked me as I walked around the table and stood to Johnny's right. My fist clenched the Beretta, pointing it at Killer's chest. However, I didn't repeat my earlier mistake and ignore Jade. I waved it toward her just so she'd know I remembered. The looks they gave me clearly said I would not receive a Christmas card.

"Okay bastard, what do you want?" Jade asked. Her tone of voice echoed the look she gave me. "I told him ten thousand, and I want it. All of it. Today."

"Nope, you've got all you're getting until we see negatives and video tapes."

Her mouth opened, but I cut her off. "Not only that, but there are certain documents and pictures involved."

"What? You want what?" she demanded, and again Killer began to rise.

"Killer, don't disappoint me. Try something so I can blow your ass away. With your track record, everybody in Texas will believe me when I say self-defense."

Killer settled again, but continued to shred me with his eyes.

"Here's the deal," I said. "You'll sign a full confession to your blackmail scheme. Only, it will identify me as your mark, not Johnny. He will serve as a witness to your signatures, just as I will. Oh, he's also a notary so it'll be properly notarized." The last part was a lie, but I figured neither of them would know. "You'll also sign a confession to the theft of the BMW in El Paso and the robbery you two pulled. In other words, if I ever see you again, I'll have enough to put you away for a few years. Plus, if we reach that point, the police will probably file a few more charges against you."

I raised one foot onto the bench and leaned forward in a relaxed position, keeping the pistol pointed across the table. "That's my deal. You have no choice, but to take it."

Jade laughed. "You're crazy, you know that?" Her head swung toward Johnny. "Where'd you find this nuthouse reject? He's been reading too many Cat-in-the-Hat stories. Either you produce the ten grand now or I'm going straight to your mother-in-law."

"Ace," Johnny said nervously, twisting toward me.

I patted him on the shoulder with my left hand while my right squeezed the Beretta a little tighter. "It's okay, she's only blowing smoke."

"Blowing smoke? You sonnavabitch, I'm headed straight to Ms. Evans' place. You damn sure won't shoot me in the back." She started to rise.

"Oh, I don't think you'll have to go that far. Just look around."

Jade's head made a circuit of the parking area, "What are you talking about?"

"I tried to explain this to you before, before your gorilla got nasty. Ms. Evans knows more about Johnny than you do. That includes the night he spent with you. You see, she's not a very trusting soul so she has him followed. While you and he played hide the weenie and other assorted games, her man camped outside your place. Hell. I bet she has better quality pictures than you do."

"Shit. Who do you expect to believe that crap?"

"Okay, look around again—slowly. See that red Ford SUV about ten cars down. There's a man behind the wheel, kinda scrunched down with a hat pulled low over his eyes."

Her head swiveled in that direction.

"Now, look the other way. There's a black Caddy, same scenario. Somebody behind the wheel, sitting low. Also, while we've been here a blue Toyota pick-up has come through the parking area twice."

She looked toward the Caddy, then back to me. "This is crazy. What you said don't prove a thing. You probably planted them."

"Nope, they're not mine. But you don't have to believe me. You can talk to Ms. Evans. But remember, she's a well-respected matriarch in Van Zandt County and knows the sheriff well. She also knows as much, maybe more, about your background as I do. You won't make it halfway down the hall before the sheriff has you in handcuffs."

She swelled, her mouth started to work, then she wilted while Killer continued to glare. I hoped he'd kept up with the conversation and believed me, too. But that might be asking too much of his brainpower.

"Pictures, you said something about pictures," Jade murmured.

"Oh thanks. How could I forget? We'll take several pictures of you singly and together holding the license plate on the Chevy you're driving, also pictures showing the car's serial number with you two. I know the plate came from the BMW you stole, and you probably got the Chevy the same way."

"You're out of your frigging mind, Edwards. Nobody will buy that crap. Even if we cooperate." Jade's eyes gave her away. They reflected defeat.

"Ah Jade, dear Jade," I said. "Look at Killer. He'll do fine in prison. He's big and mean enough to take care of himself. But you, you're small, a beautiful and desirable woman. You'll be somebody's piece of meat, and when she's through with you, you'll get passed around until you're all worn out. Also, it's rumored that certain male guards have been known to take advantage of their situation. By the time you get out of prison, you'll not only be an old hag, but you'll be burned out, wrinkled as a prune. No man will ever want you again. But that won't matter so much. You'll think sex is dirty, hurtful, and only for the satisfaction of another. For all practical purposes, your life will be finished."

That did it. Her neck sagged and the fire went out of her eyes. When she looked at me again, there was a feeble attempt at defiance. "We'll, we'll talk it over and let you know."

"Okay, talk it over, but in the meantime, sign this." I handed her a blank sheet of paper, blank except for their typed names and signature lines at the bottom. Kit had prepared it for me before she left Dallas.

"What the hell are you trying to pull?" she said, surliness slipping back into her voice.

"Nothing much. Just sign, and I'll fill in the content later. Don't worry, it'll be something you're guilty of."

"Suppose we refuse?"

"I think you know the answer. I'll call Sheriff Galoway and hold you until he gets here. There's still a warrant out for you in El Paso. Need I say more?"

"Money, we'll need more money to get out of town. How about fifty grand? We give you everything you want, then we're history?"

I looked at Johnny who was sitting with a glazed look on his face. His eyes kept cycling from Killer to Jade to me, then back around the circle. "Whaddaya say, Johnny? How about five grand, and they're gone forever?" I wanted him to feel some pain since it was his philandering that had created this situation.

"Five grand," he gulped. "I suppose I can come up with that."

"Good. It's a done deal." I turned my full attention back to Jade and Killer just in time to thwart another move by Killer. "You heard him. Five is as high as he'll go. Take it or leave it."

"We'll take it," Jade said. "When and where?"

"Same time, same station, three days from today," I said. That'll give you time to make your travel plans. I'll call if Johnny gets the money earlier. In the meantime, you get all the stuff together for delivery. I'll have the documents ready for signatures. We'll also take pictures. Now, sign the blank paper."

They did.

CHAPTER THIRTEEN

"You must have been born under a lucky star," Kit said. "That's the most hare-brained scheme I've ever heard, and you're telling me they bought it?"

"Yep, the whole *brilliant* plan."

It was seven in the evening, and I relaxed with a Killian's while explaining the day's events to Kit in Dallas. "Actually, I should say Jade bought it. I suspect Killer does whatever she says. He's like a pit bull. Vicious to others, but loyal to his mistress."

"Yeah, and you won't get off so easy if he gets his hands on you again. He'll rip your lungs out. Have you switched motels?"

I sat up so abruptly I spilled my precious Killian's. "Ouch, I hadn't thought of that. The solution to their problem is to take me out, isn't it?"

"Of course it is, you idiot. Damn, who does your thinking when I'm not around? Now, get out of there—fast. Check out and tell the desk clerk you're headed for El Paso, Los Angeles, or even New York City."

"No, can't do that. If they think I left the area, they'll go straight back to Johnny, and he'll fold like a cheap shirt. But I will check out and leave address unknown."

"Good. Now do it. Call me when you're re-located." Kit hung up, mumbling some unintelligible sounds.

I immediately packed—I use the term loosely—and headed for the motel office. When I gave the young man my name and announced my checkout, he said, "Mr. Edwards? If you leave now, you'll miss your friend."

"What are you talking about?"

"While you were on the phone, a call came in. When I told the man the line was busy, he said he'd come right over."

"Just check me out." My knees attempted to cha-cha their way around the room without consulting the rest of my body. The caller could have only been one of two men. I didn't think Johnny made night calls.

On the way to another motel along Interstate 20, I pulled over to the side of the road and dialed Jade's number on my cell phone. It did its mandatory four rings, then Jade's voice on a microchip kicked in.

My knees took my feet to the dance floor again—this time in an up-tempo tap number. "Jade. Ace Edwards here. Just want to remind you of our deal. Don't screw this up. It could cost you more than money." *That ought to do it. That'll remind her of the jail sentence hanging over her head.*

I hung up wondering where they were, hoping I didn't know, and drove to the new motel. After checking in, I called my old place. "Hi, this is Ace Edwards. Did my friend show up?"

"No sir. Guess he changed his mind."

That left me feeling better—and worse. Why hadn't the caller come, or had he, and found me gone? If he hadn't shown, why not? I knew Jade and Killer weren't home, or didn't answer the phone. But that could mean any of a hundred things. Probably, they were just out spending the thou they'd gotten from Johnny. Or, maybe they were looking for a new mark, or maybe they'd skipped town, or maybe— I gave up on the maybes.

I gave Kit my new location, then crawled into bed. Things had come together nicely. I should be back in Dallas by the weekend with everything locked up. I fell asleep thinking about where I'd take Kit for dinner—if she'd go.

* * *

My day started like so many recently—a phone making its grating noise. I rolled toward it wondering who'd discovered my new lair. The list was short. It had to be Kit, although it was too early for her to call unless there was an emergency. Could be Ms.

Evans who undoubtedly knew exactly where I camped. I hello'd the handset.

"Ace, it's Bob Galoway. How're you doing?"

"Fine," I stuttered in surprise. Bob's the sheriff of Van Zandt County. We worked together during the earlier case I handled there. "How'd you know I was here?"

"It's my job to know who's coming and going in the county— especially the famous ones."

I laughed. "So? I repeat my question."

"Chip told me you had a case in Grand Saline. Said your old buddy, Jake, told him."

Here we go again, I thought. *My buddy Jake, my own private PR firm.* "Bob it's good to hear from you, but I repeat my question, how'd you know how to reach me? I just arrived last night."

"Like I said, it's my job to know who's in my county—and where they are."

"Okay. I probably don't want to know any more on that subject, but I suspect this isn't a social call. What's up? Need some help?"

"Yeah, kinda. Can we meet for lunch? I need to talk to you."

"Sure, love to, but I've got a better idea. I haven't had breakfast yet. Why don't I meet you in—oh, say an hour at that nice little restaurant on South Buffalo in Canton."

"You must mean Maizie's. It's a date. I just realized how early it is. I probably woke you, didn't I? Sorry, but I lost track of the time. I've been up most of the night. Make it an hour and a half. Still have a couple of things to check here."

I set the handset down and stared at the phone. Right-brain screamed that something wasn't right while left-brain encouraged me to take a shower.

I climbed under the hot water rerunning every word of our conversation, but could find no hidden meaning. Surely, he hadn't gotten word of the blackmail scheme or he'd be looking for Jade and Killer, not setting up a breakfast date with me.

After dressing, I still had forty-five minutes so I gave Jade another call. My biggest worry was she'd find wriggle room and come back with a new hook. The phone rang three times, and I prepared to hang up if the next ring produced her recording. As it ended, I heard, "Hello."

I hesitated, expecting to hear more, but the silence that followed convinced me it was a real person. "Ah, hello. May I speak with Jade?"

"She's not here right now. Who is this?"

The voice wasn't familiar, but I continued, "Is this Killer?"

"No, he's not available either. Who is this?"

Right-brain protested that something was strange. This time, I listened. "Uh, it's not important. I'll call back later."

As I replaced the handset, I heard, "Who is this? Answer me, who—"

A ripple ran up my spine. Something definitely was not right.

* * *

I walked into Maizie's at eight-thirty on the nose, exactly an hour and one-half after Bob and I spoke. Promptness is one of my virtues, especially when I'm hungry. Passing through the doorway, I scanned the small dining room. Bob sat at a table against the back wall.

I started toward him, but was taken aback by two guys sitting at the front of the restaurant, near the entrance—Dub Jones and Bull Gardner, two of Bob's deputies. As my left-brain led me toward Bob, my right-brain asked, *Why aren't the three of them sitting together?*

I detoured and said, "Dub, Bull, how're you doing?"

They looked up, uncomfortable expressions on their faces. Dub replied, "Great, Ace, just great. Uh, Bob's waiting for you."

Right-brain screamed that this peach had a worm in it, but left-brain led me past their table to the rear.

Bob stood as I walked up. "Ace, good to see you again. Your coffee should be right here. I didn't order breakfast yet, figured I'd wait for you. Last time I saw you tear into breakfast, it was Annie's cooking, and you ate like you hadn't seen food for a while."

He referred to Chip Jamison's cook, housekeeper, and all around nursemaid. Anything she prepared had a special taste. That last meal at her table had been something special, but it also brought back an unpleasant memory—my breakup with Wanda, Chip's lovely sister.

"Good to see you, too," I replied, pulling out a chair and dropping onto it. "Let's eat before we talk business. I'm famished." Actually, I wasn't quite that hungry. But a moment to study Bob was in order. Why had he set this meeting? "What's good?"

"Eggs, pancakes, bacon, and grits," Bob replied, chuckling. "What else is there?"

"Sounds good, let's do it."

The waitress, her nametag read Barb, delivered a country breakfast that would do Texas proud—huge portions. Hard to get food like that in Dallas, or any other city.

"Okay," I said, finishing the last of my pancakes, "what's up, why'd you call?"

"Hugo and Jade Noble. You know them, right?"

My antenna, which was already up, quivered as signals slammed into it. "Noble, hmmmm. What makes you think I know them?"

"Because they're dead."

He stared.

I stared.

His mouth was closed.

Mine hung open.

"Dead?" I paused, struggling with what he said. "When, how?"

"Last night. Execution style. Someone shot both in the back of the head, just like the big boys. A couple of kids out necking found them."

I digested that for a moment. This was too weird—dead, executed. "Where?"

"Clark's Ferry." He took a sip of coffee. "Suppose you tell me about your connection with them. Why are you here? What're you doing? Who for?"

I leaned back in my chair, my brain spinning, wondering how to answer his questions. This was one of those times I envied smokers. A smoker could have fiddled with a cigarette. You know, shaking it out of the pack, tamping it down, lighting it, blowing smoke at the ceiling. All those things you see in the old movies. It would have provided valid stall time. But as a non-smoker, all I could do was sip my coffee.

"What makes you think I have a connection with them? In fact, what makes you think I know them?"

Bob's laughter answered my questions even before his words came out. "Don't try to bullshit me, Ace. We both know you're involved up to your ass. Telephone answering devices are wonderful inventions, don't you think? Those little electronic chips store all that's been said to them."

That definitely answered my question. I struggled to remember what I'd said last night even as the mystery of the morning was solved. I now knew who had answered Jade's phone. A deputy.

Bob picked up a pad that lay on the table, flipped it open and read, "Jade. Ace Edwards here. Just want to remind you of our deal. Don't screw this up. It could cost you more than money." He lay the pad down. "Interesting message." He tapped his fingers on the table. "Don't make this more difficult than it has to be."

"I'm afraid you have an advantage on me," I replied, desperately looking for a way around the phone message. "You think I left a message on her machine." Suddenly I had a brainstorm. "What makes you think it was me? Might have been someone using my name."

Bob shook his head. "Are you saying it wasn't you?" he asked, a small smile licking at the corners of his mouth. "You want me to run a voice print on you and the tape? That lack of cooperation might make me unhappy, maybe even suspicious." The smile had disappeared, and his eyes had taken on a hard look. The hand holding his coffee cup was white knuckled.

"Easy, Bob. I simply asked a question."

"Yeah, I know. A smart-assed city question to get out of answering mine."

When I worked with Bob previously, he proved he was a hard-nosed cop and a straight shooter. But he could get nasty if he didn't get cooperation. In spite of that, I had to try. "You know I can't talk about the case I'm working—not what, and certainly not who."

His face got uglier.

I grinned. "You know, doctors, lawyers, and PIs—we all take confidentiality oaths." Along with my integrity, I figured Ms. Evans would rip my legs off if I said anything that caused Johnny's behavior to go public.

"Crap. Don't play games with me or I'll run your ass in. The cooler will make you a little less confidential. This is my damn county, and you *will* cooperate."

I didn't like the emphasis he placed on *will* so I slowly removed my billfold, pulled out a twenty, and lay it on the table. "I'll be leaving now. That should cover the bill. It was a pleasure having breakfast with you."

As I stood, he nodded. A hand clamped hard on my shoulder. Turning, I saw Dub and Bull standing directly behind me. Bull's big hand gripped me. I shifted my look to Dub and saw his hand hovering near his police revolver. I should have listened to right-brain when it warned me. All it said now was I was hip deep in pig stuff unless I defused this situation quickly.

Gently, I reached up and took Bull's hand off my shoulder, surprised that he allowed it. "I'd appreciate it if you'd put that paw away, Bull. It's probably registered as a lethal weapon." That drew a grin from Bull, but he didn't relax, just flexed his fingers.

"Okay, Bob, I'll give you what I can. But you've got to understand there are certain rules I won't break. If I do, I may as well go out of business. My credibility will disappear. Clients will run from me. You ask, I'll answer if I can. Fair enough?"

"For now," Bob growled. "But if you get cute, you'll pay. Understand?"

"Yeah. Ask away."

"Are you still carrying that Beretta? Do you have it with you? Is it legal?"

Strange questions. Not what I expected. "Yeah, I still have it," I replied, tentatively, "and yes, I have a license for it. Right now, it's in my motel room." I switched on a grin. "You might remember I don't really enjoy lugging it around."

"I want it."

"For what?"

Bob leaned forward. "To run through the state lab in case the doc says a nine mil killed the Nobles. The wounds are such a mess, we might never know what size round it was. I'll test every weapon I can lay my hands on that could have been involved. Yours is first." He sat his coffee mug down with a bang, "Dammit, this is Van Zandt, not Dallas."

"Would you like some more coffee, Sheriff?" a meek voice asked. I looked up and saw the waitress approaching the table with a pot of coffee.

"Huh? Oh, thanks, Barb. Sorry about banging the mug, but this tourist is not making me happy," Bob replied, grinning. "Bring us a check, please. He's paying. Here's a twenty," he added, handing her my money.

She refilled his cup, ignored mine, and walked away after giving me a blistering glare.

While she poured, and he sugared and stirred, the seriousness of the situation caught up with me. Bob really thought I might have something to do with the murders.

"It was a blackmail scheme," I said. "The Nobles were trying to shake down my client. We worked out a deal, and I called to remind them not to double-cross me. That's all it was—blackmail. I had nothing to do with their deaths."

"Who was your client? Maybe he knows more than you do."

"Sorry, but that's something I won't tell you. I'll talk to my client, and if that person gives me permission, I'll get back to you."

Bob scowled. "I'll ride with you to the motel to pick up your gun." He took a sip from his fresh cup of coffee. "Soon's Barb brings your change."

I stared at my empty cup. "All right, but I need to borrow a piece. It's not safe in this county."

Bob ignored my humor. "While we're riding you can tell me more about this case you're working and where you were last night."

CHAPTER FOURTEEN

I parked in front of my motel room, glancing at Bob as the car came to a stop. He'd quit asking questions about halfway from Canton and now sat quietly, a frustrated look on his face.

"Here we are," I said. "No place like home."

"Yeah," he grunted. "Let's get the gun."

A Do Not Disturb sign hung on the outside knob of my door. When I inserted my key, the door swung open. I stared in. Bob did the same. In today's economy, it's tough for motels to hire competent maids, but what I saw went far beyond incompetency. The mattress and bed coverings were off the bed, the drawers in the nightstands and bureau were out, chairs were upside down, and my clothing decorated the place.

Bob elbowed me aside and stepped in, gun in hand. He quickly checked the bathroom, then holstered his pistol. "I guess you didn't ask for early maid service?" he said, grinning.

I stood in the doorway scanning the area, looking for anything appearing out of place, other than everything. Maybe my visitor had dropped something. Nope, nothing I could see.

"I don't suppose you left things this way," Bob said. "Don't come in until I get a team in here to dust for fingerprints. Then we'll check to see if anything is missing." He looked around. "Where's the gun?"

"In my overnight bag, the one upside down on the mattress."

"Uh-huh. So you say. Wanna bet it's not there now?" Using his handkerchief, he carefully looked under the bag. "Nope. No pistol."

He walked to the doorway, knelt, and examined the area around the lock.

"No jimmy marks," I said. "I looked while you were John Wayneing the bathroom."

"Uh-huh. Maybe we should step outside. Dub might be in the parking lot."

Sure enough, he was. Watching Bob and him whisper while surreptitiously glancing in my direction caused me to think of Batman and Robin. With those two plotting, the bad guys had better watch out. They'd be caught before the next commercial break. Of course, I wasn't exactly sure where Bull, Bob's second deputy, fit into that scenario. He didn't fit the build of Alfred Pennyworth, Bruce Wayne's erstwhile butler, but he was doing his part—keeping a close eye on me as Bob had instructed.

Bob's fingerprint man showed and began his routine while Dub and Bull kept the curious back. Bob and I walked to a nearby restaurant for a cup of coffee.

"Ace, I'm bothered by a couple of things," Bob said after we'd settled into a booth. "What time did you leave to meet me this morning?"

When I looked at him, he appeared serious. My stomach flipped. "About eight, maybe ten after. Why?"

"Uh-huh." He concentrated on stirring his coffee. "What time did we get back to the motel, about ten wasn't it?"

"Yeah," I said.

Left-brain sounded off. *He can't be thinking what I'm thinking he's thinking.*

Right-brain responded, *Oh yes, he can be thinking what you're thinking he's thinking.*

The rest of me just wished they'd both shut up. "Bob, where are you headed with this?"

"The ransacking of your room bothers me, Ace. If you left at eight, and we were back at ten, it means someone went through there during those two hours. In broad daylight, while the maids and custodial staff moved around. Doesn't that seem a bit strange to you?"

"Sure, but—"

"And the Do Not Disturb sign on your door. Why? To keep the maid out so we would discover the mess?"

"Yeah, but—"

"Gotta be one gutsy burglar to do something like that, don't you think?"

"Okay, Bob. Lay it on the table."

"Let me just say if I didn't know you, I'd think this was a strange set of circumstances. Roll with me a minute. There are two bodies, each shot through the head. When we search their place, we hear a telephone message containing a threat. I contact the guy who made the call and tell him I want to chat with him. We talk. He has no alibi and is uncooperative. He takes me to his motel to pick up a weapon he has a permit to carry, but is not carrying, and we find his place tossed." Bob sipped his coffee, but his eyes never left my face. "Now, Ace, here's the real tire-shredder. The alleged search had to take place in a two-hour window in broad daylight. The gun is missing." He fiddled with his spoon, then lay it on the table with a tap. "Would you buy a story like that?"

Told you so, right-brain said.

Shut up, left-brain replied.

I was too busy staring at Bob to pay much attention to their banter. He'd painted a picture I couldn't disagree with—on the surface. I searched for something to say, something that would assuage Bob's suspicions.

"Well? What do you say?" Bob asked.

I grinned. "You have a logical mind. Bet you'd make a good cop." I killed the grin. "This time, though, you're out in left field— way out." I let a bit of my frustration show. "And, I'm getting a bit irritated at your insinuations."

"Tough. Real tough." He shrugged. "Who knows? Country cops might even solve this case." He sipped his coffee, then let out a sigh. "Look, this is difficult. We've worked together, and I don't think you'd do something like this. But I'm a cop, and my gut says follow the leads. Before you leave Van Zandt County, you'd better check in with me. I might have other plans for you." He stood, took out his wallet and removed a five-dollar bill. "Pay the lady for the coffee and give her what's left as a tip." He walked out.

Damn. I knew I was in trouble. Cops never pay for their coffee.

* * *

While Bob pulled away in his clearly marked Sheriff's car, I worried. His case summary left no doubt things had taken a definite turn for the worse—my worse.

Bull and Dub were busy with the break-in. Dub had rounded up the maids and other service personnel while Bull went door-to-door. He didn't seem to be finding anyone so I opted to watch over Dub's shoulder.

I walked up behind him in time to hear him say something in Spanish. So much for that idea. My Spanish was as bad as my Swahili, and I speak no Swahili. After a moment of listening to Dub ask questions in Spanish and get only *no, señor* for an answer, I walked away. Maybe Bull's luck was better.

Wrong. He still banged doors with no response. This was probably a waste of everyone's time. Whoever trashed my room was too good to have been seen, or had enough money or muscle to insure silence. There were things I needed to do, and do quickly. Any cut-rate cop knows the older a crime, the tougher it is to solve. While Bob and his boys might find the Nobles' killer, I knew I'd better not sit around and wait, or my waiting area might be confined to a hospitality suite in the Texas state penitentiary.

I ducked under the yellow crime scene tape strung across the door to my room. Bob's print man industriously spread dust around. He said he'd finish in a couple of hours.

"Have you found my Beretta?" I asked.

"Nope, but the dust bunnies under the bed are collectibles."

No place to go, but my car. I dropped the top, sat in the front passenger seat and pulled out my notebook. *Damn. Could that be what they were after?* My case notes were in the room. My last meeting with Jade and Killer had completed the small binder I carried. The one I now held was blank. I'd picked it up before meeting Bob. A trip back to my room confirmed my worst fear. The notebook was not there.

Damn, damn, double damn. This was the screwiest case I'd ever handled. Finally, I controlled myself and made a list: 1) Call Kit. 2) Call Tom Roberts. 3) Call Ms. Evans. 4) Call Johnny.

My call to Kit went quickly if not smoothly. I asked for help. She commiserated with me, chewed my butt, and commented on my ability to walk and chew gum at the same time. Then she promised to help twenty-four hours a day if I needed it.

The call to Tom was almost a repeat of the one to Kit. Since I've known him longer, he felt free to be more descriptive of my ignorance, my lack of professionalism, and suggested in no uncertain terms I find a new line of work—if I survived. However, in the end, he also promised to help. It's great to have friends who know you so well.

The third call was the most uncomfortable. After the customary delay and one-upmanship, she was on the line.

"Ms. Evans, this is Ace Edwards. I—"

"Mr. Edwards. I have explained to you previously that I prefer Mrs. Evans. Kindly use it or I shall find it necessary to terminate this conversation."

Ouch. I felt like I'd been bitten by a fire ant. She was in a feisty mood.

"Excuse me, Mrs. Evans, but once you've heard my message, you'll understand my breech of etiquette."

"Undoubtedly, you are calling about the much deserved demise of the Nobles. I am surprised you took this route, but I applaud its effectiveness."

"Excuse me?"

"Frankly, I never expected you to have the courage, how did you say it, to take them out. I shall insure that Jonathan sends you a check for services rendered."

That told me three things right away. First was, as usual, she knew more about my life than I did, and second, she knew as much about what happened in Van Zandt as Sheriff Galoway. The third was the shocker though. She assumed I'd killed Hugo and Jade.

"You're right on only one count. I am calling about the murders. I had nothing to do with them. I'd like to come by and talk to you. Also with Johnny, Louise, and Matthew Thomas."

"I shall not speak for Jonathan. He disobeyed me when he hired you. However, I assure you that Louise and I have nothing to discuss with you. Matthew Thomas has nothing to say to you either. Now this conversation is at its end."

"How can you be so sure they don't want to talk to me?" I said quickly before she could hang up.

She sighed. "Not that it is any of your business, but we discussed it at breakfast, and they told me. You should be pleased to know they approve of your resolution."

I blurted, "Mrs. Evans, you can talk to me now or the Sheriff later. Your choice."

"My dear young man. If Robert Galoway should happen to come by, I shall, of course, speak with him. Especially since I was the largest contributor to his campaign fund. I also gave him considerable public support during the last election. I suggest you leave the area before he puts it all together. He is a very good sheriff, you know?"

"This is absurd," I said. "Again, I'm telling you I had nothing to do with their murders. But someone around here did, and your family—"

"Mr. Edwards. The Evans family is above such Machiavellian activities. That is why we employ persons such as you. Now, I have better things to do. If it will make you feel better, I will not tell how cocky you were about removing them as a threat to my family."

"What? Cocky?"

"Surely, you remember how you assured me they posed no threat to the Evans name. Now, unless you have something more important than this incident, please do not call again."

The phone clicked in my ear, but it didn't matter. I was speechless anyway. It was hard to believe I'd not only been dismissed with a wave of her fingers, but set up for a frame. This lady played rough, rougher than I'd expected, and I already had high expectations.

The conversation with Ms. Evans sent me back to my scratch pad. As accurately as I could, I recorded the exact words we'd exchanged. I suspected I might need them later.

After my exercise in shorthand, I flipped back to the first page and stared at items one, two, and three. My eyes lingered on number three. Since Ms. Evans was so willing to declare me guilty, did that mean she had a part in the murders? I preferred to believe her innocent, but until the killer or killers were found, I couldn't rule out anyone.

I flipped to a new page and headed it: Possibilities and Motives. Down the left side of the page, I listed Ms. Evans, Johnny, Louise, Matthew Thomas. I finished the list with double question marks. Those were for all the people I didn't know who might have good reason to kill Jade and Hugo. After all, they hadn't exactly led lives that elicited love and understanding.

For motives, I didn't do as well. Only Johnny had a clear motive, and I took care of that before the Nobles were murdered. The others? Certainly no motive that would justify murder. After all, this was Texas and most families have at least one scandal in the back of the closet.

Item two on page one seemed to be my best bet to start the process of winnowing out suspects. I called Tom Roberts again.

After bringing him up to date, I said, "Tom, can you run a complete trace on the Nobles? I need every scam they ever pulled, and who they pulled it on. I need every enemy they ever made, and how. I need—"

"Slow down, Ace. I get the picture. Remember I was a cop, too. Okay, I'll find every stain they left anywhere. It might take a few days so try not to get arrested while I work it."

I rang off feeling better, but still worried I might get a knock on the door any moment. I considered bolting to Dallas, but knew that was no good. I'd have to trust that Bob Galoway would give me the benefit of the doubt and not obtain an arrest warrant. The more

I thought about it, the more I knew I needed to encourage that line of thinking.

I dialed the phone again. "Bob, Ace Edwards. Just so you'll know I'm playing straight, I'm checking in." I followed by telling him of my conversation with Ms. Evans, and what I'd asked Tom Roberts to do. I didn't tell him about Kit. Somehow, one small ace in the hole felt right.

"Ms. Evans? Was she your client?"

Before I could answer, he continued, "No, I don't think so. She's not the type who'd turn to someone like you. That means it had to be Johnny. What kind of crap was he in this time?"

I cut in. "We've already been there. You know I can't answer those kinds of questions."

"Okay, have it your way. Maybe I'll have Dub stop by and chat with Johnny. What are you going to do now?"

"Any problem if I check the crime scene?"

"Not with an escort. Clark's Ferry. You know it?"

"No, I—"

"Just head north out of Grand Saline. When you run out of road at the Sabine River, you're there. Don't expect much, it's just a wide spot in the road. Dub will meet you at five."

CHAPTER FIFTEEN

I lay the cell phone down, my mind in turmoil. This case was getting weirder by the moment, and the weirder it got, the more I felt like a hooked fish. I lay the front seat back and pulled my hat low over my eyes, forcing all thoughts from my mind. I closed my eyes and floated.

The blackmail material. Did the killers take it from Jade and Hugo before murdering them? If not, it might be good for me to have it. If Ms. Evans wanted to play hardball, a good catcher's mitt was a necessity.

I popped the seat forward and drove to the trailer park where Hugo and Jade had lived. After cruising the area to find the right trailer—and none of Bob's deputies—I parked about two hundred yards away. A woman in tattered jeans hanging wash on a clothesline glared at me and called to someone out of sight.

Her actions caused me to move the car and risk parking in front of the Nobles' trailer. From the trunk, I took a battered briefcase. It's there for those times when it pays to look official. Walking to the front door, I surveyed the immediate neighborhood. There were no people in sight and no drapes or blinds revealed spying eyeballs. While knocking, I examined the lock. It was a simple one. If necessary, it could be picked in a few seconds. However, remembering an embarrassing episode from earlier in my career, I tried the knob. In that earlier case, I'd consumed twenty valuable minutes before the place proved to be unlocked. This time, the lock was broken.

Sticking my head through the opening, I called, "Anyone home? Jade? Hugo? Got that stuff you wanted." The last was for the benefit of any neighbors who might be within earshot. "I'll just leave it inside."

I pushed into the room and closed the door. A quick look told me the place was a dump. No wonder Jade took Johnny to a motel. This place would kill a rabbit's lust. The briefcase went onto the floor where it would topple if the door opened. Then I moved toward the bedroom.

A quick survey told me there were few hiding places. *Where would Jade keep incriminating photos*? I slipped on a pair of rubber gloves and walked to the chest of drawers. The top drawer revealed she liked to wear sexy underwear, thongs and pushup bras. The second drawer held Hugo's briefs and T-shirts. Thank goodness for the gloves. The third held shorts and tops, again for Jade. The fourth was another drawer of Hugo's briefs. Shoving it closed, I looked around the room for other likely hiding places.

Wait a minute, right-brain said. *Does Hugo strike you as the type who'd have that many pairs of skivvies?*

Not a chance, left-brain answered.

I pulled open the lower drawer again and pushed Hugo's stuff out of the way. Something about the drawer bothered me, other than Hugo's briefs. Its depth didn't look right. I took out a one dollar bill and opened the one above. Moving Jade's shorts to the side, I measure its depth. Six inches. Then I checked the bottom drawer—only three inches. There must be a false bottom.

Looking around for something to use as a shim, I spotted a metal nail file. It took me twenty minutes and two broken fingernails, but I finally broke through. Five minutes later, I walked out of the trailer with my briefcase packed with a digital camera, videotapes, an envelope containing pictures, and a Zip disk for an unseen computer. Slung over my shoulder was a video camera. Hopefully, I had everything and had left no evidence of my visit.

Driving back to my motel, I debated what to do with the material. Johnny had hired me to recover it, but the game had changed. Ms. Evans' behavior told me the rules were different now, rules she made. It would be smart to play by them.

I swung by the post office and mailed all the material to Tom Roberts. Inside the package, I put a note asking him to hold it for me and not to examine it—but when he did, not to blush.

* * *

It was two o'clock, three hours before meeting Dub at Clark's Ferry. Kit still did not answer her phone, so I accepted the invitation of her electronic chip and left a message.

The next call was the one I'd been ducking, and I wasn't sure why. Normally, the client is the first person called when a case turns south. This time— Did I suspect Johnny of killing Jade and Hugo? Yes? No? No decision. The blackmail material would be my secret though. There would have to be a drastic change in attitudes before my mind switched on that. I don't like double-crosses, especially when they are pointed at me.

"Johnny," I said when he came to the phone. "I suppose you've heard about Killer and Jade."

"Yeah."

He sounded noncommittal, almost bored. "We need to talk."

"Uh, look, Ace. Just send me a bill. I can't be involved in this anymore. I'll—"

"Oh no, it doesn't work that way.

"You don't understand. I . . . I . . ."

His voice trailed away leaving silence. "Is someone with you?" I asked. "Is there a problem on your end of the phone? Look, I'll meet you in thirty minutes at the restaurant where we had our first meeting."

"No, I can't do that. Just bill me. I'll send you a check."

"Johnny, hear me, and hear me good." I let my irritation show. "Because of you, the Sheriff suspects me of murder. Because of you, your mother-in-law is assisting the Sheriff in that suspicion. Maybe because of you, two people are dead. Your choices are limited. You'll either meet me in thirty minutes, or I'll track you down and sit on your chest. Whichever, we're gonna talk. Your call. Which will it be?"

"You don't know what you're asking. Things are, things have changed. I—"

"Thirty minutes. Be there." I slammed the phone down so hard the handset might have broken. When I checked, it hummed merrily. Made in China.

Thoughts swirled through my head. Right-brain screamed, *Frame, frame, frame*. Left-brain didn't contradict it.

I paced for a moment, then walked to the dressing area. In the mirror, a worried man stared at me. I engaged in one of those techniques the experts say no one does. I talked to the guy in the mirror. "What the hell's going on here? This was a simple case, and now a murder charge hangs over me. Why didn't Johnny ask about the photos? Does he think removing the Nobles removes the threat? Nothing fits."

The stupid-looking reflection just stared. I noticed bloodshot eyes. Great. If Bob saw those, he'd accept them as proof I didn't sleep much last night, and if not asleep— I didn't allow that thought to continue.

I splashed water in my face, dried with a motel towel—very thin—and headed for the door. I wanted to be there first if Johnny showed. At this point, everything and everyone was suspect.

Fifteen minutes later, I peeked around the back edge of the restaurant. My car was hidden behind the building. If Johnny showed, I was in position to spot him. The wind swirled making me wish for a different location. Serious Dumpster halitosis.

My Timex vibrated along, counting off the seconds, then minutes as my mind spun worse than the Dumpster smells. Twenty-eight minutes had passed since I'd given Johnny the deadline.

A Mercedes convertible pulled in front of the restaurant with its top down. Johnny drove with a second person in the passenger seat. He parked, handed the keys over, then walked into the restaurant. The passenger looked around the lot as he shifted to the driver's position. I wasn't surprised when he moved the car to the far end of the lot and parked between two huge SUVs. They effectively hid the Mercedes from the world. He entered the restaurant. I didn't recognize him behind large sunglasses and a hat pulled low.

After waiting a few more minutes and seeing nothing of interest, I relocated my Chrysler to the front of the restaurant where the air was fresher. A space near the entrance enticed me to park, and I walked into the restaurant.

Johnny sat in a booth in the right rear of the eating area, and his friend in the left rear, still wearing hat and sunglasses. He stood out like a computer nerd at a Harley-Davidson rally. When I turned in his direction, he quickly averted his eyes to the menu that concealed the lower half of his face. There was a familiarity, but nothing clicked.

"Good morning, Johnny. Glad you could make time for me."

"Morning, Ace." His eyes flicked toward his friend, then returned to me. "What do you want? I told you I'd mail you a check."

"Yes, I heard that." I was in my Joe Cool mode. "But I don't consider that enough." I moved into the booth across from Johnny, not liking my back being to the front. However, it did position me where I could keep an eye on his friend. "Perhaps you didn't understand when we talked. Jade and Killer are dead, and I'm a suspect. Someone broke into my room, turned it upside down, and stole my gun. The Sheriff is checking to see if my gun killed them, and suddenly, you have no interest in the case you hired me to solve. Makes me curious, Johnny, very curious." I stared at him.

He refused to look me in the eyes. Instead, he looked at the table top, probably checking flyspecks. Then he picked up the menu. "Want something to eat? I'll buy."

I said nothing.

"The chicken-fried steak is good, and it comes with extra gravy."

I continued to stare.

He fumbled with the menu. "I'm not too hungry. Think I'll just have some pie and coffee. Had a late breakfast—"

The waitress arrived with water and two coffee cups dangling from a forefinger. "Coffee?" she asked as she deftly slid the glasses and mugs onto the table.

"Yeah," Johnny replied. "Just fill it two-thirds though."

She shot him a knowing look as he glanced toward the other side of the restaurant.

He leaned against the back cushion. "I'll have a double wedge of hot apple pie with vanilla ice cream. Ace?"

"The same." I didn't relax my stare-down. "Except fill my cup and a single slice of pie."

Johnny looked everywhere except at me. He checked the ceiling, the table top again, fingered the dusty curtains, even leaned over and made sure the floor was clean. The ketchup bottle received special scrutiny.

I stayed mute.

The waitress returned with a coffeepot and filled our cups, following Johnny's directions. When she'd finished her chore, he fished in his jacket pocket, pulled out a flask and topped off the cup with a generous dollop.

"Brandy?" He held the flask toward me.

I stared.

"Dammit, Ace. What the hell do you want?"

I stared.

"Look, I tried to tell you on the phone that things are different. I said I'll pay you. Hell, I'll give you the whole amount if that's what you want. It's over. That's all. It's over."

"Where were you last night, Johnny? Did you have a late breakfast because you slept late? Did you sleep late because you were out late? Were you out late killing Jade and Hugo?"

"No. I didn't, I couldn't—" He broke eye contact and looked at his coffee cup, but not before quickly glancing at the man with whom he'd arrived.

I looked that way also, but only saw a man in a hat and sunglasses tearing into a huge chicken-fried steak. He sat angled toward us.

"While you think, I'll hit the restroom," I said. The door to the men's room was behind our friend's booth.

Crossing the floor, I stared at Johnny's passenger and searched my mind for identity. He was clean shaven with a light scar diagonally across his left cheek. As I passed his booth, I reached over and plucked off his oily western hat. "Didn't your momma teach you to take your hat off inside?" I said with right-brain screaming, *It's Billy, Ms. Evans' bartender.*

I looked closer and saw that right-brain had scored again. "Why Billy, why don't you join us? Sit on Johnny's side. I'll be right back." I took a step, then turned back. "You look better with the beard."

He looked at me, hesitation and confusion in his eyes. "Ah, I cain't. I mean—"

"Oh, it's okay," I said. "Tell Johnny I sent you."

I entered the men's room and waited. When I thought Johnny and Billy had had time to recover, I peeked out. Across the room, I saw them, heads together, on the same side of the booth. The waitress transferred Billy's food.

"Now, isn't this much better?" I said, sliding onto the seat. "All three of us together like this. Much cozier."

Both of them looked uncomfortable, but it hadn't stopped Billy from eating. He busily chewed while looking like he'd rather be someplace else. Not an easy task, but he accomplished it. Johnny stirred a fresh cup of coffee. I suspected it carried a fresh load of brandy.

"Any others around we should invite to lunch, Johnny? I'd hate to think they have to sit alone or wait outside in the weather."

"Now, Ace," Johnny said. "This ain't what you think. Billy needed a ride, and I was—"

"Yeah, that's it," Billy said through another mouthful of food. "I jist come along for the ride."

"Interesting," I said.

The clatter of Johnny's spoon in his coffee cup reminded me of shaken dice. Billy continued to eat. I settled back into my stare routine with Johnny.

"We have to go," Johnny said.

Billy's head snapped up. "But—"

"I mean, I gotta go," Johnny corrected. "If you want to finish, Billy, maybe Ace will give you a ride. I can't stay any longer. I have to, have to, uh, go up to the big house. Yeah, Mrs. Evans said for me to come up this afternoon."

"Okay, Johnny, you can go," I said. "But, before you leave, tell me one thing. Why'd you have Jade and Hugo murdered?"

"Me? I didn't do it. You, you did it. Mrs. Evans said—" His mouth stopped, but his eyes continued to dance. "I gotta go." He rose.

"Take Billy with you. You've told me all I need to know."

He looked at me unsteadily as Billy crammed a big hunk of his chicken-fried steak in his mouth.

Even as I stared, Johnny's resolve appeared to solidify. "Send me a bill," he said. "I don't want to get in trouble with Jake. I'll pay you like I said." He turned toward Billy who ate as if it might be his last meal. "Get up. Let's get out of here."

Billy gave me a scowl over stuffed cheeks. He didn't look happy, but I wasn't sure whether he was unhappy with me or at leaving his plate.

"Leave the waitress a nice tip," I said. "And tell your mother-in-law I don't go down easy. If this frame works, you can bet Matthew Thomas will never be President. In fact, when I'm finished with the news media, he won't be able to get a job in Miami. Look behind you frequently, Johnny. I'll be there. Billy, have a nice day."

I rose and walked out of the restaurant while Johnny fumbled with his wallet, and Billy crammed more food into his face. I thought it best to get out before them. An ambush was not high on my wish list.

* * *

My drive back to Grand Saline was thoughtful, but uneventful, and provided no answers to explain Johnny's behavior. None I wanted to acknowledge. The only one that made any sense was Johnny was not only involved in the murders, but was also part of my frame. He'd done little in the past to earn my respect, but I preferred to believe he would not use me as a patsy. However, he'd made himself my primary lead, one I'd have to watch.

I debated between seeing where Johnny headed and being early for my rendezvous with Dub. Dub won. I took State Route 19 to US 80, then 80 west through Fruitvale. It saved a few minutes.

The road to Clark's Ferry was not the best type for my Sebring. The lack of a stabilizing roof causes convertibles to make strange squeaks and other noises not known to sedans. The Chrysler made all of them.

Finally, I sighed as I viewed the end of the road. The Sabine River lay in front of me. It wasn't much of a crossing. Where did the name Clark's Ferry come from? On my side of the stream, it was nothing more than a well-rutted clay turnaround and the other, East Texas forest.

Yellow police tape encircled an area along the bank. That was my goal, and that's where I headed. As I lifted the tape to step inside, I heard a car bouncing up the road behind me. Holding the tape over my shoulder, I turned to see a police car coming toward me.

The car, a Ford I think, came to a halt behind my Chrysler, and Dub stepped out. "Hey, Ace. Wanna slow down there?" He laughed, and slapped his hat against his thigh. "Bob said you'd be early. Dammit, I owe him a box of donuts."

I groaned and dropped the tape. Diplomacy was my best bet today. "I got bored so I thought I'd come on out and wait for you."

"Sure, Ace, sure," he said between chuckles. "That's what Bob said you'd say."

I definitely needed to do something about my *modus operandi*. Apparently, it was a bit obvious. "Did he tell you your tape had fallen? I was holding it up."

"Yep. So I see." He chuckled some more. "We always have trouble with tape staying in place." He stared behind me.

I turned, chagrined to see the yellow tape merrily stretched three feet above the ground. So much for my story.

I went for the light-hearted approach and laughed. "Okay, you got me. I came out early to look at the crime scene before you could steer me away from the good stuff." I forced another chuckle. "You've ruined that plan."

Dub stuck out his hand, and I took it, positioning my palm so he couldn't crack my knuckles. "Ace, you haven't changed a bit. You're still as wacko as you were when you saved Joseph's hide." He squeezed.

I squeezed. "Yep, I never change." I squeezed as hard as I could, but he'd positioned his fingers deep inside my palm. The only thing that prevented it from being a Mexican stand-off was, we weren't Mexican.

"I shore am sorry 'bout this morning. I can't believe you killed those slime-balls. Did you have to?"

"Dub, I didn't kill anyone. I'd finished my dealings with Jade and Hugo. One more meet, and they would have been history."

"Yeah, that's what I figgered. You're too smart for two rejects like them. But, you know something, didn't nobody else 'round here have no reason to kill them."

His comment opened a gate I cared not to enter. "Show me where they were killed, where the bodies were."

I spent the next hour working the site. Bob's people had been thorough, and all I really saw was the residue of their activity. Hugo and Jade had apparently knelt on the embankment facing the river. When the bullets slammed into the rear of their heads, they pitched down the slope to the edge of the water. Other than some dark brown and grayish stains, no evidence of their demise remained. Dub said no shell casings were found, and no footprints had been visible. The clay around the site was drought-dry and brick-hard. I had learned almost nothing.

I looked at Dub. "I'm about finished. I—"

He stared into the woods, his head turning slowly from side to side as if mesmerized.

"Hey, earth to Dub. Are you with me?"

"Oh, yeah. Sorry, I was just remembering something that happened when I was a kid."

"Want to share with me?"

He looked at the ground, trying to dig the rock-hard clay with the toe of his boot. Then he pulled his hat off while wiping his arm across his brow and staring into the sky.

"Quit fidgeting, Dub. You don't have to tell me if you don't want to."

"Promise not to say I'm nuts?" he asked, giving me a serious look.

"Sure—no more than usual."

"Not sure that's an improvement," he said, a smile cracking the seriousness of his face. "Craziest damn thing, though." He hesitated and took a deep breath. "You know this place is haunted, don't you?"

"It's what? Sounded like you said haunted."

"I did. Ghosts. You know, like Casper, except not so friendly. Didn't Bob tell you?"

"No, he didn't. You telling me you believe in ghosts?"

"I don't know. All my life I've heard stories about Clark's Ferry, funny things happening. I always figgered they was just tall tales. Then, when I was a teen, a bunch of us come here one night to drink beer and make out." He pointed at a six-pack of empties laying alongside a log. "Just like they do today. Anyway, we bought a case and drove up here. We was sitting around telling stories, necking a little, and drinking cheap ones when it happened." He stopped and stared at the tree line again, then said quietly. "Dam'dest thing I ever heard."

I waited a moment, but my patience ran out quickly. "Heard what?"

"The ghosts."

His voice was still quiet, so quiet I had to strain to understand his words.

"They started screaming and didn't stop. Then the lights rushed out of the woods at us. It sounded like women screeching, babies crying, men cussing, whips cracking. The lights bobbed and weaved, jerked up and down and sideways. It scared me half to death."

His voice had risen in both volume and timbre with each word. "C'mon, Dub," I said. "Are you jerking my chain? Do I look like a tourist from New York?" Even as I said it, I knew his answer.

"I'm serious, Ace, serious as a preacher on Sunday. The screams were horrible, and the lights were like nothing I ever seen before."

I took a hard look at him. Here was a guy that normally looked like he could take on a stampeding herd, and now, he was pale, his eyes were wild, and I could see sweat beads on his forehead. Tentatively, I said, "Okay, I'll bite. What did you do?"

He looked around the area, especially at the trees. "Got the hell out of here. Left the beer, the blankets, everything. We piled in the cars and put this place behind us, and I ain't been back out here after dark since that night."

"So?"

"So if you're finished, I'm ready to leave. It'll be dark soon enough, and I want to be far away when the sun goes down."

I gave him the once-over again. The normally cool Dub was pale. There was a ripple to his body like a shudder.

"Yeah, I'm finished. Good story." I forced a laugh.

He didn't laugh.

We walked to the cars, and Dub gradually returned to his normal form. "Bob said for me to tell you not to worry too much. We'll help you if we can 'cause he don't think you did it. So you need anything you call me, okay?" He opened the door to his squad car and got in. "Hey." He leaned his head out the window. "He also said you're still the best suspect we got."

I watched him drive away knowing I needed a miracle. The Edwards family tree might end with me dangling from the last limb.

CHAPTER SIXTEEN

My mind was in turmoil as I bounced toward Grand Saline. I had no idea what was happening around me. It's embarrassing to find you're tied to a railroad track before you learn there is a right of way. I've always found that doing something simple helps when things are about to overwhelm me. Maybe investigating Dub's story about Clark's Ferry might settle my mind.

Once back in town, I parked on Main Street and walked into the offices of the *Grand Saline Sun*, the local newspaper. An attractive young woman greeted me.

"Hi, I'm Ace Edwards, an investigator from Dallas," I said, handing her a business card.

"Hey, yeah, I've heard of you. You're that guy who's out here to get Johnny Nichols out of trouble again. Did you really kill those people? I'm Janie Blackman." She stuck out her hand.

I sighed and shook hands with her. What else could I do? The rumor network in a small town is faster than CNN can ever hope to be. "Yep, that's me, and no, I didn't kill them." As an afterthought, I added, "Or anyone else."

"Good," she said. "I don't think it's nice to kill people."

I hesitated to mull that over while she plowed on. "What can I do for you? I'd sure like to get the story on who really killed those jerks. Ought to be worth a front-page byline. People like that give Grand Saline a bad name."

No way could I disagree with that. I'd never view the town the same. "I'm interested in Clark's Ferry, its history, why it's called that. Do you have any info on it?"

"Yeah, let me think. You know, somewhere back there," she nodded toward the rear of the building, "there's a paper that has the whole story. A high school kid wrote it. Give me some time. We close at six. Come back before then."

I thanked her, then wandered outside to kill time. The Sabine Café beckoned. I knew I couldn't get a Killian's, but I was sure there would be sugar-laced iced tea. I was right. Mabel, the friendly waitress, kept my glass filled, and thirty minutes later, I'd eaten a grilled cheese and updated my journal.

At five before six, I pushed through the front door of the paper again. Janie greeted me with a smile. "Where've you been? I was beginning to think you were pulling my leg. Here's the paper."

As I reached for it, she said, "That'll be fifty cents."

After I fumbled and produced two quarters, she handed me a copy of the November 11, 1999 edition. "Look on page 4A, the article by Josh Crain. Zack Ingrim, and Lindsay Stewart worked with him. That article will tell you everything about Clark's Ferry."

I thanked her and opened the door.

"Give me the exclusive when you find out who killed those creeps," she said.

She showed more confidence in me than I felt right then. Back in the car, I opened the paper and read the article entitled *Students Investigate the Legend of Clark's Ferry*. Janie's prediction was correct. My curiosity was sated. On one hand, the article left me chuckling, but on the other, I never challenge the supernatural. Dub's story could well be true.

* * *

I drove into the motel parking lot and smiled when I saw a blue Geo Metro convertible. Kit had gotten my message and, like I'd asked, ridden to my rescue. I parked and let myself into my room. A flashing light on the telephone greeted me.

There were two messages. The first told me Bob's people had released my old room, and I could get the rest of my stuff. The second said Kit had checked into Room 118—next door. The first brought a sense of relief, but the second generated a smirk. I wondered if she had some poor guy evicted. Wouldn't surprise me a bit.

I knocked on the door between our rooms, flipping the lock on my side. On hers, something clicked, and the door cracked open. Kit slipped through wearing jeans and a T-shirt, the most beautiful sight I'd seen since leaving Dallas.

"So, what kind of trouble did you get into this afternoon?" she asked, smiling.

"Nothing serious. Just the same old suspicion of murder."

"Actually, I'm surprised to see you," she said. "I was looking up the number to the county lock-up. Figured you'd be sleeping over." She punctuated her sarcasm with a grin.

"Did you drive up here to make me feel better or put another pinprick in my ego?"

"Both—and to bring your cats."

She opened the door wide, and Sweeper and Striker peered around the corner. They looked at me, ran in my direction, then stopped to check the room. Cats are smarter than humans. They never rush into a strange situation where something could lay in ambush. Me, I do it routinely.

After thoroughly sniffing everything in sight, they came to me, and rubbed between my ankles. I picked them up and sat on the edge of the bed. Striker promptly curled in my lap while Sweeper moved to his customary position on my left side. He didn't appear happy there was no chair arm to use as a perch.

Kit took the only chair in the room. "Okay, fill me in. Your phone message was rather cryptic."

"Looks like I'm being set up to take a fall on the murders. I met with Johnny, and he's ducking big time. Funny thing was he brought along Ms. Evans' bartender. Not sure whether he was there to protect Johnny or to make sure Johnny didn't tell me anything. Did you bring what I asked for?"

"Yeah. So what else have you been up to this afternoon? If I know you, you were off someplace stirring the pot."

"Visited the murder scene and made a trip to the local newspaper. That's it."

"What'd you find?"

I handed her the newspaper opened to page 4A. "Here's the scoop on the place. It's called Clark's Ferry. Where's my toy?"

Kit went into her room, returned with a small gym bag and handed it to me.

In it was my throw-down, a snub-nosed, six-round, .32 caliber revolver rolled in two towels, the inside one lightly oiled. I'd had it for years, obtained when I first joined the Dallas police force. While going through the academy, the word went out to find one, unofficially of course. It carried no serial number traceable to me. With the advice to get a throw-down, came the instructions on when to use it.

For all you criminal-rights activists, I quickly add that the Dallas Police Department never condones any officer planting a weapon on anyone. But a cop who hesitates is too often dead. So if the perp points something at you, shoot and examine the body later. If that something was other than a gun, use a throw-down.

The moral question here is simple: Which is better, to be dead or for the sleaze-bag you were chasing to lay on the sidewalk oozing blood? For me, that was and still is a no-brainer.

I eased off my right boot and strapped on the ankle holster. I remembered from years ago how uncomfortable it was. Today, it felt right. When I put the boot back on and dropped the revolver in, it lay heavy against my ankle, but raised my confidence level considerably. I took it out, flipped the cylinder open and laid it on a towel.

From the gym bag, I took out a cleaning kit, a can of oil, and a box of .32 caliber bullets. Ten minutes later, I closed the cylinder, clicked it a couple of times, and then inserted six rounds. I smiled as I filled three speed loaders. That gave me twenty-four rounds ready to use with minimum delay. My mood had improved considerably.

"You caress that gun like a woman would love to be handled. Makes me jealous."

Kit's words surprised me. I'd actually forgotten she was in the room. But there she sat with the boys curled in her lap, napping, or catnapping, if you prefer.

"Sorry. Guess I got carried away. It's been a while since I prepared a gun expecting to need it."

Kit stood and walked into her room, but returned a moment later carrying a package. "From what you said, can I assume you won't be using that peashooter as a throw-down?"

"Correct, my dear Watson."

"In that case, here. I think you'll like this. Clean it up."

I instinctively caught the package she tossed toward my vulnerable lap. "What? Oh yes, it's my birthday. How nice of you to remember."

"Bull. Your birthday's in August. I just can't afford a funeral wreath because some guy walks through that peashooter of yours and puts a real slug in you. So I picked this up."

I unwrapped the package and saw Smith and Wesson markings on the case. When I opened the box, a hammerless revolver in black and gray softly gleamed. "A Centennial. Nice, but it doesn't bring much more to the table than my .32, and it's one shot less."

"Look again, cowboy. That's a .357 and light as a feather. It's all new."

I followed her instructions and grinned. It weighed about the same as my .32, but packed a lot bigger wallop.

"Scandium. That's the key," Kit said. "Makes the alloy strong enough to kick up the caliber without adding weight."

"Nice, and there's no hammer to catch in my boot. I don't suppose you cleaned it."

"Didn't want to spoil your fun. Here're the speed loaders." She tossed a package of four. "If you hit someone with that baby, he won't be coming back for a second try."

I cleaned and loaded the .357 while she read the newspaper article.

* * *

"Do you buy this story?" Kit asked, waving the paper at me. "I kept looking for the part that said it was a put-on. Was it late for Halloween, or something?"

"Yeah, I know what you mean. Apparently, they printed it as a serious article. If not, I missed something."

"Clark's Ferry. I suppose if all things were right, you could sink a ferry by blowing holes in the bottom, and, if it sunk, I suppose people could drown." She hesitated as if searching her memory. "Haven't there been stories about ferries sinking in Indonesia or somewhere, drowning hundreds of people?"

"It's happened, but the Sabine River is hardly as wild as the Pacific Ocean," I said.

"Uh huh. So, do you buy it?"

"Don't know. Ghosts are one of those things I don't make judgments on." I thought for a moment, remembering ghost tales from my youth and what Dub had told me. "There's lots of strange things in this world I don't understand. Why not ghosts?"

"Sure," Kit said, shrugging. "The part about the ferry sinking and drowning all the students could be real enough. Especially, if you throw in old-man Clark going nuts and shooting holes in the bottom."

I grinned, waiting for more.

"The KKK? Yeah, I can believe that. Bunch of mini-Hitlers hiding under sheets, hanging innocent people whose only crime was being black or brown. African-Americans and Mexicans didn't have a chance with them. Yeah, if I was one of their victims, I'd haunt those woods until I got justice."

"So, what's the problem with the story?" I asked. "Goat lady bothering you?"

"Don't laugh at me," she said, chuckling. "A woman gets her head cut off so she grabs the head of a goat, then kills her husband? Come on, Ace. That's a bit of a stretch, even for you."

"You left out the dancing lights, screaming banshees, and the lady's husband with the ax," I said.

She folded the paper and lay it on the bed. "Okay, I'll keep an open mind, how about that? But I hope we don't have to find out. What say we stay away from Clark's Ferry—especially after dark." She shuddered.

"Deal. We'll do our investigating during daylight hours only. That'll leave us the evenings for in-depth research of one another."

"Oh. You've forgotten all about Terri?"

Sweeper jumped into my lap saving me from having to answer. He gave me a couple of licks then checked out the gun cleaning equipment. I stroked his back, and he rewarded me with a contented purr.

"You know, Kit. We have a ghost expert in the place," I said. "All we have to do is ask Sweeper. He'll tell us."

"Sure," she replied.

Striker entered the room and looked up at Sweeper's position. He promptly jumped into Kit's arms.

"So what do you think, Striker?" she said. "Should we ask Sweeper about the ghosts of Clark's Ferry?"

Striker looked at her, arched his back and rubbed under Kit's chin.

"Is that a yes or a no?" she said.

"Looked like a yes to me," I said, stroking Sweeper. "Okay, big guy, here's the question. Is there a Goat Lady out there?"

Sweeper looked at me and purred.

"Hear that. Sweeper says there is a Goat Lady," I said to Kit. "That's one for one." I turned my attention back to Sweeper. "Does the Goat Lady's husband haunt Clark's Ferry?"

Sweeper purred.

"Two for two. We're on a roll."

"Sure," Kit cut in. "You rub him, he purrs, and you say that means yes. Even a bad carny wouldn't pull that scam."

I held Sweeper out in front of me. "Hear that, big guy. She still doubts us. Sorry, but it looks like I'll have to turn you loose before she'll accept your words."

I put him on the floor where he promptly sat back on his haunches and began to wash his face.

"Now, listen carefully," I said. "Are there strange lights and ghosts that scream at Clark's Ferry?" I stared at him, expectantly.

Sweeper finished his face, looked first at me, then Kit. He slowly stood, then leapt into the air, let out a bloodcurdling yowl, and raced around the room before flopping onto his side at my feet as if unconscious.

Striker jumped from Kit's lap, ran to Sweeper and licked him. Sweeper reached up and cuffed him. One of their pretend fights began.

"So, what do you think of that?" I said. "That proves my case."

Kit watched the two of them a moment, then said, "Humph. Proves the whole Edwards family is nuts."

I laughed and scooped the boys up. They promptly assumed their normal positions, Striker in my lap and Sweeper on my left. I stroked them, and they rewarded me with loud purrs. Soon they tired, jumped from the bed, and headed for the food dishes.

By mutual consent, we stayed away from the subject of Clark's Ferry, but continued to talk in the way close friends do. Mostly, it was about the case, but occasionally, the conversation drifted into personal territory. Once, I mentioned Terri. Kit stood and threatened to return to Dallas if her name came up again.

While Kit and I munched a pizza, the boys resumed examining the rooms. They seemed satisfied, especially after discovering Kit had brought expensive cat food.

"Hey guys," I called. "What's your theory? Who killed Hugo and Jade?"

Kit chuckled. "You still think those cats have ESP?"

"Probably not, but remember what Sweeper did for me on the Cisco case." I turned toward Sweeper. "Talk to me, guy."

Looking at me, he hunched his shoulders, then tilted his head so he stared down the length of his nose. After prancing around on his tiptoes a few steps, he relaxed and galloped to his food dish.

Kit watched him. "All I see is a cat with a bottomless pit for a stomach. That reminds me. You owe me for the cat food. That stuff's expensive."

The phone rang.

"Must be for you," Kit said. "No one knows I'm here."

"Ace Edwards," I said, picking up the receiver.

"Aceman, what the hell's going on," a female voice said into my ear. "I hear you got yourself bullshit deep in trouble."

The bullshit did it. "Candi, how are you?" I asked, suspiciously. The last thing I needed was a man-hating female lawyer on my case.

"I'm fine, Chip's fine, Joseph's fine, and Wanda misses you. Now, can we move on to this bullshit trouble you're in?"

Chip was Chip Jamison, my client in the case I worked in Canton. Joseph was the kidnappee. Wanda was the beautiful woman who assisted me in the case and almost made me forget Terri. Almost, but not quite. Candi was the lawyer who started out as a bitter adversary trying to clean Chip out with a civil suit.

"Nothing much to tell," I replied to her question. "Bob thinks I might have killed a couple of people, and my gun is missing. Other than that, I'm having a good season."

"Yeah, that's what I heard. Okay, here's the deal. You keep your mouth shut. Don't volunteer anything to Bob, Dub or anyone else until I find out what Bob's got on you. I'll work on him tomorrow—missed him today."

"Wait a minute, Candi. You're talking like a defense attorney. Are you my lawyer, or just a nosy bitch?"

"Both, but mostly I'm your bullshit lawyer. Hell, can't you keep up with anything?"

I grinned in spite of myself. Candi used bullshit to season her language like a good chef adds spices. Also, the look Kit gave me was one of absolute puzzlement. "All right, Malady, slow down and tell me the whole story. How'd you become my lawyer?"

"Dammit. You know my name's Maladay, not Malady. So knock it off. Either that or I'll give you a malady."

I had to laugh. Candi hadn't changed a bit since I'd last seen her. "So—"

"Chip and Jake hired me to represent you. They agreed you'd take the long course in Huntsville if you didn't have a good attorney. With your bullshit track record, Bob would have no choice, but to turn the DA loose on you."

"How'd Chip and Jake get into this?"

"Bob called Chip. Chip called Jake. They talked it over, Chip called me. Don't sweat the fees. They're paying me well."

Just what I needed. Another obligation owed to Jake—but this time I was glad. "Okay, mouthpiece, what do I do?"

"You do what you do best. Find the real killers. I'll keep Bob off your back, but you'd better hurry. I hear he's real upset that a double murder occurred in his county. Is your chickie from Dallas with you?"

"Chickie? Not exactly safe to call her that, but yes, Kit's here."

"Good. Tell her to keep you on a tight rein so you don't get into any more trouble. Oh, don't let her near Wanda. She's ready to scratch her eyes out—and might take yours with them."

I was familiar with Wanda's temper. "I won't. But Kit's a partner, not a lover."

"Sure, Aceman, sure."

The phone went dead as her witch's cackle echoed around the room.

"Candi?" Kit asked as I settled the handset back into its cradle. "Not Chip's Candi, the one you told me about?"

"Yep, the same. Seems like Jake hired her to keep me out of jail. Wish he'd asked me first." I reflected a moment. "I can't fault his choice, though. She's tough."

CHAPTER SEVENTEEN

Morning arrived and I invited Kit to join me for breakfast. We drove into Grand Saline to the Sabine Café. It was eight-thirty when we walked in, and we sat at the only free table.

I examined the crowd. They weren't especially handsome, well dressed or exceptional in any way, but they exuded a quality that at first eluded me. Then I realized what it was. They were at home and obviously liked it. Homeyness hovered around them like trouble follows me.

In the rear of the restaurant there was a large round table occupied by six older gentlemen. They spoke easily with one another, and friendly laughter passed among them. I noticed their coffee cups were different from the others in the place. Whereas the restaurant cups were white mugs, theirs had printing on them.

The waitress walked over. Her nametag still read Mabel. Fits, doesn't it.

"Hey, you back all ready. I figgered since you didn't drink all your tea yesterday, you didn't like this place. Whyn't you finish it?"

Huh was the first response that popped into my mind, but I managed to squelch it in favor of, "I had to run. The paper was about to close shop for the day."

"Yeah. Know what you mean. They close kinda early, don't they?"

"Can we see a menu?" Kit asked.

"Honey, you don't need no menu here. Just say what you want. If we ain't got it, I'll tell you. Think about it while I get coffee." She surveyed Kit. "You probably want cream with yours." With that, she walked back to the counter.

"And a glass of water," Kit said to her retreating back. "Wipe that smirk off your mouth," Kit said to me, then chuckled. "Good, isn't she?"

"I like her," I said. "You gotta love life in small towns. Before she gets back, you'd better decide what you want for breakfast. If you don't, she might decide for you."

Kit laughed again. "You're right."

Mabel sat two mugs of coffee, a small pitcher of cream, and one glass of water on the table. The water went in front of Kit. "Ready to order?"

"How about some water for me?" I asked.

"You ain't the type. Drink coffee. It's better for you. How you want your eggs, over easy?" She gave me a smile that could boil water or keep me from disagreeing with her.

"Over easy sounds good. Bacon and grits okay?"

"No problem. I already wrote that down. See."

She shoved her pad in my direction. It was blank.

"Ah, sure," I said.

"How 'bout you, miss? We got some fresh bagels this morning. You look like you'd enjoy a bagel and cream cheese."

Kit shot her a look, but must have been satisfied with what she saw. "Not a bad idea, but just toast me an English muffin with eggs over easy and grits on the side."

"You got it, sweetie. I'll bring you a bagel and cream cheese just in case, though."

I hid my snicker by coughing into my fist. Kit glared after Mabel.

"Who does she think—" Kit started, but stopped as her laughter interrupted her. "Like you said. You have to love small towns."

"Mr. Edwards. It's good to see you again. Find the killer yet?"

I looked toward the voice and saw Janie Blackman, the reporter from the local paper, headed our way. I stood, proving once again that down deep, I'm a gentleman. I noticed a shocked look on Kit's face, but ignored it. "Good morning, Miss Blackman. Nope, no killer yet. I save things like that for after breakfast. Got any clues for me?"

She grinned. "You came to the right place. If anyone in Grand Saline knows anything, the word will be here. I get most of my stories by just drinking coffee and listening." She turned toward Kit and stuck out her hand. "I'm Janie Blackman. I work at the local paper. I met your husband yesterday when he came in looking for an article."

"Husband?" Kit said, a shocked look on her face. "Me, married to this character? Not a chance." She shook hands with Janie. "I'm Kit Levitt from Dallas. I rescued him from a homeless shelter and told him I'd buy breakfast if he could find a restaurant they'd let him in. This was as close to Dallas as he could find."

Janie's mouth dropped open as she cut her eyes from one to the other of us. Then she smiled. "Okay, I know when I've been had. Score one for you. You a private cop, too?"

I quickly shook my head at Kit.

Her eyes filled with question marks, but she answered, "No. Just a casual friend. I knew he was here, and I was on my way back to Dallas from Longview so I cut through to have breakfast with him. I'll be heading on after we eat."

Janie gave her a look, and I wondered if that secret language between women was saying, "I don't believe a word of their fairy tale." Aloud, she replied, "Too bad you can't hang around. Ace promised me an exclusive when he captures the murderer."

"Sit down," I said. "Breakfast will be here—correction, it is here, and you can join us."

Mabel placed our orders in front of us. True to her word, she'd brought Kit a bagel and cream cheese. "Janie, you're not fishing these two for a story, are you? Take a look at'm. City-slickers. Ain't nothing there worth printing. I'll get your breakfast."

Janie laughed. "Mabel says that about anyone I sit with. She only reads the obits. Guess if you're alive, she doesn't think there's a story."

All three of us enjoyed a good laugh. Like I said, you have to love small towns.

"I read the article you gave Ace," Kit said. "Give us the long version on Clark's Ferry. Is all that hocus-pocus for real?"

"If you lived around here, you'd show more respect. The old-timers take the legend of Clark's Ferry quite seriously. I remember when Josh researched that story for his school paper, the one we printed. He stirred some strong feelings. We got several nasty letters after running it. This is a small town, and—"

"Janie Blackman, are you telling these strangers 'bout Clark's Ferry?" One of the men from the round table stood by her. "You know them ghosts ain't something we talk about."

"Yessir, Mr. Abercrombie. That's just what I told them. We don't talk about Clark's Ferry."

"Good. Keep it that way," the man said, walking away and out of the restaurant.

"Whew. See what I mean," Janie said. "It's a touchy subject." She leaned forward. "But I will tell you that every word in that article is as true as Josh and the others could find out. Things like that aren't often documented."

"But it's so strange," I said. "How can anyone—"

"Hey. Can we change the subject? Have you been to the Salt Palace?"

"The what?" Kit asked.

"It's a museum here in town. The outside wall of the building consists of salt crystals. You oughtta go look at it. Mighty interesting for a couple of city-slickers."

* * *

The Salt Palace appeared as advertised. Off-white lumps of something crystalline covered the walls. I was willing to believe it was salt, and later, the curator substantiated my belief.

A historical marker in front of the building bragged that Wiley Post, a pioneer in aviation, was a native of Grand Saline. My dad said he'd known Post and had flown with him during Post's barnstorming days, maybe between his two round-the-world flights.

We entered the one-room building and signed the guest book. While I signed in, the lady explained the different sections of the museum: the Wiley Post section, the salt-mining section, and the historical section featuring Grand Saline. Kit expressed surprise to find that the town sat on top of a huge salt dome reputed to have enough salt to last twenty thousand years. When I pointed out that might have something to do with its name, she pinched me.

"Playing the tourist with you is fun," Kit said, "but don't you think we should get serious. There's still a killer out there."

"Thanks. I was hoping to forget that. Let's go back to the motel and plot our next move."

* * *

"Ms. Nichols, Johnny can talk to me now or he can talk to me later, but we're going to talk." I was on the phone with Louise Nichols, Johnny's wife. His performance from the previous day still grated on my nerves, and I was determined to pin him down. "This whole mess started— Well, never mind how it started." Sometimes my integrity just plain pisses me off. But I couldn't break the confidence between Johnny and me. He was still my client, even if he didn't exactly act the part.

"Mr. Edwards, I know why you came to Grand Saline. Mother told me all about it. Don't be embarrassed. Jade Noble's not the first woman Johnny's been with, and I doubt she'll be the last. He's just that kind of man. In any case, I don't know where he is— probably looking for a replacement for Jade. Mother says we can't talk to you so I'm hanging up."

Her voice was cold, unemotional, almost detached. "Ms. Nichols," I said, but it was too late. I heard a distinct click in my ear.

"No progress on that front," I told Kit, replacing the handset.

"That was obvious," she said. "Are you ready to get serious about this case? Unless something's changed, you're still the number one suspect."

"What do you suggest?"

"I'd like to see the scene, the killing ground. Maybe we can spot something that'll help us."

"Okay, but let me try Johnny's cell first. He has to be the key to this mess." I punched in Johnny's cell phone number and listened to it ring four times before the answering service cut in. "Johnny, it's Ace," I told the microchip. "It's eleven-thirty, and I'm headed out to Clark's Ferry. Meet me there and come alone. I'll give you one hour. You still have questions to answer."

"Did you really want to tell him where we're going?" Kit asked. "He may be the one who offed Jade and Hugo."

"Naw, not Johnny. He doesn't have the guts. Of course, I don't expect him to show up either."

* * *

We stood on the embankment over the Sabine River. The yellow police tape was still up around the scene, but Kit and I ignored it. We couldn't track up the place if we'd wanted to. The ground was so hard I couldn't have scuffed it with a pick and shovel.

"From what Dub said, Jade and Hugo knelt here, facing the river. They were shot from behind," I told Kit. "The bullets struck them in the back of the skull, apparently from close range, execution style. They pitched forward down the slope." I looked toward the river. "See, you can still see some stains—"

I've read you never hear the one that gets you, and I can vouch for that. I felt something slam into my shoulder at almost the exact moment my legs were swept from under me, pitching me down the incline. Then the sounds of the shots reached my ears.

Even as I slid, I realized Kit was with me. She grabbed me, stopping my slide toward the water, then fumbled in my right boot. Two quick shots boomed from where she lay beside me.

"Ace, where the hell are the speed loaders?"

BOOK TWO — KIT'S STORY

CHAPTER EIGHTEEN

Kit spun, recognizing the sound of gunfire and dived, grabbing at Ace as he fell down the short incline toward the river. "Ace, Ace, are you okay?" She stopped his slide, jerked up his pant leg, and fumbled in his boot for his throw-down. "Don't go away. I'll be right back." She scrambled up the slope, and fired two quick shots into the trees.

Bits of clay kicked up to her left as two booms echoed from the tree line. She crabbed to her right, then popped up, and fired again. "Ace, I need a speed loader."

The woods went quiet. Keeping her head down, she slid back to Ace, and patted his pockets. "Don't tell me you didn't bring them." Risking a peek at the woods, she thought, Can't see anything. Have they gone? She glanced toward Ace.

He didn't move, lying face down with his head toward the water. Blood covered his shoulder, and thigh.

A rustle from the trees attracted her attention. She took a quick scan of the area. Something moved. She sighted and pulled the trigger, the .357 slug kicking a large chunk of bark from a pine tree. *Crap. Only one more bullet. I'd better not miss next time—if there is a next time.*

"Oh damn, that hurts. Look, I'm bleeding." The words came from the forest. "Somebody's got a damn cannon over there. I ain't hangin' around for this shit."

Kit listened, hoping she'd hear sounds of departure. She heard only a muffle of voices, then quiet. *Damn, what are they up to? Trick? Maybe they're trying to make me think they're gone. Show a target, you bastard, an ear's enough.* Gradually, she relaxed. "Ace, answer me, Ace. Do you have the speed loaders?" The tree line stayed silent.

She returned to Ace's side. "This is a five shot, remember?" She crossed over him as quickly as possible, keeping her rear end down, then lifted his wounded shoulder. "It passed through, Ace. That's good—I think . . . isn't it?" She felt his neck for the carotid artery. A strong pulse answered her fingertips. "Okay, you just rest, I'll check our friends again."

She glanced, but neither saw nor heard anything. "Wish I knew what those guys are doing." She crawled back to Ace, and quickly tested each pocket without finding a speed loader. "Okay Ace, I guess you don't have one. Now, let's see what I can do here. How you feeling, fella? No problem. You'll either make it or I'll kick your dead ass all over Texas." She forced a smile, but Ace did not reciprocate. Nervously, she undid the scarf from her neck and tore it into two pieces. "Okay, this might hurt." She crammed one piece into the front of his shirt, placing it firmly against the exit wound. The second went onto the entry hole. Blood continued to flow. She knew she had to apply pressure.

Desperately, she looked around the area, seeing nothing she could use to put pressure on the makeshift bandages. Sighing, she slumped in defeat resting her head on Ace's stomach — on the belt buckle of his wide western belt.

She unfastened the belt. *You'd love this if you were awake.* After tugging it from his jeans, she placed it around his upper chest. It was short, but by pulling hard, it fastened in the first notch, fitting snugly over the pieces of scarf and applying pressure on the wounds. With the shoulder wound bound, She sat back and grinned. "Shit, those bastards."

She scrambled to the edge again, seeing nothing except trees, but hearing murmuring from the same spot as before. "Don't know what they're talking about," she said settling beside Ace, "but I'd better examine your leg." She stopped. *C'mon, girl, think. There's a big artery in the thigh. Bright red blood pumping out would mean it was hit. Looks red to me, but it's oozing more than pumping. Hope that means it missed. I'll use a tourniquet anyway.*

She looked at the trees again and heard another noise. Straining, she recognized the sounds of someone moving through the trees away from her. The sounds grew fainter . . . fainter, then faded away altogether. She relaxed and grinned. They were gone—she hoped. If it was a trick, they could come at her from another angle.

She looked at Ace wondering what to do. Inspiration struck. Laying down the pistol, she peeled off her T-shirt, then unhooked her bra. "Okay Ace, I've been wearing one of these since I was eleven. Now you get the pleasure." She slipped it around his thigh above the wound, stretched the elastic, tied it as tightly as she could, then sat back and admired her handiwork. *Looks funny, but the bleeding seems to be slowing.*

The shooters. Again, she eyed the woods. All quiet, no murmuring, no movement. As she squinted, trying to penetrate the shade of the underbrush, a rabbit hopped into the clearing from where they had been. "Thanks, little buddy," she said, relief flooding over her. "Hope you get lucky tonight."

She shuffled to Ace's side, picked up her shirt and wiped his forehead, seeing a trickle of blood. She moved a large rock. "I see why you're not talking. Did you have to crack your head, too?" She lightly rubbed the lump and was gratified to see the bleeding had stopped. "Looks like we're in the clear. Don't go 'way while I scoot up to the car, get my cell phone, and call for help. It's either that or I'll have to drag you out of here."

"Damn, ma'am. Always said Clark's Ferry has some beautiful sights. Those prove me right."

Kit flung her shirt aside and grabbed for the revolver. Before she could retrieve it, someone seized her wrist.

"Hold it, ma'am. I'm the law. Name's Dub. Ask Ace. He knows me." He stared at Ace. "Ah, crap. Might wanna put your shirt on. We're gonna need some medics here."

Kit blushed, trying simultaneously to grab her T-shirt, cross her arms over her breasts, and turn her back to Dub. She accomplished two out of three.

* * *

Kit lost track of time over the next few hours. Her memory came back fragmented. Dub had radioed for an ambulance, and they arrived with lights whirling and siren wailing. The EMTs unloaded and worked on Ace like he'd been wounded in a war zone.

She remembered a medic punching an IV into Ace's arm, then saying, "Dam'dest tourniquet I ever seen. Worked, though." He lifted his eyes and stared at Kit's T-shirt. "George Killian's Irish Red. Nice, very nice. Only a two-pack, but nice."

She crossed her arms over her chest.

Sheriff Galoway was close behind the ambulance and stomped around, cussing. A medivac chopper landed, loaded Ace, and airlifted him out. Kit tried to follow Ace on board, but there was not enough space.

As the helicopter gained altitude and turned west, Sheriff Galoway asked Kit, "What happened out here?"

"Where are they going? I didn't ask." Tears welled in her eyes. "Dammit, not now." She swiped her arm across her face.

"Dallas. He'll be okay. They're the best." He looked back toward the departing helicopter, now lost behind the tall trees. "Now, you and I need to talk. Tell me what happened."

"Not now, Sheriff," Kit answered. "I'm going after Ace."

"Oh no, you're not. You're in no condition to drive."

Kit walked toward Ace's car, determined to follow. She pulled on the door handle. Locked. "The keys, Ace. The keys are in your pocket." She rested her head on the soft-top, tears quietly plopping onto the canvas.

Sheriff Galoway had followed her to the car. He watched for a few seconds, then sighed, gripped her by the shoulders, and turned her to him, letting his arms slide around her. "Cry it out, missy. Get it out of your system. Can't be bawling like this around Ace. Might upset him."

Kit felt good nestling against his chest. She felt small and safe, like she had when she was a youngster, and her father had comforted her after skinning a knee. Gradually, tears changed to sniffles, then stopped.

Over her head, the sheriff said, "Dub, call in Bull and Brogan to secure the scene. You're headed for Dallas." He lifted her chin. "Miss, a man's damn lucky to have a woman to cry over him. In my book, Ace is double-lucky to have you. Go with Dub. I think you need Ace more than he needs you right now."

Later, Kit recognized the wonderful truth in what he'd said. Medical personnel treat the injured, but who takes care of those who love them? She needed Ace to treat her wounds. She accepted that Ace was in her bloodstream, and she would never bleed him out.

Dub radioed for the backup, then walked over to the sheriff. "You sure about this? Didn't know providing taxi service was part of our job descriptions."

"Not taxi service. You happen to be going the same direction. I want you to stand by in case Ace decides to make a statement." The sheriff turned his attention back to Kit. "Miss, when Ace wakes, tell him I'll fill Chip in on this mess. Give your statement to Dub. I'll talk to you and Ace in a couple of days."

* * *

It was three in the morning, the day after the shooting. Dub had delivered Kit to the hospital in Dallas and stayed with her. They sat in a refrigerated waiting room on uncomfortable plastic chairs somewhere in the cavernous medical facility.

During the drive from Clark's Ferry, Kit had filled Dub in on what happened, or as much as she could. She held back the information about the call to Johnny's cell phone, deciding that information was for her use only. Johnny would make his explanations directly to her.

She idled over the ambush, analyzing, and organizing each event. Suddenly she looked at Dub, her brain clicking furiously. How had he managed to walk up at precisely the right moment? Could he one of the shooters? She sat up straight. "What were you doing at Clark's Ferry?"

"Whoa, ma'am. I don't like that look in your eye. I drove out there because Sheriff Galoway told me to. He said Ace would probably go back to the scene, so he put out the word that any deputy in the area should swing through. It just happened to be me. Could have been Bull or any of the other guys." He grinned. "Shore glad it was me though. I wouldn't have missed sitting here all night for nothing."

Kit stared at him, then relented. "Sorry, Dub. I'm just screwed up in the head right now. Wish someone would let us know what's going on."

Even as she spoke, the door opened, and a man in scrubs walked in. "Are you here for Arthur Edwards?"

Arthur? Kit thought. Oh, he means Ace. "Yes."

"I'm Doctor Win, Mr. Edwards' surgeon. He should recover nicely. He's weak right now, still under the anesthesia. We repaired the damage to his chest and leg, a lot of tissue and muscle. Fortunately, the bullets didn't hit anything vital. He has a mild concussion, but nothing to be concerned about. He's really quite lucky. I've seen two bullets and a crack on the head do a lot more damage."

Kit listened intently, her eyes dry. Even though the news was good, almost as good as she could have hoped, there was a burning in the pit of her stomach, an aching for revenge. The son-of-a-bitch who shot Ace would pay, and pay big.

"How long's he gonna be in here?" Dub asked.

"Few days, no more than a week. After that, we'll move him down to the rehab ward for another week or so. I can't say for sure. Depends on how quickly he regains his strength. He'll be flat for a few days. Then, they'll push him onto his feet and put him through physical therapy. He won't be running marathons anytime soon."

Kit laughed, maybe because she was giddy with fatigue, maybe because of the relief the doctor's words brought. Or maybe because the picture of Ace running a marathon was beyond her. On many occasions, she'd invited him to join her in 10k charity runs. He always found an excuse.

Doctor Win looked at her, concern showing on his face. "Are you okay, miss?"

"Fine," she said through a grin. "Just relieved. I don't envy you trying to keep Ace down. When he wakes, he'll be hard to handle."

He chuckled. "Oh, we're quite experienced in treating rambunctious patients. We get a bunch of cowboys here. Most of them want to leave earlier than we recommend. Now, if you'll excuse me, I'm off duty. Doctor Sism will take over." He left the waiting room.

"I gotta call Sheriff Galoway." Dub looked at his watch. "He said wake him when I had news, no matter what time it was."

He dropped coins into the pay phone and brought the sheriff up to date. After listening for a moment, his head swiveled toward Kit. "Don't know. I'll ask her." He cupped his palm over the mouthpiece. "Ms. Levitt, wanna ride back with me?"

"How soon are you leaving?"

"Anytime. Certainly within an hour."

"Good, I'm ready now. Ace's car is at Clark's Ferry. Ace's cats are in the motel, and the shooters are in the area."

"Uh, Miss Kit—"

"Don't waste your breath, Dub. I'm going to find that bastard. If you and Sheriff Galoway want him, you'd better stay near me. You can have what's left."

Dub shrugged, then spoke into the phone. "She's coming with me, and she's breathing fire."

CHAPTER NINETEEN

Dub and Kit left Ace in ICU—recovering nicely, according to his nurse—arriving at Clark's Ferry about eight in the morning. They walked to the Ace's Sebring, Kit with his keys in her hand.

Bull, the senior deputy on the scene, stepped forward. "Sorry, ma'am, but you can't take the car. Sheriff said nothing can be moved without his permission."

"What do you mean?" Kit exploded. "I—"

"Easy, Ms. Levitt." Dub lay his hand on Kit's arm. "Let me take care of this." Turning to Bull, he said, "I'll take the responsibility. This lady had her friend shot, was a target herself, and spent the night in an uncomfortable hospital waitin' room sittin' on a plastic chair. She needs rest. She can take the car."

Bull stammered, "But, the sheriff—".

"I said, it's okay," Dub said in a firm voice. "I'll brief him myself."

A few minutes later, Kit drove away with no desire to look back. Sleep was foremost in her mind—that and relief that Ace would be all right. At the motel, she was greeted by Sweeper and Striker who dashed in from the adjoining room. "Hi, guys," she said, leaning down and stroking them. "Give me a moment, and I'll tell you about your dad."

She filled their food and water dishes and cleaned out the litter box. Sweeper and Striker watched from Ace's pillow, then promptly curled together and went to sleep.

"Okay, we'll talk later." After putting the Do Not Disturb sign on both doors, she flopped onto the bed in her room, fully clothed—except for her blood-soaked bra. It rested in a plastic bag on the back seat of the car beside Ace's jacket, where the speed loaders resided.

* * *

Kit awoke about one p.m. She was rested, but still felt sluggish, a lack-of-sleep, hung-over feeling, her head throbbing slowly to an unheard beat. Gradually, she sat up, slipping her legs over the edge of the bed.

Striker and Sweeper bounded from Ace's room and leapt up beside her. "Easy, give me a moment." She stood, stretched, then fixed a pot of coffee. While it brewed, she returned to the cats. "Okay, if you'll be patient until I get some caffeine, I'll bring you up to date."

The two animals waited, staring as if they understood every word she said. A few minutes later, she was back, sipping from a Styrofoam cup. "Ace was shot, hit twice, but he's going to be okay. He's in the hospital in Dallas. Sorry, but they don't have cat visiting hours."

Striker pawed at his eyes. "Meow."

"Meow," Sweeper echoed in a mournful tone.

"We don't have time to feel sorry for ourselves. It's up to us to find the people who hurt him." She sipped her coffee, carefully studying them. "Ace says you might have psychic powers. If you do, I need help. Give me a clue."

Sweeper looked at her, yawned, then stood. "Meow," he said again as if calling for her attention. He hunched his shoulders and walked on tiptoes, tilting his head so he stared down his nose.

"Sorry, little buddy. If that's a clue, I don't get it. Ace said you did something like that for him, and he didn't understand it either." Kit stood, stretched and eyed the bed. She was still tired, not recovered from the night's adventure. "Nope, that will have to wait." She looked back at the cats. "Hang on. I'll check on Ace."

After her call, she told the cats, "The nurse says he's doing as good as can be expected—whatever that means."

Sweeper and Striker gave her a long look, then curled up on her pillow.

Kit thought for a moment, then picked up the phone again. She dialed Tom Roberts' number. She knew Tom from the cases she'd worked with Ace and had used him when she needed computer support. However, she also knew Tom had a talent that did not appear on his business cards. He could acquire unregistered weapons, often without serial numbers.

Tom answered on the third ring. After he and Kit exchanged the necessary amenities, she briefed him on Ace.

"So, what can I do to help?"

"I need an automatic handgun, nothing too heavy, but something that will bring down an elephant with one hit."

"Oh, sure. Not a problem," he replied, chuckling. "I'll check under the cushions on my sofa."

"Obviously, you're not taking me seriously. Make it two pistols, one for my waistband and a second for my purse. I need stopping power—and they need to be lightweight."

"Have you thought through this?" Tom asked, his voice serious. "I thought you were the anti-gun PI, never carry. You're hooked on Ace, but there's a better answer. Back off and let the locals handle it."

"Look, I won't deny you usually offer good advice. But this time I need a handgun and my .22's not up to the job. Just get me the weapons. I'll take care of the rest." Kit paused.

Tom said nothing.

"I know you're there. I hear you breathing. Can you meet me at the hospital tonight?"

After a few more minutes with Tom losing every argument, he agreed to do his best. Kit replaced the handset, feeling better. She knew Tom would come through, or bust his butt trying.

She lay back. "Okay, what should I do next? Maybe I'll collect phone numbers and start shaking the bushes."

Sweeper and Striker snoozed on.

She retrieved the phone book from the nightstand and thumbed through it, stopping three times to write down numbers. The first call went to Sheriff Galoway. "Any progress?"

"Depends on what you mean. I checked Ace a few minutes ago, and he's coming along. Dub just came in so I sent him to Clark's Ferry to take charge of the scene. Bull and Brogan came up with shell casings from the edge of the woods, two nine-millimeter and two .32s. Haven't found the slugs that dropped Ace."

"What about the shooters? Anything on them?" Kit reviewed the incident. Yeah, two guns sounded right.

"A few stomped-down weeds, two cigarette butts. Looked like they'd only been there a few minutes. Must have showed up just before you two. Did anyone know where you were headed?"

Kit remembered the call Ace had made to Johnny's cell phone. Since they'd been in no hurry and had stopped for gas, Johnny would have had time to contact someone, pick him up, beat them to the site, and set up an ambush.

"No, no one I know of," she said. "It was a spur of the moment thing. We simply decided to drive out."

"Why do I find that hard to swallow as the whole truth?"

"You wouldn't accuse a lady of lying, would you, Sheriff? I have to run now. I'll—"

"Miss, I'd appreciate it if you'd call me Bob. This is a little county in East Texas. First names go farther here."

Kit smiled at his small-town friendliness. "That sounds good. Call me Kit." She paused. "But being on a first name basis isn't going to stop me from bringing those bastards down. I hope you understand that."

"No, I don't understand. Those bastards, as you call them, citizens as I'm forced to call them, are my responsibility. Better if you go home to Dallas and take care of Ace. I'll get the guilty bastards, uh . . . excuse me, the citizens who shot him."

"I'll stay out of your way," Kit said. "I'll be so far in front you won't even see my dust." She hung up the phone with a smile dancing around her eyes.

She looked at her list of numbers, then dialed Johnny Nichols' house.

A woman answered.

"Is this Ms. Nichols?"

"Yes, who is calling?"

"Ms. Nichols. My name is Carsen Levitt. Most folks call me Kit. I'm working with Ace on the case he took for your husband. I'd like to speak with Johnny, please."

"Johnny left a note to take no calls from Ace. I am sure that applies to you, also. I—"

"Listen. I don't care what message he left. Someone shot Ace, and I'm going to find out who did it. That will involve talking with your Johnny whether he wants to chat or not. Tell him I expect to hear from him soon."

"Ms. Levitt, you do not understand. I am not Johnny's secretary, and I do not have to—"

"That's right. You don't, but you will. I'm going to be all over you and your husband. When you buy tomatoes, I'll be there to squeeze them for you. When Johnny buys gas, I'll be at the next pump. You two are going to have me on your backs every minute of every day until I find the bastards that shot Ace. Now, write that on your mirror and stare at it." Kit slammed the phone down. *Hey, you're good. You even spooked yourself with that.*

After looking at the last number on her list, she said, "Later," and crossed into Ace's room.

Sweeper and Striker marched beside her, new looks of respect on their faces.

From the nightstand, she picked up the notepad and added Johnny's cell number to her list. Sweeper and Striker escorted her back to her room. On her cell phone she punched in Johnny's number. The cats curled at her feet.

Johnny's answering service picked up, requesting she leave a message.

"This is Kit Levitt. I work with Ace and need to talk to you. If you have doubts about me, you might want to touch base with your wife. Give me a call. It will be easier on you if we approach this on a friendly basis." She added her phone number and hung up wondering if she'd been strong enough to elicit a response.

She looked down at the cats who snored. "Okay, one more call, then I'll leave you for a while. Ms. Evans and I need to chat. If she's half of what Ace described, she'll probably be too high and mighty to talk to me."

Sweeper and Striker continued to snooze.

They looked so comfortable she was tempted to nudge them awake, but instead dialed Ms. Evans' number.

"Evans residence," a male voice said.

Kit took a deep breath. "Hello, my name is Kit Levitt. May I speak to Ms. Evans?"

"I am sorry, Miss, but Mrs. Evans is not available."

"Does that mean she's home and won't talk to me or that she's not home, and I should call back later?"

"I stand by what I said, Miss Levitt. She is unavailable."

"Thank you, and what is your name?"

"I am Marston Coker, Mrs. Evans' butler."

"Well, thank you, Mr. Coker. Your eagerness to help is well beyond the norm. Please inform Ms. Evans she and I will talk." Kit hung up, frustrated. "This case gives stonewalling a whole new meaning."

She leaned back again and closed her eyes, taking deep breaths while flexing her fingers. This was a habit she'd nurtured for those times when she was about to lose control. Gradually, her body relaxed, the tension draining away. Her mind searched the case, but came up with nothing new.

After a few moments, she sat up and swung her legs to the floor. "Okay, little buddies, I'm headed for Dallas to check on Ace. When I get back, I might swing by Ms. Evans' estate. Probably have to pay her a visit before this is over. While I'm out there, I'll check Johnny's place. Somebody knows more than they're willing to say. Besides, I don't like people who brush me off. Makes me damn curious."

She replenished the cats' food and water supply, checked the lock on Ace's door, then stroked the cats good-bye. They gave her the same acknowledgment they always gave Ace. They ate.

* * *

Ace was still in ICU. The nurse on duty, Ms. Harper, said he was under heavy sedation, all vital signs were excellent, and he was looking better. She opined he might move to a room the next day.

When Kit saw him, she thought his appearance was terrible. He had as many wires and tubes attached to him as the early astronauts. "You said he looks better," she told Ms. Harper. "His color is not normally mottled-white."

"You should have seen him earlier, all mottles, little white," Ms. Harper said, grinning. Her look turned serious. "He's been mumbling periodically. Do you know anyone named Terry or Sherry or something like that?"

Kit gasped, then tried to cover it with a cough. *Dammit, even when he's out cold, she's still at the front of his mind.*

"Sounds like a name, but I can't be sure," the nurse continued. "If it's a person, it might be nice if he or she would visit. It could help his progress."

"Terri," Kit said.

Ms. Harper gave her a questioning look.

"She's dead."

"Who was she, his wife?"

"No, just someone he loved very deeply." After a moment, Kit added, "She died in his arms. He's never gotten over her."

"I'm sorry," Ms. Harper said. She gave Kit a sympathetic look. "And I'm sorry for you. Must be tough loving a guy who chases a ghost."

Shit. Am I that obvious? Kit opened her mouth to reply, but a tap on her shoulder cut her off. A nurse said, "Excuse me, ma'am. If you're Kit Levitt, there's a man in the waiting room looking for you."

CHAPTER TWENTY

Kit thanked Ms. Harper for her time and walked out of ICU admonishing herself for wearing her feelings so transparently on her sleeve. What she needed was a full body flush, to get Ace out of her system.

Tom Roberts leaned against the doorframe of the waiting room. "How's he doing?"

"The nurse says okay. He looks like hell to me. But they might move him to a room tomorrow." She looked around, then asked in a quiet voice, "Did you get them?"

"In my car. I found a dark corner. That'll give us time to chat."

"Won't do any good, Tom. You can't change my mind. Some sonnavabitch is going to pay."

"I agree, but that doesn't mean you have to play vigilante."

Kit shot him a determined look.

They started across the parking lot. "Why don't I drive over to your car?" Kit asked. "It's been too tough a day for long walks."

They shifted direction. After crossing several rows, Tom said, "Ace's Sebring? That'll get him out quick. You know how he loves that car. Did your roller skate die?"

"No, but I'm driving it less this way. It has over two hundred thousand now. I don't want to run up the mileage."

Tom chuckled as they entered the car, and Kit pulled out of the space. On the other side of the parking lot, in the darkest corner, she pulled alongside Tom's vehicle. He got out and popped the trunk. Inside were two rolled towels. Looking slowly around the area, he picked up one and held it against his chest. "Sure you won't change your mind?"

"Not a chance. Don't waste your breath. My mind is made up."

"Okay. I have two nine mils, lightweight subcompacts. Unloaded, they weigh about a pound. The magazines hold ten rounds, and you can keep one in the chamber, although I don't recommend it. They're double action, and the recoil's not too bad. Should be exactly what you need."

"Sounds good. Let me see one."

Tom checked the parking area again, then opened the towel. An automatic weapon gleamed in the faint light.

Kit fingered it, then balanced it in her hand. "Nice. Feels good." She pointed the weapon away from Tom across the lot.

"Hey, don't do that. There are rent-a-cops all over the place. The last thing we want is someone calling 9-1-1."

Kit grinned and handed it back. "Fits like an expensive pair of jeans. You done good."

He rolled the automatic back into its towel, picked up the other, and they walked to Ace's car.

Two hours later, after late night coffee with Tom and his ineffective arguments for her to let the local police handle the investigation, Kit parked in front of her motel room. Carefully checking the area for lurkers, she entered.

Sweeper and Striker slept on her bed. "What's up?" She sat beside them, running her fingers along their backs.

They opened sleepy eyes, stared briefly, and went back to dozing.

"Okay, if that's the way you feel. Hang tight, I have to get something from the car." She watched them briefly, rose, and walked out the door. She paused, looked around, then returned to the car, and retrieved the two towels. Once back in the motel, she stripped the automatics and cleaned them carefully. After she was satisfied they were in perfect working order, she undressed for bed. "Remember, you two," she said as she scooted between the sheets, shoving Sweeper and Striker aside, "I've earned a late morning. Take care of yourselves and be quiet about it."

The cats woke, glared at her, jumped down, and ran into Ace's room.

* * *

Kit woke at 8:30 to find Sweeper and Striker snuggled close beside her. She grinned. *My first time with two males.* She remembered other nights when it had been Ace with whom she had cuddled—with nothing between them.

Suppressing a yawn, she slipped from bed, showered and dressed in her standard jeans, T-shirt and boots. After taking care of the cats' needs for the day, she sipped a cup of coffee as she dialed the hospital. Ace was doing better and would be moved later in the day.

Feeling good at the news, she called the sheriff's office.

His response to her question punched a hole in her euphoria. "Nope, haven't come up with anything new. How about you?"

"Nothing, but I'm still digging. I'll let you know what I find out."

"Yeah, I just bet you will." Sheriff Galoway punctuated his comment with a wry chuckle. "Remember to call before you get yourself into trouble."

After replacing the handset, Kit thought for a moment, then spoke to the cats sitting on their haunches watching her. "If there are any rumors floating in Grand Saline, they'll probably find a home in the Sabine Cafe. I bet Mable knows everything that happens around here. If she doesn't, Janie Blackman at the newspaper will." After pondering another few minutes with no better ideas coming to mind, she stepped to the mirror and applied lipstick.

"Okay, guys, you're in charge," she said, her hand on the doorknob.

The phone rang.

"Hello."

"Is this Kit Levitt?"

"Yeah, who's this?"

"Candi Maladay, Ace's lawyer. Can we meet for breakfast? I heard what happened, and we need to talk."

Kit didn't reply.

"Hey, you there? Ace has friends, and we want to know what bullshit is going on."

"Meet me at the Sabine Café in Grand Saline if you want to help. How long will you be?"

"I know the place," the voice replied. "Give me a half-hour. I don't know what you look like so watch for a blond in a black pantsuit carrying a black briefcase. That'll be me."

Kit signed off, wondering if she really wanted to meet with Candi. Ace's description of her had been derogatory. Of course, he'd also said he was happy she'd been hired as his lawyer. "Guess she can't be all bad," Kit told the cats, picking them up. "What do you think?"

Striker purred, his reaction to being picked up.

Sweeper squirmed out of her arms and leapt to the floor. He spent a moment washing his face, then looked at her and purred. His eyes were slitted making him appear happy, but devious.

"I'll take that as a good sign."

* * *

"Hey, I heard your hunk got shot. How's he doing, hon?" Mabel said as a greeting while Kit seated herself. "Figured you'd be gone by now."

"He's recovering, and I'm hanging around to find out who did it. You hear anything?"

"Only that he was making some folks uncomfortable. Now what can I get for you?"

Kit stared at Mabel who kept her attention on her pad. "If you know something, I wish you'd tell me. Ace could have been killed, and so could I. They were flinging lead all over the place."

Mabel picked up the menu and studied it. "I recommend a bagel and coffee. Want cream cheese with that?"

"Hold the bagel. I'm meeting someone. Just bring coffee for now."

Mabel walked away with Kit wondering what she knew, if anything.

"You must be Kit Levitt. You don't look like you grew up in Grand Saline."

Kit turned toward the voice and saw an attractive, well-dressed blond in a black pantsuit carrying a briefcase. She glanced at her watch and saw that twenty-eight minutes had passed since her phone conversation. "You're Candi?"

"Yes, but the question was are you Kit Levitt?"

"That's me." *Damn, this can't be the woman Ace described. She looks great.*

"You look surprised. Let me guess. I don't look like Ace's description. I bet he used terms like fat, terrible dresser, frowsy hair, red-frame glasses. Did I miss anything?"

Laughing, Kit replied, "You're close. He did say you were smart, though."

Candi hooted, a witch's cackle just as Ace had said. "I'll bet he had some choice things to say. He was right. When we met, I'd let myself go. Gained weight, didn't care what I wore, never colored my hair." She pulled out a chair and sat. "All I wanted was revenge on Chip Jamison. In a way, Ace saved me." She paused. "Hey, Mabel. What do I have to do to get a menu?"

"You can't leave me dangling with a line like that," Kit said.

A smile lit Candi's face, enhancing her beauty. "Okay, when Ace solved Joseph's kidnapping, the case he took for Chip, it brought us back together. Getting a second chance gave me incentive to take off the weight. The rest of what you see is store-bought—hair, clothes, make-up, contacts." She'd pointed at each as she enumerated it. "I'm sure he also told you my favorite word is bullshit. See, I'm even trying to use it less. Haven't said it once since I walked in."

"Wish I had a camera," Kit said. "Ace will never believe me."

"That's enough of the bullshit." She grinned. "Let's get down to business." She looked toward the waitress station where Mabel stood, head down. "Mabel, bring me a grapefruit and some coffee, please."

"I'm working on it, hon," Mabel said, looking up from her work. "Knew you'd want one. Now, if this damn thing will quit spitting at me. When you gonna start eatin' normal again?"

A few minutes later, the grapefruit and coffees were served along with a bagel and cream cheese. Kit chose not to comment.

Candi proved she was serious about her weight. She drank the coffee black and sprinkled artificial sweetener on her grapefruit. Popping a section into her mouth, she said, "Catch me up on Ace. I know he survived the surgery, but what's his status now? How soon can he get out here? Getting shot should take the pressure off as far as the sheriff is concerned, but he needs to get to the bottom of this bullshit."

"He's doing great. Later today, he'll be shifted from ICU to a room. Now, tell me what you know about the Evans family. They must be involved some way."

"You're twirling a big lasso there, honey. Lottie Evans is a powerful woman out here. I don't know what would bring her down, but the deaths of a couple of creeps like the Nobles probably won't do it."

"Suppose she's behind Ace's shooting?"

"You don't want to know. Ace is big to you, and I love him dearly, but out here, he's no bigger than a flea on a Great Dane, and Ms. Evans is definitely the big show dog in this part of Van Zandt." She sipped her coffee. "Okay, what do I do? How about the Nobles?"

"Sounds like you're dealing yourself in."

"You better believe it, sweetie. Like I said, I owe Ace, and that's uncomfortable for me. When this is over, I will have paid my debt. Somebody's coming down for the bullshit they did to him."

"Leave some space for me."

"Sorry, I don't mean to crowd." Candi frowned. "I'm just so damn pissed off. I'll handle the legal end of things. That's my forte."

Kit stirred her coffee, then spread cream cheese on the last bite of bagel. "Candi, if you really want in, skip the Nobles. Somebody's already on them, and they're so transparent, they'll be easy. Go after Ms. Evans and Johnny Nichols. Dig out everything you can find, and, if you happen to stumble across some dirt along the way, that's even better."

Candi nodded.

"While you're doing that," Kit continued, "I'll dig around and see if I can uncover any shallow graves. Maybe there's a skeleton or two that wasn't buried deep enough."

While Kit spoke, Mabel arrived with a fresh pot of coffee. "Hon, I don't want y'all to get hurt. There's some folks 'round here that won't hesitate rearranging your pretty faces."

"Yeah, who?" Candi asked.

Randy Rawls

CHAPTER TWENTY-ONE

Mabel looked around before responding to Candi's question in a quiet voice. "'Bout fifteen years ago, a man come to town. Said Ms. Evans was gonna sell him property along highway eighty for a shopping center. Later, he said she changed her mind, but it wouldn't do her no good. Said he had enough on her to get the land. I never saw him again. Some folks say he gave up and left town." She scanned the room again, then whispered, "I was with him the night before he disappeared. I know he didn't just quit on the deal. You girls be careful. Ms. Evans don't let nothin' stand in her way." She refilled the coffee cups.

A voice from the rear of the restaurant called, "Mabel, you working today? My cup's empty."

"Remember what I said." She shook her finger at them, then moved toward the complaining customer.

Kit stared after her, then turned to Candi. "What do you think?"

"Mabel's a good waitress. For all the years I've eaten here, she's never been a gossip. I trust her, and that means I believe her story."

Candi and Kit talked for another half-hour, discussing Ace and whispering about Ms. Evans. Mabel refilled their coffee cups twice more while ducking their questions.

After paying and leaving a generous tip, they walked from the cafe. Candi went toward her black Mercedes while Kit turned toward the newspaper office.

She entered the lobby of the *Grand Saline Sun*, and a lady with a smooth Texas accent greeted her.

"Hi. Is Janie Blackman in?"

"Have a seat, and I'll find her. We have fresh coffee if you'd like a cup."

Janie came in from the rear of the building. "I remember you. You were with that PI from Dallas. Just traveling through, you said."

Kit smiled, sticking out her hand to shake. "Ace and I stretched the truth a bit. At that point, we hoped I could snoop without attracting too much attention. Guess you heard what happened. Now, I don't care what I attract."

"I suppose not. Three shootings in a few days. That's a ten year supply for Grand Saline. Do you think they're connected?" As she spoke, she led the way to a private office.

"Can't see it any other way," Kit said, seating herself. "Have you heard anything?"

"Nothing I can print."

"And just what does that mean?"

"Ms. Levitt, do you know who owns this paper?"

"No and the name is Kit." She paused. "You mean, Ms. Evans?"

"Yes. We got the word right after the article about the death of the Nobles that we were to write no more on the subject, and anyone who did could look for another job—in another state."

"Sure, but what about Ace's shooting?"

"Same rules." Janie looked at her hands. "Ms. Levitt, uh, Kit, I've probably already said too much. I have a six-month old baby, and my husband is a native of Grand Saline. He doesn't want to leave. I need this job."

"Understood. I promise not to let anyone know where I obtained the info. Have you heard anything?"

She sighed, examined her nails and then looked at the ceiling. "Some people whisper that Ms. Evans does not tolerate people who make a nuisance of themselves. I can't say it's true, but if I were in your shoes, I'd be careful."

"Janie, I already know that. I need specifics."

"Like I said. I need this job."

Kit's frustration was near the surface. "Two murders and one attempted murder—two if you count the shots at me. Do you want to raise your baby in a town filled with outlaws? Do you want to write about the flower club while assassins walk the streets? Is that the legacy you want to pass on?"

Janie's eyes misted and her head dropped. "No, but . . ."

Kit waited, exuding patience, but never looking away from Janie. *Tell me what you know.*

"Ms. Evans is a crusty old bitch who's determined to have her way. She'll throw money around and buy anything and anybody in sight. However, I can't see her as a murderer. A control freak, yes. A conspirator in murder, no." Janie sighed and bit her lower lip. "But be careful of the people around her. They'll be watching you." She stood and walked from the office.

* * *

Kit drove to the motel. Her breakfast with Candi had left her feeling frumpy in jeans, boots, and T-shirt. She slipped into black slacks and a simple white blouse.

Sweeper and Striker sauntered in from Ace's connecting room. They sat on their haunches, watching her change clothes.

"What do you think? Is this better?" she asked.

"Meow," Striker said and rubbed against her leg.

Sweeper continued to stare, not moving.

She hesitated, then left her boots in the small wardrobe, slipping on sandals. The ankle holster came off to be left behind with Ace's .357 in the dresser drawer.

Sweeper stood, stretched, shook his head, and walked toward the connecting doorway.

"Hey, I'm not unarmed. Look." She took one of the nine mils and dropped it into her purse with an extra magazine. "See. I'll be okay."

Sweeper stopped, walked toward her, then lay down, and began to lick his fur.

"I assume that means you feel better." She stepped in front of the mirror and ran her fingers through her hair. "Nothing I can do with this. Short is short." After a fresh application of lipstick and a good-bye to the cats, she left.

She'd decided to run Johnny to ground if she could. She suspected that calling him in advance would be counterproductive so she drove to the Evans estate. As she pulled past the huge mansion, Kit wondered how lonely the old lady's life must be with no one except her hired guns and her grandson when he was in town.

About a quarter mile farther down the driveway, there was a large cottage. This must be Johnny and Louise's home. It faced away from the big house with a large porch across the front. Comfortable rocking chairs and a swing gave the house a country feeling. Kit rang the doorbell. An attractive, mid to late thirties blond opened the door. Kit noticed tiny worry lines around the eyes.

"Hi, I'm Kit Levitt. Is Johnny here?"

The smile disappeared, replaced by a look of disapproval. "Where were you when I went shopping this morning? I had to squeeze my own tomatoes. You said you'd be there to help me."

"Sorry about the other day, Ms. Nichols. I was rather nasty, wasn't I?"

"Yes, but I now know it was after you spent the night at the hospital with Mr. Edwards. Your apology is accepted, but that still does not mean I choose to talk with you."

She began to close the door, but Kit stuck her sandaled foot into the crack. "Ouch, would you mind letting up a bit? My foot's getting crushed."

"Oh, is that what that is?" Louise Nichols replied, sweetly. "I thought the door was jammed." She gave another push.

"Can we call a truce a moment while I get my foot out?" The pressure lessened. "I'd really like to talk to Johnny. Do you know where he is?" She massaged her toes.

"No, I have not known where he is for a long, long time." A look of sadness settled over her attractive face. "Not since he sold out to my mother."

Kit put her foot down and looked at Louise. She saw sadness. "My guess is you need someone to confide in. Maybe a stranger would be best, and I'm about as strange as they come." She grinned with an open look. "If Johnny's not here, I don't have anything to do. Plus, I'm a good listener."

Louise appeared to reflect on what Kit had said. She looked around the front yard, hesitated, then opened the door wide. "Come in. Some tea would be nice."

"That sounds like an excellent idea." Kit followed Louise into the house.

Louise put a teapot of water on to boil. "Would you like to see the house?"

"Sure," Kit replied. At this point, she'd do almost anything to gain Louise's confidence.

They moved from room to room with Louise making small talk, and Kit responding with appropriate comments. What she did not say was she found the place to be cold and sterile, like a hotel suite. The only pictures were of Matthew Thomas, and each showed him with his grandmother. There was nothing reflecting a loving home where a family had lived, loved, and raised a child for over twenty years.

"Miss Levitt, you said you are a good listener." Kit and Louise sat at the kitchen table, steaming cups of tea in front of them. "Do you mind?" Louise continued. "Some days I get so lonely I want to scream." She stood and opened a cabinet. "How about a cookie with your tea?"

"Call me Kit. Are they chocolate chip? Produce one of those, and I'm yours for the duration."

Louise laughed, a delightful, full-throated chortle. "Okay, I'm Louise, and you can be my captive." She brought out a package of soft cookies, opened it, and spread them on a plate. "Have you heard the saga of my storybook marriage? I see your ring finger is bare. This could stop you from ever walking the aisle."

"I've heard a little about it, but no details." Kit wanted Louise's confidence. "Talk. I'm in listening mode."

"I met Johnny while we were in high school. He was a junior, and I was one year behind. He was something to see in those days—star athlete, played trumpet in the band, president of his class. Every girl in school had her eye on him. When he showed interest in me, I was in heaven." She paused and took a sip of tea. "Of course, that was before I told Mother he asked me out."

Her eyes took on a faraway look as she lapsed into silence. She took a cookie and nibbled on it.

"What happened?"

Louise sighed. "Before I tell, you need to know I have never been my mother's favorite." Her eyes were downcast, her voice soft. "Her favorite is the precious son she could never have. When she was pregnant, she openly prayed for a boy, and when I came along, she was disappointed—very disappointed."

"How do you know this?" Kit asked. "Perhaps—"

"She told me. Not once, but many times. She wanted a male to carry on in the Adams tradition—not Evans, mind you, but Adams, her family name. After I was born, she could have no more children. She said I destroyed her ability to have that son. So I grew up yearning to be loved by my mother and doing everything I could to earn it." She frowned, examined her nails, then continued. "When Johnny asked me out, I was a mess. I wanted to go with him, but did not wish to disobey Mother. She forbade my having anything to do with him. She said I must save myself for a rich man, preferably someone with heavy oil holdings. In her world, a woman uses her body to capture a rich husband. Johnny did not qualify." She laughed, a small sardonic laugh. "You see. Even though I was not the child she wanted, she still chose to control my life."

"Where did your dad fit in?"

Louise sipped her tea and took another bite of cookie. "Dad? The bright spot in my childhood. He loved me, nurtured me, told me I was his little girl. He was one of the best, maybe *the* best. But he could not stand up to Mother, no more than I could. He loved her, that I believe, but he also held her in awe. She was so incredible, had such a commanding presence that everyone moved out of her way—my father included." Again, she chuckled, a laugh with no happiness. "You have not met her yet, have you? When you do, you will see what I mean. Remember, she is now seventy-two years old. Try to picture her at thirty, forty, fifty. You may understand what I mean."

"So, how did you and Johnny end up together?"

"Sorry, I got off on a tangent." She sipped. "First time I disobeyed her. Then, in my junior year, Johnny's senior, I became pregnant. Johnny, and I— Well, I do not need to go there, do I?"

"No, I understand how that happens," Kit replied with a smile, hoping to lighten the mood.

Louise ignored it. "Mother went berserk, saying no Adams had ever involved themselves in such a contemptible situation. Daddy did all he could, but she refused to listen. She called Johnny in, and, after several private conversations, demanded we be married in a quiet ceremony. She had this house built for us, and we have lived here since. Not as a family, more like two strangers under the same roof."

"That's so sad," Kit said. "What happened? How did you go from a loving teenage couple to Johnny's reputation of ignoring the connubial bed?"

Kit's comment about Johnny's lack of marital fidelity brought a flush to Louise's face.

"True, Johnny has led a randy life. But, when I look back, I am not sure who is at fault." She sipped, bit into a cookie, then chewed with a thoughtful look on her face. "The whole time I was pregnant, Mother talked to me. Johnny was a freshman in college, and I stayed with Mother to have the baby. Every day, she told me Johnny was partying here and partying there, that he went out with this girl and made love to that girl. She made it sound like he was with a different female every night. Kit, I am not proud that I believed her, but please remember, I was only seventeen. I loved Johnny with all my heart, and the things she told cut me so deep I still have scars. Anyway, to shorten the story, at the time Matthew Thomas was born, I hated Johnny, or thought I did. When I came home from the hospital, I moved into the guestroom and told him to never cross that threshold. He cried, he pleaded, he told me how much he loved me and how much he loved Matthew Thomas. I say with no pride that I told him my mother would take care of our son. I also told Johnny he would never touch me again."

"And?" Kit asked.

Louise turned her head from Kit, then said softly. "No man has touched me since."

CHAPTER TWENTY-TWO

Kit and Louise talked for another hour. Mostly Louise talked and Kit listened. It was like a floodgate had opened releasing a torrent of words.

"One of my mother's favorite lectures is that she bought me a husband," she said, "not one that she chose, but one I selected. She loves to say, 'You made your bed. Now lie in it with all the dirt and thorns he brings in.'"

Kit set her teacup on the table and moved beside Louise, putting her arm around her. "I'm sorry. I had no idea. But this is why I need your help. If Johnny doesn't talk to me—"

"How can I help you? He will not talk to me either. We have not talked in too many years. If only I had not believed Mother. If only I had let him know how much I love him. If only, if only . . ."

"It's not too late, Louise. If we get Johnny to help us find the killers, it could change his whole life. If we don't, others may die."

"But, Kit, what can I do? Mother says he is lazy, unreliable, and a philanderer. She says he will never take responsibility for his actions." Tears flowed.

"We must find a way," Kit said. "Anything else is unacceptable." She took a box of tissues from the end table and handed them to Louise. "Blow your nose. It's time for us to work together to change things. Your mother may or may not be involved in shooting Ace. Also, the death of the Nobles was convenient for her. Was it a coincidence or—"

"Please, not that. She is still my mother. I may have differences with her, and I have considered what you say. I cannot believe she would participate."

"Don't dismiss it out of hand," Kit said. "Whoever did it will kill again. They *must* be stopped."

The talk continued until the pile of teabags in front of Kit had climbed to four, and Louise had replenished the chocolate chip cookies twice.

Finally, in exasperation, Kit said, "Louise, if you don't help, Ace will probably die. Whoever shot him won't be satisfied, and what about Johnny? This all started when he walked into the Nobles' blackmail scheme. Now it looks like someone is determined to wipe the slate clean of everyone involved. Jade and Hugo are dead. Ace is lucky to be alive. Even now, the killers may be stalking me because I'm stirring the pot. What makes you think they'll ignore your husband? Someone is eliminating everyone who knows about Johnny's shenanigans and the blackmail."

Louise stared at Kit. "If what you say is true . . ." She sat for a moment while Kit held her breath. "I will do what I can. Enough people have died."

Louise stood, walked to the kitchen counter, and took down the cordless phone. After consulting a list, she punched the number pad. "Louise Nichols here . . . Yes, I am fine . . . Johnny is being difficult. He refuses to level with Ace or to talk to Kit Levitt, Ace's co-investigator. Please speak to him."

Kit relaxed, listening to Louise's end of the conversation, wondering who was on the other end. It went on for a few more minutes, but the gist of it was Louise asked someone to intervene.

When Louise turned the telephone off, she said, "That was Jake. He told me to call him if I ever needed anything. If anyone can get through to Johnny, he can."

* * *

Kit left Louise's house at four, sloshing with tea, and sated on cookies. *No dinner tonight—just a long walk.* She stared at Ms. Evans' house, fighting an impulse to bang on the door and force a confrontation. She was accustomed to taking the shortest route, not pussyfooting around until another day. However, she had agreed Louise could talk with Ms. Evans first. Kit had serious doubts it would change anything.

Climbing into Ace's convertible with the top down, Kit marveled at the story Louise had told of her relationship with Johnny, her mother, and her father. A soft wind ruffled her short blond hair. *This bunch redefines dysfunctional. They don't meet Texas standards.*

As she drove out of the driveway with a last glare at Ms. Evan's house, she made a mental schedule. *First, I'll check on Ace, then take a walk. After that, a nap will be in order. By midnight, I'll be ready to find out if the Goat Lady is for real.*

* * *

Kit parked three spaces from the door to her room. With the way the case was going, she figured nothing should be trusted, even her parking space. She let herself in. Sweeper and Striker ran in from Ace's room.

"Anybody been here while I was out?"

Sweeper gave her a strange look, then jumped onto her bed. "Meow."

"Okay, other than the maid. I can see she rearranged the dust and straightened the covers." Kit stood and surveyed the room, breaking it into quadrants for close scrutiny. Everything appeared to be in order. She checked the zipper on her makeup case finding the hair she'd placed there still laying as she left it. The same applied to the hair hanging from her suitcase zipper.

Both cats were now on the bed, alternating looks between her and one another.

"Meow," Sweeper said.

"Meow," Striker echoed.

"Oh, shut up," Kit said, walking into the adjoining room. "I don't have as much faith in you as watchcats as Ace does."

They followed.

"I guess you were right," she said, rising from looking under the bed. "Nothing under there except a collection of dust bunnies deep enough to support vegetable life."

The cats lay on their bellies and crawled under the bed before quickly backing out, sneezing.

"See, I told you it was dusty."

The three of them returned to Kit's room where she saw the blinking light on the telephone. "Let's see who called." She dialed message retrieval and listened.

The first call was from Candi. "Give me a call. I have news."

The second was also from Candi. "Chip called. You'll love what he had to say."

The third call was from Johnny. It opened with a chuckle. "Kit, this is Johnny Nichols. Jake just finished chewing my ass. Obviously, you got through to my loving, loyal wife who told Jake a cock-and-bull story." He chuckled again. "But, I guess you're not interested in my home life. You want to talk, we'll talk. Meet me at Harvey's Steak Saloon on Route 80 tomorrow morning at nine. We'll have breakfast, and I'll answer your questions, or as many as I can. Bring a big appetite. Harvey serves a great breakfast buffet." There was another chuckle as the line went dead.

The time stamp was four o'clock. Kit listened to his message again trying to hear behind his words. She had the feeling there was something she was missing—or maybe her paranoia was in full gear. The fourth time she listened, she thought there were sounds just before he hung up. On the fifth, she decided there was a quiet squeak, then a click. They reminded her of a door opening and closing.

There were no other messages so she dialed Candi's cell phone, then hung up quickly. "Uh-oh, looks like Candi's smarter than me. The night Ace checked into Grand Saline, the motel operator broke into our call because he was afraid of Ms. Evans. Not a good idea to call her on the house phone." She picked up her purse, took out her cell, and dialed Candi again.

After she'd gotten past the secretary and had Candi on the phone, Kit said, "I'm all yours. What do you have?"

"Are you on your cell?"

"Yes."

"I'm making good headway on putting together a list of Ms. Evans' holdings. She owns things I would have never thought of. No wonder she sweeps with such a big bullshit broom in this part of the county. But that's not the big news. Chip called."

"So you said on the message. What's he up to?"

"Hush, honey. This is too good to be interrupted. Chip said Jake called him. Seems Louise called Jake asking for help with Johnny. So, Jake called him and chewed his ass. Those were Jake's exact words according to Chip—chewed his ass. I love it. Chip says Jake can be very persuasive."

"I guess so," Kit said. "He—"

"I said hush. This is my story. Johnny promised to get in touch with you and help all he can. How about that?"

"He called already."

"Well, why didn't you tell me? What'd he say?"

Kit chose to ignore the response that jumped to her lips. "We're meeting in the morning, some place named Harvey's Steak Saloon."

"Can I go?"

"No, I don't want to spook him. I'd better take this one alone."

"Call me as soon as it's over. I'm dying to find out what he has to say."

Kit rang off, grinning. She knew Ace would curse a blue streak at another obligation owed to Jake.

She dialed the hospital and connected to Ace's room.

"Ace Edwards, perfect patient here."

"Telemarketer Levitt checking in. Great to hear your name."

"'Bout damn time you called. Last I remember we were downrange on the stationary target course alongside the Sabine River. All the nurses could tell me was a cute blond was here with a tall cop during my surgery. They said the same person visited a couple of times while I was napping in ICU. I could only hope it was you and not one of the many other women who dog my steps."

Kit laughed. "Your disposition is back to normal, but you're hallucinating on the drugs. Women definitely do *not* follow you around. On the contrary, your sex life is preparing you for the priesthood." She cut off any protests from Ace. "I'm damn glad you're awake and as clear-headed as you ever get."

Kit brought him up to date on everything that had happened since the Sabine River. He interrupted with laughter when she told him she'd bound his thigh with her bra. His volume increased when she admitted Dub had walked up while she bent over Ace wearing nothing from the waist up except a frown.

"Quit it," he exclaimed. "I'll bust these stitches. But I do envy Dub. It's been a long time since you and I—"

"Drop it, Romeo. Won't happen, and you know why—Terri Hart."

That sobered him. "Any progress on Johnny?"

She quickly told him of her meeting with Louise, and the ensuing phone calls, loving his under-the-breath cursing at Jake's intervening.

"You be careful with Johnny," he said. "I don't know how much we can trust him. Ask Bob or Dub to go with you. I'm sure whatever Johnny has to say will be of interest to them."

"Are you nuts? First, he's mine. I set it up, and I'll reel him in. Second, he'd probably clam up around a cop. Your hunch was he knew more than he was letting on. I have no reason to disagree, and, since he's proven himself a pushover for a wily female, I'll have him eating out of my hand."

"Just make sure he doesn't eat your hand." Ace paused. "Be careful. I've grown accustomed to having you around."

"I will."

They chatted for a few more minutes, then Ace announced, "Gotta run. My vampire nurse is here to draw a gallon of blood."

Kit hung up feeling good. "Hey," she called to the cats. "Ace feels much better."

They celebrated by running to the food dishes.

Maybe someday soon, Terri will fade far enough into the background for us. She reflected over that thought. *Then again, maybe not.*

* * *

"Candi," Kit said into the phone. "Want to go spooking tonight?" After she'd pictured Clark's Ferry at midnight, she decided to find an ally. Candi was her first choice. If any spook came after her, she'd bullshit it back to its grave.

"Sure. Who're we going after? Johnny?"

157

"No, Clark's Ferry."

"Huh. Why? I know that bullshit story, and I haven't lost a thing out there. Now, don't get me wrong, I'm not scared of man or beast, but ghosts, well, that's different."

"Come on, Candi. You don't believe that stuff. There's no such thing as spooks and haunted houses."

"Bullshit. That's easy for you to say. I know good people who've had some strange experiences—a couple of them at Clark's Ferry."

"So, prove me wrong. Go with me tonight. I want to spend the bewitching hour there." Kit had sized Candi up as having an impenetrable shell. *If Candi's scared, maybe I should reconsider.*

"I'll drive. I want control in case we need to get out of there in a hurry. Pick you up at eleven."

Kit set her clock radio to alarm at ten, then lay down, her mind filled with trepidation. She pushed it aside to rehearse questions for Johnny and fell asleep.

* * *

A screeching sound filled the room, forcing Kit awake. She hit the off button on the clock radio and swung her legs around. The sound reverberated again, and she tapped the button again, looking at the red numbers on the face. Nine o'clock. As she questioned the time, the noise repeated itself. It was the phone.

"Hello."

"Ms. Levitt, can you come out here right away? Ms. Nichols is real messed up and wants you."

"Who is this? Go where? What's wrong with Louise?"

"It's Dub, Deputy Jones. The sheriff and me are here at Johnny's, and things are bad. Louise locked herself in her room and won't come out. She's says she wants to talk to you. The sheriff asked me to call. Ms. Evans is raising hell with everybody."

Dub's voice was in full motor-mouth without telling Kit much. She interrupted. "Slow down and tell me exactly what is going on. Why is Louise asking for me, and why are you and Bob there?"

"Johnny's dead."

CHAPTER TWENTY-THREE

Dub's call sent Kit tearing from the room. Scrambling into the car, she'd seat-belted herself in before remembering Candi. Quickly she dialed her cell phone. "Meet me at Johnny's. Might need legal advice."

"What's up?"

"I'll fill you in when you get there."

When Kit arrived in front of Johnny's house, the place swarmed with official vehicles. There were six patrol cars parked in the front yard, four with blue lights twirling.

An officer she did not recognize said, "Sorry, ma'am. This is a crime scene. You'll have to move on."

"Tell the sheriff Kit is here. He'll clear the path—oh, there's Dub. Over here, Dub."

As Dub hustled her toward the house, she said, "Make sure Candi gets through the picket line. I'd hate for her to break that young cop's face."

"You got it. Now, we'd better hurry. Louise locked herself in her bedroom and won't come out. The sheriff's back there talking to her through the door, or trying to. She quit responding after asking for you."

"You must be Miss Levitt. You look like the type woman with whom Mr. Edwards would associate."

Kit turned toward the voice and saw an attractive, well-dressed, elderly woman with every hair in place. *So, this is Ms. Evans.* She repressed an urge to counter the implied insult. "Good evening, Ms. Evans. Yes, I'm Kit Levitt. Ace has told me about you. I'd love to stand and chat, but I have business with Bob."

Turning away from her, Kit said to Dub, "I know the way. When Candi gets here, send her back." She started down the hall, then stopped. "Dub, does Louise need a lawyer?" With all that Johnny had put her through, it was possible Louise had done him in.

"Young woman, your effrontery is unacceptable," Ms. Evans snapped.

Dub stood between the two women, a look of consternation on his face. It was obvious he had a serious quandary, which woman to honor. After a moment of hesitation, he said to Kit, "Don't know, ma'am. Looks like a suicide."

Kit continued her walk toward the bedroom Louise had shown her earlier in the day.

"Deputy, stop that woman," Ms. Evans demanded.

Dub shrugged.

"Your career in law enforcement in Van Zandt County is concluded. Leave my house." Ms. Evans' voice carried the unmistakable edge of one accustomed to authority.

Kit turned a corner in the hallway, wondering how Dub was reacting. She saw Bob at the door to Louise's room, his ear pressed firmly against the upper panel. "Are you sure that's in your job description?" Kit asked, tapping him on the shoulder. "Let me get up there. Women are much better at eavesdropping. We get more practice. Besides, you'd better go back and rescue Dub. Ms. Evans just fired him."

Bob stepped aside. "I'm glad you're here. She hasn't said a word for close to an hour. Dub can take care of himself."

"Louise." She knocked on the door. "It's Kit. Open up, please. I'm here to help."

There was noise from the other side, like feet shuffling on a soft rug. Then there was the click of the lock.

"Ms. Levitt, I want you out of my house," Ms. Evans said brusquely. She had come down the hall and now glowered at Kit from a few inches away. "We Adamses have never required the likes of you to assist in our personal matters. We do not wish you now. Leave my house."

The lock clicked.

"Now, Lottie—"

"Sheriff, I strongly suggest you remember your place. I am not and have never been Lottie to you. Move out of my way. This interloper is only here to destroy the Adams heritage."

Kit was stunned silent.

Bob's mouth hung open. "Ms., Mrs.—"

"Maybe I can help here," a new voice said. "Mrs. Evans, you should come with me."

"Candi," Kit said, delight reflected in her voice.

"Please excuse us," Candi said. "We have legal matters to discuss." She had Ms. Evans by the arm and was gently moving her away from the doorway. "We'll go into the kitchen where it's quieter. You may be in need of serious legal advice. I don't think you want Kit and the sheriff to hear."

Mrs. Evans turned her glare on Candi. "If I want legal advice, my lawyer will supply it." In spite of her comments, she allowed herself to be led away.

Kit spoke through the door again. "She's gone, Louise. Sorry, I didn't know she was behind me."

For the third time, the lock clicked and the door swung inward an inch. "Come in, Kit. Sheriff, you stay out there."

Bob nodded, and Kit moved into the room. Louise looked terrible. The hair that had been so perfectly coifed earlier was now a series of tangles falling in every direction. Mascara had washed down her cheeks leaving dark streaks. The jeans and white blouse she wore had lost their expensive look. Deep red-brown stains discolored the top.

Louise was an emotional mess. She opened her mouth to speak, but tears poured instead. Kit sat beside her, holding and consoling her, handing her tissues. Eventually, Louise's tears slowed, and she began to talk. Her words were driven by emotion, often incoherent with little continuity. One refrain appeared repeatedly. "I love him. Why did this happen? I love him."

A man stuck his head in the door. "I'm Dr. Jurgens. Mind if I take a moment?" He moved in beside Louise and quickly gave her a cursory examination. "I'll give her a sedative. Her psyche has had terrible jolt. It needs time to recover, to repair itself. I'll stay with her for a while, then I'll arrange for a nurse. She'll be out for six to eight hours."

Before Kit could ask him where he came from, he ushered her out the door where Bob grabbed her arm and walked her away. "Let the doctor do his thing. I have something to show you."

"Sure, but first, catch me up on what happened here."

Bob stopped and faced her. "Looks fairly simple. Johnny took a nine-millimeter and put a hole through his heart. Doc," he nodded toward Louise's room, "says death would have been almost instantaneous. Very little blood although I see Louise managed to soak some up."

"Was she here when it happened?"

"Apparently not. She was pretty messed up when we arrived. I didn't have much time to talk to her before she bolted for her room and locked the door. What she said was she was at her mother's. When she came home, she noticed the door to Johnny's room ajar and walked in. He was slumped in his chair—dead."

"How long was she away from the house?"

"Not sure, maybe an hour."

"What was the time of death?"

"Wild guess—between noon and eight."

Kit frowned. "That's rather vague."

"Easy. Doc only had a moment to examine the body. Once he determined Johnny was dead, he was more interested in Louise's condition. She did act rather peculiar, locking herself away and all. What did she tell you?"

Kit reflected on Louise's almost garbled words. "Mostly, she said what a fool she'd been, how much she loved Johnny and . . ."

"And?" Bob asked. "Don't stop on me now. I have to talk to her when she wakes up. The more I know, the easier it will be for her."

Kit let out a heavy sigh. "She told me how much she hates her mother for what she did to Johnny. She blames Ms. Evans for the kind of bum he was. In Louise's current state, he'd have been the perfect, caring husband and father, if her mother hadn't corrupted him with her money."

"I see."

Something Bob had said detonated in Kit's head. "Nine-millimeter? Tell me it wasn't Ace's Beretta."

"Wish I could. I don't know yet, but I did wonder the same thing. It's probably good that he's in the hospital—and in Dallas."

"Yeah. Isn't there something about the darkest cloud having a silver lining? Heck of a way to find out." She thought about Ace, his gun, then Johnny. "Was there a note?"

"Two. One for the world and one for you and Ace."

"Nothing for Louise?"

"Not that we found."

That bastard, Kit thought. "Why one for me?"

"You'll have to tell me." Bob walked her into Johnny's bedroom where Dub and a fingerprint man were busy. The body had been removed. "Where're the notes?"

Kit stared at the recliner, the blood spot on the cushion obvious. She looked away.

"Yeah, that's where Johnny did it," Dub said. "The notes're in the same spot. We ain't got to them yet." He pointed to the table beside the chair.

Kit locked her hands behind her to remove any temptation to pick the note up. She leaned over the paper, noticing there were two notes, one to Ace followed by a second to her. She read both.

"Looks like it came out of a computer printer, and neither is signed." She looked back at the paper, something nagging at her. She gave it a moment, but it did not resolve itself. "Bob, when your man is finished with this, I'd like a copy, please. I want to show it to Ace. He'll be thrilled to know he's ten grand richer." She again stared at it. There was definitely something nibbling at the back of her brain. "What about the other one? May I see it?"

"It's under the one to you and Ace—like Johnny stacked them together before he killed himself. Dub, move the top one for Kit."

Dub stepped forward and with a pair of tweezers shifted the top message. Underneath was a second which appeared similar to the other. Again, Kit locked her hands behind her and read. It also looked like it had come from a printer, and it, too, was unsigned.

"Interesting," she said. "I'd like a copy of this one, too."

"Sure," Bob said. "Swing by the office tomorrow. I'll give you duplicates. Now, why don't we get out of here so my officers can do their jobs?"

Walking into the front room, Kit said, "So, is the case closed?"

"Not my call. The DA will make that decision. I only make recommendations."

"And, your recommendation will be?"

"I'll let you know when I know."

Candi sat on the sofa talking to a large policeman. "Bull, this is Kit Levitt. She's Ace's associate."

"We've met," Kit said. "Bull was under the impression I should not move Ace's car from Clark's Ferry."

He rose from the sofa, towering over Kit. "Oh, I was hopin' you'd forgotten that," Bull replied, blushing. "I didn't know who you were then."

"Is this something I need to know about?" Bob asked.

Kit chuckled. "No. We worked it out. Right, Bull?"

"Yes, ma'am," he replied, a look of gratitude on his face. He shook Kit's proffered hand, his huge paw swallowing it. "Dub and I checked on Ace tonight before things went to hell. He's doing good." He waved his arm around. "What do you think of all this? It's more excitement than we've had in Van Zandt in years."

"Typical day in Dallas," Kit said, a smile taking the sting out of her words. "How well did you know Johnny?"

"Only by reputation. He cut a wide swath in the county." Bull grinned in that special way males do when alluding to sexual exploits.

"Hey, you two," Candi interrupted. "Don't you have anything better to do than bullshit? If not, we should talk, Kit."

Candi steered Kit out the front door. They sat in two porch chairs.

"What's going on?" Candi asked.

"In a nutshell. Johnny committed suicide leaving three notes. Louise found the body and went to pieces. Her mother was acting like a total ass, and that's where you came in."

"Do I hear something in your voice?"

"My gut says Johnny had help with the notes, and, if he had help with the notes . . ."

They sat in silence, each lost in thought.

Candi broke it. "I haven't been able to pin anything down on this mess yet. My women's intuition tells me there's something going on with Ms. Evans. Everybody ducks my questions, like they're afraid to say anything. It all sounds like bullshit to me."

"That's not surprising. From what I hear, she's dominated this area for years."

"Perhaps," Candi said. "But it seems more than that. One person told me to look into her oil holdings, then clammed up tight."

"What do you think? She bought herself a politician?"

"Don't know yet. If I had to guess, though, I'd say something underhanded took place." She paused, then laughed her witch's cackle. "This is the kind of bullshit I love. I'll find out."

Kit stood and walked around the porch, hands in her hip pockets, deep in thought. *This just seems too strange. Three people dead, Ace shot from ambush, possible political payoffs, suicide notes that may be forged. What the hell is going on here? This is hardly the small-potatoes blackmail case Ace bargained for.* She stepped into the yard and stared at the sky, saying, "Lots of stars out tonight." A moment later, she added, "Okay, Candi, your intuition is good enough for me. I'll ask a computer guy I know to look into Ms. Evans' finances."

Kit sat on the top step and took deep breaths while fluttering her hands. After a moment, she said in a more relaxed tone, "Let me chatter a bit. It may bore you, but sometimes an idea will slither through if I talk enough. Be my sounding board."

"Let fly. Chip's on a business trip tonight. I have nothing better to do."

"Ace walked into a blackmail scheme that functioned only because Ms. Evans is determined to protect the family name, and in so doing, keep her grandson's name pure. Reason. She truly believes he can become President of the United States. The extortionists, an unsavory couple if ever there was one, are killed execution style. Ace continues to probe and is shot from ambush. I'm with him at the time and may or may not have been a target. Johnny caves and agrees to talk to me, to answer my questions. He dies—ostensibly by his own hand. You get the feeling Ms. Evans deals under the table." She pondered a moment. "Have I missed anything?"

"No, that seems to sum it up," Candi agreed.

"Given that set of facts, let's suppose she took two routes to protect her grandson and to insure his success. One, she hired someone to kill Jade and Hugo, ambush Ace, and shut Johnny up. Two, she is buying future support for Matthew Thomas. Does it fit the facts?"

Candi bounded to her feet. "Do you know what you're saying? You're accusing Ms. Evans of complicity to commit murder and political payoffs. Kit, you're talking about the matriarch of Van Zandt County. Do you have any idea what she could do if she knew what you're thinking?"

Kit met Candi's gaze. "Worse than what happened to Jade, Hugo, and Johnny? Worse than Ace?"

CHAPTER TWENTY-FOUR

Kit called the hospital and conned her way past the switchboard to Ace's room.

"Hello," Ace answered in a sleepy voice.

"It's Kit. We need to talk."

"Huh? I thought I was here to rest." The sleep was disappearing from his tone.

"You can sleep all day. It's only one a.m."

"What's up?"

"Now you sound like you're awake." She quickly briefed him on Johnny's death, Ms. Evans' behavior and her musings with Candi, closing with, "So, am I out in left field? Or, is all this being orchestrated by Ms. Evans?"

"I don't know," Ace said and went quiet.

Kit waited patiently, picturing him sorting his words.

When he resumed, his voice was angry. "But she did set me up to be hung on the wall for the Nobles' murders." He paused, then sighed deeply. "If you have doubts, run what you know by Tom Roberts. He might act like a computer nerd, but, at heart, he's still a cop."

"Glad you agree," Kit said. "I'd already decided to contact him in the morning. Do you think he can break into her accounts without getting caught?"

"No doubt in my mind. Brief him, trust him and believe in him. He pulled my ass out of trouble more times than I'll ever admit. Hell, if he'd been with me in Grand Saline, I wouldn't be lying here now."

Kit gasped, then said nothing.

"Oh shit. No insult intended," Ace added lamely.

"Sure, I believe that," Kit answered in a sarcastic tone. "So, it was my fault you stepped in front of not one, but two bullets?"

"Guess that means no sex tonight."

"You bet your sweet ass."

* * *

Kit woke to the screeching of the clock radio wondering if progress was really such a wonderful thing. *If that noise is an indicator,* she thought grumpily, *probably not.*

Striker jumped off her bed and ran into the other room.

Sweeper rolled over and resumed his snoring.

Sitting up, she mumbled, "Did I have a good reason to set the alarm for seven a.m.? What time did I kill the lights—two, three?" She looked at Sweeper. "If I have to get up, so do you." She stood and shook the coverlet.

His only acknowledgment was digging in with his claws.

Thirty minutes later after a hot shower and a cup of coffee, she began to feel more alive, not totally awake, but alive. She still did not remember why she'd set the alarm so early unless it was to have breakfast at the Sabine Café.

* * *

"You look like hell," Mabel said, stopping at Kit's table. "I've seen scrambled eggs look better'n you."

"Thanks for the vote of confidence. Just bring the coffee."

"Coffee, bagel, and cream cheese coming up."

"I don't want—" She gave up, accepting that as long as she frequented the Sabine Café, bagels and cream cheese would be in her life. At least her dad would be happy.

As promised, Mabel was back quickly, setting the food and a carafe of coffee on the table. "I got better things to do than run back and forth helping you over last night. Pour your own." She paused, stooping down to eye level. "Damn, I hope you look like that 'cause you worked real late. I never had no man cause me to look that bad after screwin' all night." She chuckled. "On the other hand, sure wisht I had."

Kit searched for a smart remark, but a voice from the rear of the restaurant cut her off. "Mabel. I need service back here."

"Keep it in your pocket. I'll get there when I have time. Hell, I know what you want. I'm gonna charge you twenty-five times what a bowl of cereal would cost you at home." She whispered to Kit. "What's wrong with these old farts? Who comes to a restaurant for a bowl of corn flakes anyway?"

Kit buried her response in the cup of coffee.

Three cups later, she leaned back feeling she could face the day. Her heart beat strongly, pushing blood through her veins. *Blessed caffeine. Could have only been created by the Gods.* Even the bagel looked good. She spread cream cheese on half.

"I must be getting good at this bullshit. When I called the motel, and you didn't answer, I figured you'd be here."

Kit looked up to see Candi dragging out a chair. She wore a brown pantsuit over a yellow blouse. Every hair was in place, and her lips glowed glossy red. She looked good—and rested. "How do you do it? What are you doing here anyway?" She took a bite of the bagel.

"Are you kidding? This is too much fun. Beats the hell out of getting drunk divers off with a speeding ticket. What's on for today?"

Kit squinted, then rubbed her eyes. "Candi, have you forgotten we were at a death scene last night?"

"Yeah, who died?" Mabel had walked up and injected herself into the conversation. "Did I lose a customer? Let me check." She looked around the restaurant, counting heads with her finger. "Nope, all mine are here. So, who was it?"

"Johnny Nichols," Candi answered. "Killed himself."

"Damn. Knowed he'd never live to a ripe old age. Too many husbands on his trail. Are you sure it was suicide? I bet somebody's man did him in."

Candi cut Kit a look, but got no support. "As far as we can tell. He put a slug through his heart."

"Now, that don't make no sense a'tall," Mabel said. "He was scared to death of guns. Wouldn't even go hunting."

"Mabel, my cup's empty," a voice from the round table in the rear said.

"I'm comin'. You ain't gonna die of thirst." She moved away at a rapid clip.

"Scared of guns?" Kit said with a close echo from Candi.

"How do we check that out?" Candi added.

"Louise," Kit answered quickly, looking at her watch. "Too early to call her now, though." Kit was awake, every nerve ending fully engaged. "Let's see if the sheriff is in." She stood, grabbed her purse, and threw bills on the table.

"Hey, what about my grapefruit?"

"You can have it for lunch. As Ace says, we're burning daylight."

"Damn bullshit diet. Now, I can't even have my grapefruit for breakfast," Candi mumbled. "Mabel," she called, "give me a cup o'joe to go. This woman wants to roll."

Outside the restaurant, Candi said, "I'll drive. I know the county."

Kit quickly agreed, looking enviously at Candi's Mercedes SLK32. A few minutes later, with the top tucked neatly into the trunk area, they were en route to Canton, the County Seat of Van Zandt County.

"Nice car," Kit said over the wind noise.

"Gift from Chip. Package deal. He hid my engagement ring in the glove box. Had to take the car to get the ring."

Kit said nothing, lest her jealousy show.

Candi drove for a moment. "I'd like for you to meet Chip. He's a wonderful man. Besides, the two of you have something in common."

"Yeah, what," Kit said, interrupting the thrill of the ride.

"Both of you think Ace is hot stuff. When he saved Joseph, he became number one on Chip's hit parade, and," she grinned at Kit, "I've watched your eyes when you mention Ace."

"Damn," Kit said. She hated being so transparent.

Candi wheeled into a parking space at the sheriff's office interrupting Kit's love affair with the SLK32. "Here we are. That's the sheriff's old Ford over there. Guess he's here." She opened the door and bounced out as if she were three years old and the ice cream truck waited.

"Better let me do the talking," Kit said. "Ace says Bob gets a bit hyper when you're around."

"Bullshit, he gets more than that. I guess I have jerked his chain a few times in the past. But I'm a changed woman now. I may even get a bullshit PI license."

"Sure, and give up your six-figure income. But you'd still better let me handle him."

"You got it, chief. I won't open my mouth."

They walked into the station, and Dub greeted them. "Mornin', ladies. You're out mighty early. Wanna see the sheriff?"

"If he's got some time," Kit said, cutting her eyes at Candi.

Dub looked at Kit, then Candi. "Well, I'm sure he'll make time. He—"

"Bullshit, Dub. This is Candi you're talking to. You can say it. You know he doesn't want to see me. But tell him I promised Kit I'd be good."

"Yes'm," Dub said, chuckling. "Mind if I watch? It'll be a first."

"You're as full of bullshit as the sheriff. Come on in, if Bob doesn't object. You'll see. I'm a reformed woman."

He led them to the back of the building, then ushered them into the sheriff's office. He had a folder open on his desk. "Take a seat. You too, Dub."

"How about me?" Candi asked. "You sure that invite counts for me?"

The sheriff groaned. "Yeah, you too." He took papers from the folder and passed copies to each of them. "These suicide notes bother me. Look'm over, and let's talk."

The room was quiet as the four of them read the facsimiles. The top was addressed to Ace, then to Kit.

Ace:

Had a long talk with Jake today. He called and ripped me a new asshole. Guess I have acted like a jerk. Sorry about that. Who could have guessed that life would throw us such a curve ball? Seems almost impossible that only a few years ago, you, Jake and I drank together at O'Malley's, or that just a few weeks ago, I was loose-footed and carefree without a worry. However, things change and now I am making another change, a change for the better. Sure hope you recover from your wounds. From what I heard, the docs did a great job putting you back together. When you find the shooter, do whatever is necessary to insure he hurts no one else. Such scum does not deserve to live among decent people.

I transferred ten thousand to your checking account. I know it is not the whole amount we discussed, but you did not exactly handle the case, did you? Give my best to Jake.
Johnny

Kit Levitt:
Guess I won't meet you tomorrow. Too bad. A care free guy like me just loves to meet honeys like you. We could have made beautiful music.
Johnny

The second note was the confession and suicide note:
To whoever finds my body
Hope you got a strong stomach cause I probably don't look too good. I can't go on living like this. I was once care free, but now I don't feel so good. Jade was a beautiful woman who deserved to live, and Hugo wasn't all that bad. I shouldn't have killed them, but I did. So whoever is looking for who murdered them, can quit. I did it, and I give myself the death sentence.
Johnny

"Is everybody ready?" Bob asked. "Kit, why don't you start?"

She stared at the note a moment. "Okay, this is quick, but they smell to me. The section addressed to Ace is more of a newsy note than an announcement of suicide. He says he's making a change for the better. Does that sound like a man ready to kill himself?

Not to me. I say it's just what he says it is. Jake called, chewed him, out, and he's trying to apologize to Ace."

"Makes sense," Bob said. "Dub?"

"Yep, I see the same thing."

"I may regret this." Bob smiled. "Candi, what do you think?"

"Bullshit, Bob. Told you I'm behaving today." She let go with her witch's cackle. "I agree with Kit. Not only that, but look a little farther. The word carefree appears in each of the sections. In Ace's part, it is spelled correctly, one word. In the other two, it's used as two words. Is this one person, i.e., Johnny, writing or two people?"

"Kit?"

"Candi's observation is valid with me. What do you and Dub think?"

"Agree" Dub said.

"So do I," Bob added. "Now, Dub, any other observations?"

"Yeah. In that last part, he says he killed Jade and Hugo, but in the first, he hopes Ace catches whoever shot them. I had it figured the same guy shot all three."

"Good," Bob said. "Same as I was thinking."

Candi and Kit chimed in with their agreement.

"Two other things," Kit said. "Notice the lack of contractions in the first, but in the next two, there are contractions. In my opinion, different people wrote the notes. Johnny probably wrote the note to Ace, planning to send it to him in the hospital. Someone else wrote the ones to me and the To whoever finds my body one, and that, my friends, spells murder, not suicide."

"You said two things," Bob said.

Kit looked at Candi. "We haven't verified it yet, but we heard Johnny was afraid of guns."

Bob ran his fingers through his thinning hair. "Wonderful. If our guesses are on-target, I have three murders and one attempted murder in my county. But you're right, all three of you. Somebody killed Johnny and did a lousy job of making it look like suicide." He looked at Kit. "There's one other fact I didn't share with you yet. It was Ace's gun that killed Johnny."

"Damn," Kit said.

"I'll be durn'd," Dub said.

"Bullshit," Candi contributed.

Heading back to Grand Saline with Candi at the wheel, Kit called Tom Roberts. "Tom, can you crack Ms. Evans' financial records?"

CHAPTER TWENTY-FIVE

A week passed slowly with Kit making little progress in finding the shooters. Ace recovered rapidly and moved to the rehabilitation wing where the physical therapists, or modern Simon Legrees as he called them, worked to strengthen his leg. The medical staff agreed that if his progress continued at its current rate, he'd be out of there in a few days—on crutches, but mobile.

Kit grew more determined each day to solve the case before Ace re-entered the perp's sights. It had happened once, it could happen again. Her frustration grew as she dashed among Dallas, Grand Saline, and Canton getting no closer to resolution. Her only victories came from the less fascinating aspects of her life, nurturing Ace's cats in Grand Saline and wrapping up the bed-hopping Barnes and Lattimore cases in Dallas.

On the latter, she spent one more day in surveillance, then compiled the reports. The reactions from both spouses were the same. Mr. Barnes and Ms. Lattimore were equally thrilled—until Kit handed them the itemized bills. The joy in their faces disappeared, and both promised to put checks in the mail. Kit said fine, fully expecting payment would be slow. That was Ace's problem. They were his cases.

As often as possible, Kit put the cats in their carriers and took them with her in Ace's Sebring, top down of course. They apparently thought it was great sport because after the second day, they ran into their cages as soon as Kit dragged them out. Their cries of pleasure were a delight as the wind rippled their hair.

When Kit handed Ace bills for the cats, he groused she was subverting his cats with the expensive cat food, litter, and kitty treats she bought. Each time, she told him to shut up and pay the bills. She added that his whining was a clear indication his health was improving.

Tom dug into Ms. Evans' financial records. He found numerous cash transactions in her household account with no viable reasons for them. The amounts were significant, however other better explained withdrawals were also large. He traced back a year where the trail petered out.

Mr. Coker, the efficient butler, deflected each of Kit's calls to the Evans residence. Bob had no better luck with Ms. Evans. She told him Louise had been with her for three hours before finding Johnny's body, and Louise confirmed the same. Clearly, the wagons had circled, and Ms. Evans was the wagon master. Their alibis did not exactly exonerate the two of them, but no one really thought Louise had killed Johnny. As for Ms. Evans, it was agreed she could have hired it out even as she built an airtight alibi.

But in all the discussions of Ms. Evans' culpability, they returned to one question repeatedly. If she had put up with Johnny's shenanigans for over twenty years, why would she risk having him killed now? If the truth came out, not only would she face jail time, but Matthew Thomas' political career would be doomed. After all, they said, rolling their eyes, Texas is not Massachusetts. However, on each occasion, they added that her delusion of power might have convinced her she could get away with it.

Kit updated Candi on everything Tom reported, but stopped short on briefing Bob. She and Candi were not sure of the exact legality of Tom's snooping, but that was only because they refused to search the statutes. Both strongly suspected they were treading heavily on one or more of the laws of the state, perhaps the country.

The week plowed along with Kit rolling up mileage on Ace's car and charges on his gasoline credit card. Her Geo rested.

Each passing day brought her closer to the end of her tether. She knew if something didn't break soon, she'd blow her stack. She'd been accused of having a hair-trigger temper before. While she'd been successful in strengthening the spring, she'd lose it sooner or later.

She sat in the motel on the edge of the bed with the cats curled beside her, doodling on a legal pad letting her thoughts float freely. The phone rang.

"Hey, kid," Ace said. "Just had to call and give you some good news. Thought it might cheer you up."

"It's more than welcome. Even the cats are down in the dumps."

"Guess who called?"

"Knock off that crap. You know I hate games—unless I'm the moderator."

"Spoil sport. I was all set for a good session of twenty questions. It gets boring lying here with nothing except gorgeous women catering to my every whim."

"In your dreams. Who called?"

"It hurts that you don't believe me."

"Who called?"

"Hope you're sitting. Mrs. Loticia Adams Evans, the queen herself, and she didn't even have one of her flunkies place the call."

"You're kidding?"

"Nope. There's more. She wants *you* to get in touch with her. Since I'm incapacitated, she decided to hire you."

"I thought they'd taken you off the strong stuff. You're clearly spacing out on aspirin. However, just in case you're on the level, what's she up to?"

"Don't know. Give her a call. She said to contact her at eight this evening. She'll let her call screener, Mr. Marston Coker, know he should put you through."

"Anything else?"

"That's it. In her own sweet, little-old-lady way, she hung up after giving me the message. I don't think she likes to talk to people in hospitals."

"Especially to you," Kit said, chuckling. "This is strange, very strange. You're sure she used the word hire."

"Her exact word. Give her a call, then get back to me. My curiosity is a twelve on a scale of ten."

                * * *

"Mrs. Evans, Ace said you wanted me to call."

"Yes, Miss Levitt. I would like for you to come to tea tomorrow afternoon at three. We have not had the opportunity to meet formally, however my daughter, Louise, recommends I speak with you. Also, Mr. Edwards and Sheriff Galoway believe you to be competent."

"Thank you, ma'am. I take that as a compliment."

"It was, but not from me. The compliments come from my daughter, your friend, and the sheriff. I will make my own judgment when we meet."

"Ace, ah, Mr. Edwards said you mentioned hiring me. For what?"

"If I judge you to be the person I need, we shall discuss it at that time. In the meantime, clear space on your calendar for matters I may or may not hire you to investigate. I shall expect you at three sharp. Dress casually, but please, not in jeans and a T-shirt. You are reportedly an attractive young lady. Try to dress like one."

The phone clicked in Kit's ear. She stared at the instrument as if it had been rude, but soon gave up. Inanimate objects refuse to be intimidated.

She sat, replaying the conversation in her mind. *Funny,* she thought. *I would have sworn we met that night at Johnny's. Guess that doesn't count with her—no formal introduction. Maybe Candi can help sort it out.*

She dialed, then summarized the call. "That's it. That's what she said. Any ideas?"

"No, but I'd love to be hidden behind the drapes tomorrow," Candi said. "What are you going to wear? Did you bring anything suitable for afternoon tea?"

"I have no idea. I do have one pantsuit, but it's pretty wrinkled. Is there a place around here I can get it pressed?"

"Sure. Larry at JJ's Cleaners. Tell him I told you to call. He'll give you quick service. What are you going to do about your hair?"

Kit hesitated. The conversation had taken on the flavor of a girls' club rather than what she had envisioned. "Candi, my hair's fine. Let's get back to the case. Do you have time tonight to go over Tom's reports on Ms. Evans' accounts? You understand them better than I. Maybe I can lead her to discuss them tomorrow."

"My bullshit pleasure. See you at your motel about seven."

Kit rang off, feeling better. Striker had crawled into her lap during the conversation, and Sweeper snuggled against her hip. "Okay, little ones. What's going to happen tomorrow? Why did she invite me? More important, is there anything I should be wary of?"

Sweeper gazed at her, blinked twice, then resumed his sleepy look. After a moment, he shook his head and looked again before jumping to the floor. He hunched up his shoulders, walked around in a circle on his tiptoes, tilting his head so he stared down the length of his nose.

"Yeah, yeah, you did that before. Get a new dance step. I don't understand that one."

Sweeper stopped prancing, glared at Kit, then sashayed to his food dish.

Striker stood, growled softly, and joined Sweeper.

Both took one last look, then began to crunch.

"Damn cats. Wonder if they really do know something."

CHAPTER TWENTY-SIX

"Good afternoon, Miss Levitt," Coker said, opening the front door of Ms. Evans' mansion. He peered over Kit's shoulder. "If you will give me the keys, I will have Mr. Edwards' car moved from in front of the house."

Kit glanced behind her at the convertible with its top down. "Why? Adds a little class, don't you think?" She tossed the keys to him. "Lock the doors." She was determined not to be intimidated.

Coker led her to the library where Ms. Evans sat in a chair resembling a throne.

"Miss Levitt, how nice of you to come and to be so prompt." She rose and stepped forward, her hand extended. "Mr. Coker, ask Mrs. Lopez to serve tea in five minutes." She swiveled back to Kit. "I have been so looking forward to meeting you. You look divine, nothing like I expected. Red is certainly your color. You must tell Louise where you bought that gorgeous pantsuit."

Kit was caught off-balance. All her carefully planned dialogue washed away in Ms. Evans' graciousness as if caught in a Texas thunderstorm. "Pleased to meet you, too, Mrs. Evans."

"Come. Sit over here. It is more intimate." She led Kit to a sitting arrangement with small comfortable chairs facing one another. A well-oiled mahogany coffee table separated them. "I do so enjoy this corner of the library when I entertain. It is much more informal."

Her hostess patter continued as Kit desperately tried to catch up—while acting the good guest. From her personal experience the night of Johnny's death, Ace's descriptions, and everything else she'd heard, Ms. Evans was out of character.

A young Latino woman rescued Kit by entering the room. "Your tea, ma'am." She sat a silver tea service on the table accompanied by two bone china cups and saucers. Small, decorated scones rested on a silver plate. Sugar, artificial sweetener, lemons and cream were each served in such delicate pieces that Kit flinched inwardly at the thought of using them.

"May I pour, Miss Levitt? Or, may I call you Carsen? That is your given name, isn't it?"

"Please, and I prefer Kit." While Ms. Evans poured, then placed a scone on one of the delicate plates, Kit studied her. Either Ace was a terrible judge of character or Ms. Evans was buttering her up for a reason. Kit reflected on those times Ace had been wrong before. She decided to ride it out, and see where it took her. "Mrs. Evans, I've heard so much about you and your family. It's a pleasure to finally meet you."

Ms. Evans smiled, a pleasant, old-lady smile. "Do not believe everything you hear, my dear. My family is not as dysfunctional as some would have you believe. Take my daughter, for example. True, she made a bad marriage, but she lived with it very well. She was a good mother and, when possible, a good wife. Unfortunately, Jonathan frequently strained the latter. Is it true you believe he was murdered?"

"What makes you ask?" *What's going on here? She's fishing for info on Bob's investigation.*

"Sheriff Galoway told me there were some doubts. I only wondered what you thought. After all, you are a trained investigator."

Kit thought for a moment, wondering whether to answer truthfully or continue the charade of suicide. She opted for a half-truth. "There are some inconsistencies, however the sheriff doesn't share his investigation with me. I really don't know much about it."

"Carsen, I suspect you are downplaying your importance in this inquiry. I know Robert Galoway respects your judgment. However, I understand your reluctance. The rift between Jonathan and me is well-known."

Kit sighed. Ms. Evans' efforts at humility were rapidly losing their novelty. "Mrs. Evans, perhaps we should quit with the party chatter and the first names and get to why you invited me here. I'm not exactly your social equal." She pushed her teacup aside. "I don't really like tea."

Kit waited. Ms. Evans' face revealed nothing so Kit continued. "That's your cue. You're the only one who knows why I'm here."

Ms. Evans smiled. "Miss Levitt, you should at least allow an old woman some dignity."

"That's what I'm trying to do. You don't need to butter me up—me or anyone else. You've earned your place. I know you're not like this."

"Was I that transparent? In years gone by, I have charmed many a visitor. However, you are correct. I deplore social chitchat. If you have finished with your tea, we can begin discussions."

"I'm ready."

Ms. Evans pushed her cup aside. "Last week, my accountant in Dallas called with two pieces of information. Neither of them pleased me. He believes someone has been attempting to gain access to my financial records. The term he used was hacking. He wanted my permission to hire a computer expert to investigate."

Kit almost gasped, but controlled it. "Probably some kid. Happens all the time around the country." *She'll never buy into that*, she thought.

"Yes, that is essentially what he said. He has three other customers who have had similar attacks."

Kit exhaled as quietly as possible. "So, is he hiring someone?"

"No. I do not welcome more people with access to my business. I have never trusted computers. I went with his second recommendation. He suggested he upgrade the firewall. Are you familiar with that term?"

"It's a security barrier, isn't it?" Kit thought of Tom and hoped he wasn't caught. "You said he gave you two pieces of information. What was the other?"

"There are inconsistencies in my household accounts. Someone may have been making unauthorized withdrawals."

"Oh?" Kit was caught off-guard. "Does he know who made them?"

"No. That is why I called you."

Kit stared at her, looking for a clue as to where she was headed. However, Ms. Evans' face was inscrutable, and Kit struggled to make hers the same. After a moment, Kit decided there would never be a better opportunity to get through to Ms. Evans. "Are we going to level with one another, or continue this Texas two-step?"

Ms. Evans laughed, a surprised look on her face. "You are perceptive, Carsen. Maybe we could be friends."

"Nice try, but let's stick with facts. May I take you back to the night of Johnny's death, and your reactions?"

She gazed at Kit for several seconds. "That is an interesting switch on your part. However, I will honor it with a reply. I was concerned about Louise, but my preoccupation was with how his suicide would affect the family name. Does that satisfy your curiosity?"

"Not satisfied, but gratified that you answered. Please continue."

"I have little to add. Jonathan was a disgrace to me and to all that I hold dear. My family tree goes back to the founding of our country. Two of my ancestors served as President. My grandson will continue in the great Adams tradition. Jonathan's actions throughout his marriage to Louise have been a threat to my plans. The only honorable accomplishment in his miserable life was fathering Matthew Thomas." She paused and poured water from a crystal carafe. "Miss, I know you cannot appreciate my feelings, that you cannot understand them. My father—" She eyed Kit. "Perhaps we should return to the reason I invited you here."

"Of course," Kit said wondering if she had choked off a confession about her family. "But before we do that, I have two simple questions." She swallowed and plowed on. "Did you kill or have someone kill Jade and Hugo?"

"Miss Levitt. Surely, you do not believe—"

"Ma'am, a straight answer would be nice."

Ms. Evans swallowed. "No, I did not. Most emphatically, I did not."

"If Johnny's death was not a suicide, did you have anything to do with it?"

"I think that is quite enough, Miss Levitt. You have outreached the boundaries of my patience."

"Seems like a simple question to me. What's the answer, Mrs. Evans?"

She glared at Kit. "No, I did not."

"Excellent. One more, and we can move on. Did you have anything to do with Ace being shot and someone shooting at me?"

The grinding of Ms. Evans' teeth filled the brief silence. "No. I am sure many people other than I find Mr. Edwards offensive. Now, can we get back to why you are here?"

"You didn't respond to my being downrange in the turkey shoot."

She sighed. "No, I had nothing to do with anyone shooting at you either."

Kit grinned. "I accept your answers and won't bother you with the questions again. Please continue with what your accountant had to say."

Ms. Evans glared, then smiled. "You are formidable," she said, respect showing in her voice. "After he told me of his suspicions, I discretely initiated my own investigation." She paused. "Is this where you interrupt? You have shown a propensity to do so all afternoon."

It was Kit's turn to smile. "No, ma'am. I'll be good."

"Thank you. I did not amass my significant holdings by allowing others to run my affairs. I always look over shoulders."

"I believe that," Kit said. "Did you find anything?"

"You said you would not interrupt."

"Sorry."

"I found enough to bother me. Someone has been withdrawing funds without my knowledge. I maintain a rather significant household account which is automatically replenished when it reaches a certain level. It is this account that shows tampering."

"Who has access?"

She moved to a desk and picked up a piece of paper. "My attorney, my accountant, the household staff, and Matthew Thomas. No one else. We can eliminate my grandson. He would never steal from me."

"Uh-huh."

Ms. Evans ignored the sarcasm. "Here are the names, and how to contact them. Of course, the household staff live here." She handed the paper to Kit. "Miss Levitt, let me emphasize that you are not to question my grandson. I assure you he is honest. I trained him that way."

Kit looked at the list, then back at Ms. Evans. "Are you hiring me to look into this?"

"Is it something within your purview, an area of expertise that you possess?"

Kit grinned at the question. "Yes, Mrs. Evans, it is within my expertise. Or, to be exactly honest, I know people who have the ability."

"Good, you are hired. Please be discrete and limit your investigation to the household accounts only." She handed Kit a second sheet of paper. "Here are the account number, passwords, and a list of the withdrawals I find suspicious. How soon can I expect you to identify the miscreant?"

"Easy, ma'am. Give me a chance to begin before you ask for a conclusion. I'll let you know as soon as I have something to report."

"All right. Remember though, your authorization is for the household account only."

Ms. Evans escorted Kit from the library and turned her over to Mr. Coker. Ms. Evans' last comments were to remind Kit of the scope of the investigation—household account only.

Gotta be a good reason for that, Kit thought.

CHAPTER TWENTY-SEVEN

Kit set up a conference call with Ace, Candi, and Tom. She had no problems with the technology. Controlling the conversation was another matter.

"So, Tom," Kit said, interrupting a side conversation between Candi and Ace, "will that information help?"

"By all means. With the account number and the passwords, no problem gaining full access. Once that happens, I can probably get into her other accounts. Did she say which firewall her accountant was installing?"

"No, only that he would upgrade it."

"I hope that's exactly what he meant. If it's an upgrade of the existing one, it'll be easier than tackling a whole new program. But in either case, I'll get there."

"How soon?" Ace asked.

"Hey, slow down, my friend," Tom replied. "All you have to do is lie around. I still have to earn a living. But a few days should do it."

"What do you want me to do?" Candi asked.

"How about you check out the people who have access to the account?" Kit said. "Find out if they've changed their lifestyle in the last year. I'll work with you on that." She thought for a moment. "Tom, can you access the accountant and lawyer's accounts? See if anyone has come into additional funds?"

"Sure. I don't suppose you know where they bank."

"Of course not."

"Why am I not surprised?" Tom's sarcasm was syrupy enough to slice with a dull blade. "I'll take that, also. Anything else?"

"Not that I can think of," Kit replied. "Ace, anything?"

"Nothing except I'm tired of missing all the fun. I'll be out in a few days. Don't solve it too quickly. I'm anxious for revenge."

* * *

A few days later the four of them gathered in Ace's room. It was his first view of Candi's re-sculpted appearance. "Damn. What happened to you? Last time we met, you looked like you could take on the Dallas Cowboys—and win. Now," he paused, giving her the once over, "you look good, damn good."

"Bullshit, spaceman. You still look like shit. But I have to admit. Getting shot improved your looks." Her witch's cackle took the sting out of the words. "If it weren't for this lovely woman who is blind to your shortcomings and all the money Chip and Jake are paying, I'd drop your bullshit ass right now."

"Careful, Ace," Tom said, settling into a chair. "My base tenet is, don't piss off a beautiful woman. Candi, I'm Tom Roberts, and you are lending beauty to this gathering."

"Ahem." Kit cleared her throat. "And what the hell am I, the local gargoyle? You two louts quit lusting, and let's concentrate on the case."

Tom recovered first. "Two beautiful women in one room. Makes me want to give up being a hermit computer guru."

"Bullshit," Candi said. "You're as full of it as your buddy." She looked at Ace. "So, how're you feeling? Ready to get your lazy ass out of here?"

Ace and Tom laughed as one.

"She's got your number, Ace," Tom said. "I like this lady."

"You would. But no need to butter her up. Her boyfriend is bigger than both of us—put together."

Kit grinned at the patter. It was typical Ace and Tom, two ex-partners, and good friends, each jousting for an advantage. Candi might not know it, but she was just the newest pawn in their game. "If you two have about finished impressing Candi, maybe we can move on."

"Tom, once again we are thrown adrift on the seas of female liberation. Kit has spoken. We must humbly obey." Ace grinned and bowed toward Kit as best he could from his sitting position in bed.

"Yes, mighty leader," Tom added. "Your wish is but my humble command. Lead us on to conquer the nemesis who plagues the fair city of Grand Saline." He stood and curtsied.

"Bullshit," Candi said. "Are these two for real?"

"Yes," Kit replied. "I fear this is as good as it gets."

All four laughed the joy of friendship.

Ace said. "We have to slow it down or I'll bust some fresh scars. Kit, lead us through our reports?"

"Since you *men* are so taken with Candi, let's here from her first," Kit said.

"Bullshit," Candi said again. "Here's what I found. The accountant is a four-eyed wimp. His office and most of his clients are here in Dallas so all I could come up with were a few general comments. From what I heard, he's harmless, no threat to anyone, and certainly not one to take a chance on jail. He'd be terrified at being stuffed into a cell with some Neanderthal who'd want him for a sex-toy." Again, her cackle filled the room.

"Comments, anyone," Kit said, a grin splitting her face as she tried to take notes.

"Fits what I found," Tom said.

"What about the lawyer?" Ace asked. "We all know how sleazy they are."

Candi shot Ace a look, but only said, "Bullshit." She flipped a page in her notebook. "Attorney Emanuel Reynolds, his friends call him Manny, is no dirtier than any other attorney, and, in spite of what Ace says, most of us are clean. Anyway, I found nothing out of the ordinary on him. He's been handling Ms. Evans' accounts for years. He had opportunity, but I don't think he's our thief. His lifestyle is simple, nothing extravagant." She swiveled toward Tom. "What'd you find?"

"I agree on both," Tom said. "Their checking accounts, savings, and stock holdings are ordinary. If either is embezzling, he's covering it well. Given more time, I could go deeper, but I'm satisfied they're clean."

Kit looked at Ace who shrugged. She continued. "That leaves the household staff." She ticked off the names of Burke and Reynolds in her notebook. "We have Marston Coker, William Lapscott, the cook, Maria Lopez, and the maid, Ismarelda Perez. Anything on any of them?"

Candi said, "I'll go first. Coker and Lapscott have worked for Ms. Evans for years. Coker runs the household, and Lapscott fills in as jack-of-all-trades. From what I could find, they are loyal, and protective of Ms. Evans. A few years ago, Lapscott got into trouble in Terrell in a bar fight. Seems someone made a nasty comment about Ms. Evans so Billy broke a beer bottle over his head. Manny Reynolds stepped in and settled the incident without any fuss. No charges filed." She flipped pages in her notebook. "No criminal record on Coker. He has been on the payroll for twenty-five years, and Lapscott for fifteen. They don't seem like likely candidates. Now, the other two—"

"Excuse me, Candi, let's stay on these two for now," Kit said. "Tom, what did you find?"

"Very interesting pair. My investigation corroborates what Candi said, however, they are not just simple country folks. Both have reps in the casinos in Bossier City. Their checking and savings accounts show large deposits and similar withdrawals. I checked with a cop I know in the Shreveport area, and he said they're high rollers. Winnings and losses could account for the fluctuations in their accounts, or . . ." He shrugged.

"They make an unlikely pair," Ace said. "I'll vouch for their loyalty though. My impression was they'd do almost anything for Ms. Evans, and it carries over to Matthew Thomas." He paused and pinched the bridge of his nose as if searching his mind. "Then there was that strange day Billy was with Johnny in the restaurant. He was either bodyguarding or making sure Johnny didn't say too much." Ace hesitated. "Not sure which."

Kit looked at Candi. "Anything more?"

"Not on those two."

"Tom?"

"I'm dry."

"Okay," Kit said, "let's move on. What about the maid and the cook?"

"No chance," Candi said. "They've only been in the country a short while and worked for Ms. Evans less than a year. Their English is only good enough to get by. No way can I picture them embezzling."

"Concur," Tom agreed. "Good, hardworking, legal, Mexican immigrants. Both send money home. If they didn't have rooms at Ms. Evans' place, they'd be hard-pressed to make it."

There was a lull in the conversation as Kit jotted cryptic notes.

Ace broke the silence. "One more. That pompous asshole, Matthew Thomas. Did we check him?"

Candi ducked her head. "Kit said Ms. Evans placed him off-limits."

"She did," Kit said. "So what did you find?"

Candi grinned. "He's spoiled, he's obnoxious, and he inherited money from his grandfather. Louise and Johnny had little if anything to do with his upbringing. Ms. Evans took him out of their hands at birth. She caters to his every whim and always has. As we all know, he'll graduate from Harvard next year, then run for public office. No need for him to embezzle funds. All he'd have to do is ask." She stopped and looked at her notes. "That's my take on him."

Kit swiveled her chair to Tom. "Your go and don't give me any nonsense about off-limits."

"I won't insult your intelligence. He was too good a target. Nothing much to add though. Except his inheritance from his grandfather was only a few thousand dollars. Most of the money went to Louise, one point two million in cash, stocks, and bonds. Apparently, he saw Matthew Thomas as we do. But, as she said," he nodded toward Candi, "no reason for young Nichols to embezzle. Besides, the amounts are only pocket change to someone like him."

Ace laughed. "Only a few thousand. Bet that frosted his ass. I'm sure he already had the money spent on his campaigns."

"Can't buy that," Candi said. "He'll expect others to pay his way into office. This is a totally selfish person who has never had to accept any personal responsibility."

Kit looked up from her notes. "So where does that leave us? We've done a pretty good job of eliminating everyone."

"No," Ace said, "Not true. We said Coker and Lapscott were loyal. We didn't say they're not embezzlers. My money's on the butler and the handyman."

"Come on, Ace," Tom said. "The butler? That's every mystery writer's cliché."

"Yeah," Ace said. "The perfect cover. Think anyone will buy it?"

"Not in this lifetime," Kit said.

The four of them enjoyed a good laugh.

When the merriment died away, Ace said, "I suggest that tomorrow, Kit and I pay Ms. Evans a visit and let her know what we've found. That'll also give me an opportunity to grill her about the murders and the asshole that gunned me. She's gotta know something."

"Ah, Ace," Kit said as Candi and Tom stared at him. "Aren't you forgetting the small fact you're still in rehab?"

"That's my surprise. I'm out of here tomorrow morning. My tormentors gave me a clean bill of health today."

Kit's emotions surged and she threw her arms around him. "You jerk. Why'd you tell us earlier? You let me sit here all afternoon playing moderator while you smugly knew you'd be taking over tomorrow."

"Wrong," Ace said, returning Kit's hug. "I'll be your assistant, your loyal Watson, Ms. Sherlock. You've come this far. I'll help you take it the rest of the way." He leered at her. "Besides, I'm still officially a cripple. Doc says I mustn't get too active—even with my leg."

"Would you two save the lovey-dovey bullshit until we finish?" Candi said. "Then I don't give a damn if you crawl up there and hump his bones."

"Concur," Tom said, smiling. "Can I stay and watch?"

"No," Kit replied, untangling from Ace's arms. "And both of you get those silly smirks off your faces. I have no intention of getting in his bed—today, or any other day."

"Crap," Ace said. "Things looked promising for a moment though."

After saying goodbyes to everyone, Kit walked through the parking lot with a grin that threatened to lift her off her feet. Ace was okay. She could hardly wait to tell the cats. They'd be thrilled.

First, a present was in order, something special to commemorate the occasion. She dropped the top on Ace's car, then sat and thought. Inspiration struck. A few phone calls later, she found what she wanted and drove to pick it up.

CHAPTER TWENTY-EIGHT

Doctor Win was in the room with Ace when Kit arrived the next morning. She lingered in the doorway while he finished his examination and proclaimed Ace well on the path to good health and laid out an exercise program.

Kit hid the gift behind her back, smiling when the Doctor mentioned exercise. She knew Ace's idea of exercise involved pulling out a barstool and lifting a Killian's.

"Good morning," Doctor Win said to Kit. "Are you here to rescue our staff?

"You? I'm the guy who's being tortured," Ace said.

"I don't know," Kit replied. "If he keeps that attitude, I may leave him here."

All three chuckled.

The doctor turned to Ace. "I know your profession encourages people to use you for target practice. However, my wife suggested you get shot in the morning. That way, I can cut on you in the afternoon and still pick up a quart of milk on the way home for dinner. I think it's an excellent recommendation."

"You hear that, Kit?" Ace asked. "From now on, schedule my ambushes no later than noon." He grinned at Doctor Win. "Will that keep your wife happy?"

"Much better," he replied, shaking Ace's hand, then Kit's. "Ah, here's your wheelchair. Good luck to the both of you." Doctor Win walked out twirling his stethoscope.

Kit took the chair from the aide. "Your chariot," she said pushing it alongside the bed.

"A present? For me?" He pointed at the long slender package she'd laid across the arms of the chair. "I didn't know you cared."

"Just something from Sweeper and Striker."

He tore at the wrappings, grinning like a little boy. "Just what every well-dressed PI needs—a cane. It's beautiful. Maple?"

"Maple burl. You'd better enjoy it. Wood like that is hard to come by."

Ace stood and tested the cane by leaning on it. "Yep, perfect. Thank you." He sat and examined it, turning it in his hands. "What's this on the handle? Looks like a toggle switch."

"Really? Push it and let's see."

He flipped the lever and a three-inch pointed blade sprang from the end of the cane. "Damn, woman. Is this thing legal?"

"It's within legal length, I'm told. Also, the maple has been finished with several coats of lacquer to make it harder. If needed, it should make a formidable weapon."

He tested the blade edge with his thumb. "Sharp, too."

"Just flip the switch the other way to retract the blade. Shove the toggle down to lock it."

Ace followed Kit's instructions. "Super." He took a couple of steps. "Do I look like a dapper English gentleman in Piccadilly Circus?"

"Close as you'll ever get. Now, after almost three weeks of lying on your lazy ass, aren't you ready to get out of here?"

"You're holding me up." He settled into the wheelchair with the cane across his knees. "Look out, Ms. Evans. Here we come."

* * *

Ace and Kit walked up onto the front porch of Ms. Evans' big house. "Are you ready for this?" Kit asked.

"Oh, yes," Ace said. "I've wanted her in my sights since I first woke up from surgery. You take the early lead. I'll jump in if I feel like it." He stepped away from Kit, out of the line of vision of anyone opening the door.

"Okay." Kit rang the doorbell.

The portal swung open. "Good afternoon, Miss Levitt."

"Good afternoon, Mr. Coker. We'd like to see Ms. Evans."

"Is she expecting you? She did not tell me you—"

Ace stepped into Coker's view.

Coker's voice faltered, then picked up. " . . . and Mr. Edwards were coming." He directed his attention to Ace. "Good day, Mr. Edwards. Apparently, your injuries are not as serious as we heard."

"Thank you," Ace said politely. "If you'll let Mrs. Evans know we're here, I'm sure she will see us."

"Very well. Please wait here."

He closed the door in their faces.

"I don't think he likes you very much," Kit said.

"Yeah, I got the same vibration. Must be my hat. He treats it like nuclear garbage." He tapped his cane on the porch. "Or, maybe he didn't expect to see me again."

They waited five minutes before Coker allowed them to enter. "Mrs. Evans will meet with you in the library. Follow me." He glared down his long nose at them, then turned and walked up the hallway. He opened the library doors and ushered them in. There was a firm click behind them.

As the sound of Coker's heels lessened from the other side of the wall, Kit said, "Thank you for your courtesy."

Ace chuckled. "Better save your sarcasm. The meeting hasn't begun yet."

They spent the next thirty minutes looking at their watches, examining the expensive furnishings and making small talk.

Kit relaxed. *It must be Ace*, she thought. *Normally, I'd be totally uptight at a confrontation like this.*

Ms. Evans entered. "Miss Levitt. I expected better from you than to show up without an appointment. However, I see Mr. Edwards accompanies you. Perhaps the explanation lays there."

"Good to see you again, Mrs. Evans," Ace said. "My wounds are recovering nicely, thank you. How kind of you to ask?"

"Save your sarcasm, Mr. Edwards. It will do you no good here. If you will remember, I warned you were not qualified. I was not surprised when you were shot." She flipped her hand toward him in a dismissive motion, then settled into her large chair.

There was a discreet knock. "Did you ring for me, ma'am?" Coker said, standing in the doorway.

"Yes, Mr. Coker. Please escort Mr. Edwards out."

"Mr. Edwards," Coker said, "please follow me."

Kit's face showed her amazement. "Ms. Evans, your effrontery is stunning. Ace is with me. You hired me. I'm here to tell you what I found. If he leaves, I leave."

Ms. Evans stared at Kit while Coker kept his eyes on Ace. Ace did not move. He stood smirking, leaning on his cane. He was clearly enjoying the confrontation. The only sound was the ticking of the ornate grandfather clock.

"Do you have a report?" Ms. Evans asked.

"Yes."

She grimaced. "Mr. Edwards can stay."

"As you wish, ma'am." Coker turned to leave. "I shall be close outside if you need me."

"Perhaps we should speak in privacy." Kit rose and followed Coker.

"Miss Levitt. Are you sure this melodrama is necessary?"

"Your call, ma'am. But it was you who gave me the list of possibles."

"Very well, close the doors."

Kit complied, insuring that they latched. "Ace, your show."

"No, Miss Levitt," Ms. Evans said quickly. "I did not hire Mr. Edwards." She scowled at Ace. "He has proven his incompetence. I hired you. I will tolerate his presence, but only if he remains absolutely quiet. Please report what you found."

Ace smiled and dropped into a chair nodding in Kit's direction. "Earn your fee."

Kit moved to a love seat by the coffee table, her brow furrowed.

"Speak, girl. I have no patience for your games."

Kit glanced at Ace, wondering if he was the reason Ms. Evans was acting like such a bitch. "As you wish, Mrs. Evans." She flipped open her notebook, slowly turning pages as she scanned. She knew the information by heart, but she was determined to regain control of the situation. "We looked into your household accounts," she said. "It appears the logical suspects are Mr. Coker and Mr. Lapscott. There are certain irregularities in their behavior." She explained the gambling in Bossier City and the fluctuations in their bank accounts. "Of course, I can't say for sure they're the ones either in combination or singly, but I'd deny them access. If you want to pursue it legally, call Sheriff Galoway." She stood. "I'll send you a bill."

"Fine, Miss Levitt."

Kit's frustration bubbled over. "Ms. Evans, you've been rude since you walked into the room. Ace and I are not accustomed to working with or for people like you. Please pay promptly." She moved toward the exit as Ace struggled to his feet.

The doors opened. "Is there a problem, ma'am?" Coker asked.

Ms. Evans smiled. "Not any more. Escort Miss Levitt and Mr. Edwards out. Do not admit them again." She did not rise from her throne-like chair.

Coker walked behind them to the front of the house. "You heard Mrs. Evans. If you return, I shall physically deny you."

Ace stared at him, lightly tapping his cane on the floor. "Uh-huh."

A few minutes later, they drove away with the top down. "Did you get anything out of all that?" Kit asked.

Ace rubbed his cane. "Not really. If she was surprised at your report, she concealed it well. Do you think she knew? Is the whole thing a sham? Maybe no money was stolen."

"Could be. But remember, Tom picked up irregularities in her household account. A lot of cash moved"

"But that doesn't make it embezzlement. Did it occur to you she might be paying someone off, even a hit man?"

"I asked her about that. She denies involvement in any of the shootings." Kit paused. "I believe her."

"Why?"

"Call it woman's intuition. I simply believe her."

Ace gave her a skeptical look. "I'd prefer hard evidence if you don't mind."

Kit glanced back at him. Her cell phone rang. She fished it from her purse without swerving too badly. "Hello."

A muffled voice said, "Miss Levitt, I know who stole Mrs. Evans' money. Meet me at Clark's Ferry tonight at midnight."

"Who—"

The phone went dead, leaving Kit with a quizzical look.

"What was that?" Ace asked.

"How about a midnight date at Clark's Ferry? I'll drive your car."

He tapped his cane. "Maybe you'd better explain."

"Simple. That was a mystery caller. He wants to meet us."

"Oh, that's just great," he said. "That place is spooky in the daytime, or have you forgotten that's where I was shot? Now, you want to go there at midnight. Remember the newspaper article?"

Kit did and a cold chill crawled up her back. "Doesn't matter. The answers will be there."

CHAPTER TWENTY-NINE

"Okay, time to get dressed," Kit said, sticking her head into Ace's motel room.

He lay on his bed fully clothed except for his hat and boots. The cats curled beside him, one on each side.

By the time they stopped for an early dinner and returned to the motel, the day's activities had taken their toll. Doctor Win would not have approved of how active Ace had been. He popped a couple of painkillers, lay down, and asked Kit to wake him later.

"It's nine-forty-five," Kit said. "You wanted to be at Clark's Ferry by eleven."

"Yes, mom," Ace said, rolling into a sitting position, disturbing the cats. "Give me ten minutes."

Kit saw how he winced when he moved. "You sure you're up to this. I can make the meet without you."

"Sure, and you can have a baby without me too, but I'm gonna do my damnedest to be there when that starts." He leered. "Nice T-shirt. Fits in all the right places."

"Oh shut up. You're in no condition even if I agreed. Hold that thought until your wounds heal. Who knows, you might get lucky?" Kit arched her eyebrows at him. "Here's your ankle holster, the .357 and the speed loaders. Put them in your jacket pocket where I can find them." She chuckled. "And, this time, keep your jacket on."

"Sure, mummy. Got anything else for me? I lost weight in the hospital. Need something to tuck in my waistband."

"We're only going for a quiet chat at midnight. You act like it's a full frontal assault."

"Last time I was too casual, and it cost me." He frowned. "Not again."

"I'm with you on that one. Here's a nine-mil with an extra magazine. If you need more than that, we're really in trouble."

Ace examined the automatic, especially the blank serial number area. "Tom's work?"

"Yeah. I have one just like it with two extra mags."

He smiled, then snickered. "With all this firepower and my fancy cane, we should be safe." He thought for a moment. "What are you thinking?"

"I'm hoping ghosts aren't real."

"No, that's not what I mean."

"Maybe not," Kit said, "but I can't get that newspaper out of my mind. What are we going to do if we're confronted by ghosts and the Goat Lady?"

"We're going to hope like hell they're on our side. Now, forget them and help me with my boots."

Kit pulled the boot onto his wounded leg. "You can do the other one."

"Thanks. Who do you think'll meet us?"

Kit forced the ghosts from her mind, concentrating on his question. "Not sure. Could be no one. Maybe a hoax. I have to believe it'll be one of the people we checked out, less the cook and the maid. I don't see either of them coming out at midnight."

"Not Matthew Thomas. Clark's Ferry is not his style. He'd want to meet in a coffee house. The lawyer, the attorney? No, I rule them out also. They'd stage it in the office so they could bill for the time."

Kit grinned at the picture. "Coker or Lapscott?"

"Only ones left. Disappointing."

"What does that mean?"

Ace picked up his boot. "Hope it's not Lapscott. He serves a Killian's chilled to perfection. A true gentleman."

"Oh, put your boot on. Your foot's ugly."

"Show some respect for an injured man, woman. I was gunned down from behind while protecting your virtue."

"You're still hallucinating. But you're welcome to protect me tonight. I have bad vibrations about this." She paused. "And that's without the Goat Lady."

* * *

The storm rolled in at ten-twenty, thunder booming, lightning flashing, the rain pounding down, a typical Texas thunderstorm.

Kit pulled back the drape and peered out. "Just what we need. That clay at Clark's Ferry will be a quagmire. We'll be lucky not to get stuck."

"Look's bad, but remember that behind every dark cloud there's a sow's ear—or something like that."

"Give it up, Ace. As a philosopher, you'll never make it." She stared at the falling rain. The black sky was sliced by a sudden stab of lightning and thunder immediately shook the motel. She dropped the curtain. "Are you sure you want to do this?"

"It'll stop," Ace said. "These storms usually blow over pretty quick. I feel lucky tonight."

Kit looked into his face, but saw only Ace's blank look. With his eternal optimism, it could be true. "If you're game, so am I. Let's make a dash for it." She threw a windbreaker over her head and opened the door into a hard wind filled with water.

Ace hobbled behind her, leaning on the cane.

She climbed into the car, slipped across as far as she could and opened the passenger side just as Ace reached it. As he got in, she flipped the jacket into the back seat and ran her fingers through her hair.

"Enough with the primping. Roll it," Ace said through a laugh. "We have ghosts, goblins, and snitches to meet."

She gave him her tough smile. "You're an asshole, you know. You're really trying to spook me."

"Nothing could be farther from the truth, my dear."

"Yeah, right." She would have said more, but lightning flashed again, this time to the east of them. The following thunder was softer, but still caused her to jump. "Looks like it's moving on. Maybe you're right. Belt up and let's get it over with. You said you wanted to get there early."

Kit drove out of the motel parking lot and headed north. By the time she reached Grand Saline, the rain had stopped. At eleven o'clock, they were on the narrow dirt road toward Clark's Ferry splashing through holes filled with rainwater. The trees were heavy with raindrops on both sides and with the headlights bouncing off them, they appeared to move to engulf them. Tree limbs looked like witches' fingers, reaching, and withdrawing. Chill bumps peppered Kit's arms while thoughts of the Ku Klux Klan and the Goat Lady ran relay races in her mind.

Ace rode, not saying a word, apparently lost inside himself. His face revealed nothing of what he was thinking, just an occasional grimace when a tire dropped into a chuckhole.

Kit couldn't clear thoughts of ghosts from her mind. *There is no such thing as ghosts. Damn, what was that? Just a tree limb, not a spook.* She peered skyward through the windshield, looking for the moon. A stubborn cloud cover refused to yield. Blackness surrounded them like the inside of the Goat Lady's heart. "You know we're driving into an ambush," she said nervously.

"Probably." Ace sat quiet for a moment, then took a deep breath. "You got a better idea?"

"No. Just wish it wasn't so damn scary."

"It's not frightening. Just dark. Wish you didn't have to be here, but I need you." Ace had dropped the jocularity he'd shown at the motel. He was serious now, his words dripping with emotion. "Stop here." There was no request in the words, only an order.

Kit had only seen him that way a few times before. She knew when it happened, somebody would lose, and it wouldn't be Ace unless he was dead. The look on his face was the one that said, "Nothing will stop me now."

"Why?" Kit said, looking around. "You can't walk from here, and I'm not going in those woods. They're dripping wet. Besides, remember that article. If I have to die, I'd rather not be scared to death."

A lightning flash punctuated her comments. The thunder boomed from the east.

"Drop the top. It'll give us better visibility and room to maneuver."

Kit reached and touched Ace on the arm. "You're sure about this? It might rain again."

"Yeah, but we'll see better with the top down, dry or wet." He opened the lever on his side, then lay his hand on her arm. "Kit, I don't know another way. Someone wants to meet us. It's gotta be the killer. I'm sure he plans to finish us off. We'll just have to ruin his plans." He squeezed. "I'm still open to suggestions."

Reluctantly, Kit flipped her lever and hit the button. As the top folder itself rearward, she imagined a ghost ready to jump into the car. "I can handle bad guys, but this is the spookiest place I've ever seen." Shudders rippled through her. The sky was slick black, not a glimpse of the moon or a star.

"The spooks will be on our side," Ace said. "They haunt because of the unspeakable things done to them. They were beaten, tortured, murdered—even the Goat Lady." He eyed Kit, a grin dancing at his lips. "Actually, I like being here with you. Understand it's a good place to make out and," He leered, "Being scared gives you a case of the nips."

"Oh shut up. I'm scared shitless, and you're thinking of sex."

"Yep. I wanna go with a smile on my face."

"In your dreams." Kit pulled the car forward, slowly. Out of the corner of her eye, she saw Ace wince with each bump. "How far do you want to go?"

"All the way into the turnaround. Point the car out in case we need to make a fast exit. Watch out for the mud though. We don't want to get stuck."

Kit agreed with him. At least it would get them away from the trees with their suggestive movements. She shivered and drove on, following Ace's instructions. A few moments and several potholes later, she killed the engine. "Ready?"

"Yeah, let's find a hidey-hole."

Kit opened her door, corkscrewed, and started to exit. Just as her left foot hit the ground, globs of mud slapped against her jeans.

Then she heard the shot. Instinctively, she jerked, tumbling from the car.

CHAPTER THIRTY

"What the hell?" Kit yelped, pushing up from the mud.

"Lay quiet," Ace whispered.

Easy for him to say. She twisted, reaching for her purse. No way could she reach it. She'd thrown it onto the back seat, her nine-mil inside. Every part of her being screamed, *Run like hell.* She felt totally vulnerable.

Ace's shuffling sounds told Kit he was struggling out of the car. She raised her head. A scruffy pair of western boots illuminated by a swinging flashlight sloshed her way. The mud covering them didn't improve their appearance any.

"Evenin', ma'am. You're early, but we expected you to be."

Kit looked toward the voice, but was blinded by the light playing across her face. It shifted, and she saw the biggest gun she'd ever seen. It looked like a howitzer.

From the other side of the car, a voice said, "Good evening, Mr. Edwards. An hour early. That fits your pattern perfectly. You are quite predictable, you know? Sorry about the rain. I'd hoped for a clear night."

The first voice was unfamiliar to Kit, but the proper English and gravelly tone of the second were unmistakable.

"Marston Coker," Ace said. "It's always satisfying to learn I guessed right. If you'll step aside, I'll finish dragging this bad leg out, and we can talk." Ace grunted. "Don't get excited, it's only my cane. You gave me this bum limb, didn't you?"

"Billy did. That is not important now. Please exit and keep your mouth shut. I have had enough of your childishness to last a lifetime—your lifetime. Give me your weapon."

"You can get up," Kit's assailant said. "Walk around behind the car." The flashlight beam showed the direction.

"I need my purse."

"Sure, lady. The purse stays."

"Hey, can't blame a girl for trying." Kit tried to see his face. Although her night vision was improving, all she could see was a western hat pulled low over his eyes. The hat wasn't as impressive as the cannon he held. "Can you point that thing downrange? You'll find I obey orders. I'm not a feminist."

Across the car, Kit saw Ace limping to the rear with a flashlight beam playing over his back. She wiped her hands on her jeans finding more mud and joined him.

Ace said, "The mystery is solved, my dear. You've met Mr. Coker. His friend is Billy Lapscott. Don't you think Mr. Coker's gun is bigger than Mr. Lapscott's?"

Kit squinted at the two weapons. She assumed Ace had a reason for his remarks so she said, "Yes. Looks like your friend has a nine-mil." She hesitated. "Oh. Isn't that what killed Hugo and Jade?"

"Yes, I believe so," Ace replied. "And, if memory serves me right, you said a nine-mil and a .32 ambushed us."

"Damn. Right again," Kit said. "Your leg might be worthless, but your brain still works."

Coker interrupted. "That is enough from you two. You—"

"You surprise me, Marston," Ace said. "I didn't think you had the guts. Or, maybe you and Billy switched guns when you killed Jade and Hugo."

"Shut up," Coker said. "I owe you no explanations. Whom have you told about the missing funds?"

Ace leaned against the car trunk and grunted. "Sorry, this leg's still pretty tender."

"Good." Coker poked it with the flashlight. "Things would have gone so much better if Billy had shot straighter."

Ace winced. "Touch it again and I'll bust your ass."

"Really? And just how will you do that, my friend? It seems to me you are at a decided disadvantage."

"Just don't touch the leg again," Ace said through gritted teeth.

"Your false bravado is touching. Again, whom have you told about the financial records?"

Ace leaned against the car, the cane only touching the ground, no weight on it. To distract Coker, Kit said, "The only important one is the sheriff. He'll have a warrant for your arrest in the morning. You too, Lapscott. He's had his eyes on you two for a long time."

It worked. Coker turned his full attention on Kit and from the corner of her eye, she saw Lapscott also showing fascination with her words.

"You lie," Coker said. "He's got nothing on us. I don't appreciate your lies." He turned and whacked Ace on the leg with the flashlight again.

Ace groaned, but held his position.

"Don't get cute with me, Levitt," Coker growled. "Your man will pay. It'd be my pleasure to work on his leg and concentrate his pain."

"Easy, Marston," Ace said, a grimace on his face. "That hurts."

Kit concentrated on Coker hoping to capture his attention. "Your grammar slipped. Ms. Evans would not approve."

Ace shifted, maintaining a poker face.

What's Ace's con? He's up to something, Kit thought.

"Leave Mrs. Evans out of this," Coker said to Kit, an even darker look clouding his demeanor. "You have no idea what a wonderful woman she is. People are so busy with their SUVs, cell telephones, and television, they have no knowledge of those who made it possible. Mrs. Evans is a true pioneer—one who paved the way for the generation of today. You and this Cro-Magnon," he pointed to Ace who leaned quietly, "and Jonathan are not worthy of being in her presence."

"I see," Kit said. "That explains why you killed Johnny. Same reason for Hugo and Jade, I assume."

He glowered at her. "Yes. Mrs. Evans devoted her life to this area. As her gift to the future, she raised Matthew Thomas to continue in her stead. Those two cretins were a threat to that legacy, as was Jonathan." He grinned a sinister grin. "As are you. I will let nothing interfere with her brilliant plans."

"Yeah," Billy said. "Johnny was a wimp. Didn't have no guts a'tall. When I heard him on the phone with that Jake guy and then to you, I know'd he was finished. The sonufabitch was gonna give us up." He chuckled, nodding at Ace. "I used your boyfriend's gun. Johnny made it easy. He'd already written a note to Ace when I walked in."

"Interesting," Kit said. "Does Ms. Evans reward you well for killing for her?"

"Not true," Coker answered, vehemently. "Mrs. Evans deplores guns. She has little understanding of what is required. Billy and I protect her without her knowledge." He waved his pistol toward the river. "It is time for the two of you to move to the embankment."

"So," Ace interrupted. "You're saying Ms. Evans knows nothing about the deaths of Jade, Hugo, and Johnny?"

"Your stupidity is even beyond my expectations. I shall make it as simple as possible. Mrs. Evans had nothing to do with their terminations."

"How about trashing my room? Was that her idea?"

"No, that was Billy operating without thinking. After we eliminated the Nobles, he panicked, thinking they might have given you something that could incriminate us. Later, I had the opportunity to explain to him how stupid he was."

"One more question," Kit said, stalling to give Ace more time, hoping he had a plan. "If you have so much respect for Ms. Evans, why do you steal from her?"

"Your naiveté is astounding. We do not steal from her. She is a wonderful woman, but very old. Many of her ideas are from her youth. One of those is wages. Her pay scale has not advanced with the passage of time. Rather than bother her, I simply take enough to boost our salaries to what they should be. It is unfortunate you told her—"

"For you and Billy?" Kit asked.

"Yes, for both of us. We earn it."

"Interesting." She paused. "How about the cook and the maid?"

"They are ignorant Mexicans," Coker sneered. "They should return to Mexico. Now, enough of this." He shifted his position. "It is time for you to take a short walk."

"Wouldn't want to reconsider, would you?" Ace said. "I really—"

A fat slice of lightning plunged downward striking a tree on the far side of the river. The thunder was so loud the mud quivered. A scream pierced the night, emanating from the edge of the woods. Then another and another. They danced and echoed from one position to the next, then from multiple spots at the same time.

Goose bumps raced one another around Kit's body.

Billy looked toward the woods, his mouth dropping open, his gun hand drooping.

"What th' hell?" Coker said, spinning toward the trees.

Ace launched himself off the rear of the car and slashed downward with his cane, catching Coker across his gun hand. The pistol spun away as Coker bellowed in pain, grasping his wrist.

Kit grabbed Billy's gun arm. He slammed her with his free hand, catapulting her backwards into the mud. Dancing lights flickered around her as she struggled to regain her feet. The brightnesses advanced and receded even as she shook her head to clear her vision. Her cheek stung from the impact of Billy's backhand and her head throbbed.

"What th' hell is them lights?" Billy screamed, firing wildly. "Git away from me."

Kit stared, glad she wasn't the only one seeing things.

Ace lunged at Billy like a fencer executing a flèche, his cane striking the upper arm.

Billy's squeal matched the ones coming from the woods as his gun dropped into the mud and slid toward Kit. He stared at the blood running from his biceps. "You done stabbed me with a dam' walkin' stick." He settled onto the ground, clutching his arm. "This don't make no sense."

The ferocity of the caterwauling in the trees increased, closing about them. Coker cracked Ace across his wound with the torch. Ace's bad leg crumpled, dropping him into the mud.

Kit grabbed at Billy's pistol even as Coker retrieved his from where it had fallen. "Hold it, you sonnavabitch," Kit screamed, trying to get a firm grasp on the muddy revolver.

Coker glanced at her, then ran, moving his large bulk across the open area, slipping and skidding as he went.

Kit sighted and pulled the trigger. Nothing happened except a dull clunk. *You idiot,* she thought. *The damn thing might be clogged with mud. It could blow up in your face.*

Coker continued his run, making little progress as his dress shoes slithered in the goo.

Ace rolled around the edge of the car, pulled his revolver from his boot and yelled, "Stop, Coker. Stop or I'll shoot."

The screams from the woods ceased.

CHAPTER THIRTY-ONE

Kit lay frozen for an instant, staring at the woods. Why had the ghosts quit screaming?

Coker whirled, fired toward Ace and Kit, then resumed his attempt to escape. His shot missed, kicking up goop to the left of them.

The wailing from the woods renewed itself, and a man's deep voice boomed over them, cursing.

Kit looked at Billy who sat in the mud, looking dazed, his hand squeezing his wound.

"A damn walkin' stick," he said. "How'd he do that?"

Assured that Billy wasn't going anywhere, Kit jumped into the car and flicked on the headlights. Coker stood out against the blackness.

The shrieking from the trees intensified. Kit shuttered, feeling the sounds echo off her bones.

Coker's head swiveled from side to side as bobbing lights flashed by. He fired again, more wildly.

"Coker, no," Ace shouted, a sound of desperation in his voice. "Stop, or I'll have to drop you."

The screams and curses ceased, and the lights disappeared into the forest.

Coker turned toward Ace and Kit, raised his pistol and took deliberate aim, the weapon in both hands, police style.

Ace pulled the trigger of the .357.

Coker vaulted backwards hitting the mud in a slide. His body convulsed, then moved no more.

A piercing cackle of laughter sounded through the night followed by complete silence. The change was as eerie as the screaming. Another chill rippled through Kit's body as a flash of lightning split the sky. No thunder followed.

"Shit," Ace said quietly. "I hate that."

Kit scrambled from the car, her nine-millimeter in hand.

"Your buddy's down," Ace said to Billy. "You're not going to give me any problems, are you?"

"No, sir," Billy answered in a whiny voice. "Would you mind gettin' me a doctor? My arm hurts somethin' awful bad." He looked toward the woods. "I guess them haints don't want you hurt. Ain't never heard them that loud before."

Kit looked around the area. A faint wisp of smoke rose from the tree on the far side of the river. "Whoever they are, I'm thankful."

"Ma'am, my arm?"

Kit pulled her scarf from around her neck. "You okay, Ace? How's the leg?"

"Yeah, for now. Check Coker. He could be faking."

With her nine-millimeter in hand, she tentatively approached Coker. If he even burped, she'd blow him away.

Ace's slug had taken him in the left upper chest. His carotid artery did not flicker.

Walking back, Kit saw Ace pull himself up and lean against the car, his bad leg out in front of him. She took the flashlight from the glove box. "Coker's dead. You sure you're all right?"

"Give me a few minutes. Leg's barking a bit." He paused. "Take care of Billy." He looked toward Coker. "Damn fool. I didn't want to kill him."

Kit bandaged Billy's arm, using her scarf, tying it off tightly, as Billy whined.

Ace watched her, a small smile flickering on his face. "Told you the ghosts would side with us."

"Yeah, right, and I told you that .357 would bring down a charging linebacker. Now, let me see your leg." She shined the light on him. "You're bleeding, I think. Hard to tell with all that mud. Got your jackknife with you?"

Ace fumbled in his pocket pulling out a clasp knife with a two-inch blade.

"Let me use it. I'll check the bandage."

"Not a chance," Ace said, amusement in his voice. "Nobody cuts that close, except me."

"Men," Kit said. "You ever think of anything else?"

"A big steak when I'm hungry." Ace sliced open his pants over his thigh.

Kit put the light on it. "You've been bleeding. Looks like it might have stopped, though."

"Might need a tourniquet," Ace said. "Word is, you wear the best."

"No way you're getting me out my bra that easy. You shouldn't have slept through the first time." She smiled, feeling good. It seemed forever since she'd felt like this. "I'll call the medics. You'll just have to bleed until they get here."

Kit reported to the 9-1-1 operator who took her report, then switched her to Dub. "Need some help here at Clark's Ferry. I've got one perp down, one bleeding, and Ace—"

"Yeah, I monitored your conversation. I'm on the road. The sheriff'll be right behind me."

The paramedics were first on the scene. One of them checked Coker while the other ran to Ace.

"You'll be fine, Mr. Edwards," the senior EMT said. "The bleeding's minor, all but stopped. I'll clean it, then re-bandage. The docs at the hospital can check it more thoroughly."

"This guy's gone," the second EMT called from beside Coker. "That slug ripped his heart out." He draped a blanket over the body.

Kit stood beside Billy, her gun daring him to move. She glanced toward Coker who only a few moments ago, had brought such terror into her being. He still lay in the headlights of Ace's car, nothing but a brown lump in the mud.

"Can somebody look at my arm?" Billy whined. "It hurts."

"I'll get him," the senior EMT said. "Get a bandage on Mr. Edwards," he told his partner, "and bring up a stretcher."

"No way," Ace said. "I came with Kit and I'm leaving the same way. Just pad it. The leg'll be fine. I'll get it checked tomorrow."

"Your choice." The EMT turned to Billy. "What'd you get stuck with?"

"A damn walkin' stick."

"Yeah," the EMT said. "I believe that."

Flashing blue lights penetrated the area as Dub slid to a halt. He jumped out of the car and rushed over, his boots squishing in the mud. "Sheriff's on the way. Everybody okay?"

"Yeah, we're fine," Ace said. "You'll need to string some tape though." He pointed toward Coker's body.

"Ain't no ghosts over there, is there?" Dub asked, starting toward the tree line.

Ace and Kit laughed.

The senior EMT gave Ace an injection and helped him into the Sebring. He sat, his head back, resting, perhaps sleeping. The sheriff and Kit walked away as the moon broke through the cloud cover. When they were out of the glare of the floodlights, Kit told him about the evening. He wasn't thrilled, but didn't seem too upset.

"Young lady, you should have called me this afternoon. You know that, don't you?"

Kit said nothing.

He sighed. "At least this case is over, and you guys are all right. Lapscott's so eager to talk, Dub had to shut him up long enough to read his rights." He surveyed the area. "Remember the last time we were here." He swung his arm, indicating Clark's Ferry. "It could have been worse tonight. You're damn fools." He rested his hands on Kit's shoulders. "Now, tell me about those screams."

CHAPTER THIRTY-TWO

The next day at nine a.m., Kit lifted the big brass doorknocker and banged it against Ms. Evans' massive front door. Her other hand was busy ringing the doorbell. Respect for Ms. Evans occupied no part of her demeanor. Ace stood at her side, leaning heavily on his cane.

Louise opened the door. "Kit? What are you doing? What do you want?"

"Sorry, Louise. Didn't know you'd be answering the door. Ace and I want to see your mother. Is she here?"

"Not sure. I arrived only a moment ago. Coker should have answered the door. I wonder where he is."

Kit looked at Ace. He nodded and said, "Coker won't be here today."

"Or Billy," Kit added.

"Why?"

"We'll explain after we talk with your mother," Kit said.

Louise looked around the foyer. "Come in. You can wait in the library. It may take a while because I must talk to Mother first."

She escorted them, walking slowly because of Ace's pronounced limp, then invited them to be seated. "I will have Maria serve coffee."

"That's not necessary," Ace said, settling on the couch with a grunt. "We'll only take a bit of your mother's time."

"As you wish." Louise started toward the door, then turned back. "Have you learned what happened to Johnny?"

"That's one of the reasons we need to talk to Ms. Evans," Kit said softly. "Louise, we're tired and would love to go through this only once. Maybe you could listen at the same time."

"Please," she said. "I was a terrible wife while he lived. At least in his death, I can be better."

Kit nodded at Ace.

He bit his bottom lip, then said, "Coker and Lapscott killed Johnny to keep him quiet. Apparently, Johnny figured out they had murdered Jade and Hugo. He was ready to tell Kit so . . ." He rotated his hand in a back and forth motion.

Louise nodded, a tear slipping from her eye. "Was he involved in their murders?"

"No," Ace said emphatically. "He tried to stop them."

"Thank you." She left the room.

"Are you sure Johnny wanted to stop them?" Kit asked.

"Why add more to her plate right now? She already seems preoccupied."

"Yeah. She has something heavy on her mind," Kit answered. "She asked about Johnny, but I don't think he's her primary weight."

"Woman's intuition?"

"I suppose so."

"Well, this time I agree. That's my impression, too."

The double doors to the library burst open. Ms. Evans strode in followed by Matthew Thomas and Louise. "It is true," Ms. Evans said. "When Louise said you were here, I did not believe her. Such effrontery."

She walked to the sofa where Ace sat, relaxed against the rear cushion. "What are you doing here?" Scorn dripped from each word. "I told you never to return to my home. If Mr. Coker were here this morning, I would have him remove you."

"Marston Coker is dead," Ace said coldly.

Ms. Evans' hand flew to her throat. Her mouth worked, but no sounds came out. She sagged and Matthew Thomas grabbed her elbow. Louise stood to the side, staring at Ace as if she'd never seen him before.

Kit said, "Louise, you might want to get your mother some water, or ring for the maid. Her color's not too good."

Ms. Evans straightened and removed her grandson's hand from her arm. "Nonsense. I am fully in control of myself. I do not need your assistance, Miss Levitt. Leave my house."

"Not yet," Ace said. "Only when we have finished our business."

"We have no business, Mr. Edwards." She swiveled on Kit. "Nor with you, Miss Levitt. I wish both of you out of here—*now*. She stood with hands on hips, defiance pouring from her eyes. "Matthew Thomas, call—"

"Mother," Louise screamed. "Have you forgotten me again— just like my whole life?" She hesitated, visibly gathering herself. "I told you I have something to discuss with you. I prefer we speak in private."

"Private, my dear? You let these, these cretins into my home, then expect to meet me in private? I am sure anything you have to say can be said anywhere." She swung her arm toward Kit and Ace. "Even in front of lowlifes such as these."

Louise swallowed, tears glistening in her eyes, then said softly, "Thank you, Mother. You have made it so much easier."

Ms. Evans strode to her throne-like chair and sat. "Go on, Louise, if you must. Whatever it is, get it off your feeble mind. Money? You need more money? I am sure we can work that out. Have I not always bailed you and your worthless husband out?"

Matthew Thomas found his voice as he moved to Ms. Evans and stood by her side. To Louise, he said, "Mother, this is not the right time. It will be best for you to return after *Grand-mère* and I have dispensed with these undesirable people. I will call the sheriff now."

He walked to the phone, but as he picked it up, Louise slammed her hand over his. "No. You will call no one. Go back to your grandmother. You made your choice. Stand with her."

Matthew Thomas' face displayed shock, but he did as Louise ordered, resting his arm on the back of Ms. Evans' chair. Once in position, a sneer caressed his lips.

Asses, Kit thought. *They sit there like Queen and Prince, rulers of all they survey. But underneath that shallow veneer, they're simply two rotten human beings.*

"Mother," Louise said, calm once again. She shifted to a position directly in front of her. "I'm leaving. I should've done it years ago, but I allowed you to dominate me. I should've sided with Johnny. Instead, I let you destroy him. I should've kept you away from my son." She glanced at Matthew Thomas, then back to her mother. "He is now what you made him—a totally selfish, disgusting jerk. I wish no more to do with him. and now, for the first time in many years, maybe ever, I've made my own decision. *My decision, Mother, not yours.* I'm leaving this house and wish never to see either of you again. With Father's money, I'll find a new home. A home away from you and your sick need to control."

Kit was shocked. Each time they'd talked, Louise had seemed thoroughly cowed by her mother. She looked at Ace and he, too, seemed to have trouble digesting what had been said. The room was pin-drop quiet except for the ticking of the Grandfather clock. Kit checked the time. Nine-fifteen. It had only been fifteen minutes since she'd banged on the front door. It seemed so much longer, a lifetime longer. In that fifteen minutes, worlds had spun out of orbit. The residue would only settle with time.

Ms. Evans recovered first with harsh laughter. "Louise, you fool. You have learned nothing in your pitiable life. Go. You will return. Just as you did after you coupled with that loathsome Jonathan. You came home crying then. You will again. I took the seed of that repugnant escapade and created something noble and proud. I will wait to see what calamity you bring to me this time. I may not accept the next one."

Louise's hand trembled as she tentatively reached toward her mother. Then it stopped—stopped moving toward Ms. Evans and stopped trembling. "Goodbye, Mother. Goodbye, Matthew Thomas." Louise spun and walked out the door.

All eyes followed the clicking of Louise's heels as they echoed in the hallway. The front door opened, then closed quietly.

"Now, Mister Edwards, where were we?" Ms. Evans said as if Louise had never existed. She rose from her chair and stood over Ace. "I believe you said Mr. Coker is dead. How did you come by such information?" Skepticism resonated in her words.

Ace calmly replied, "I killed him. I shot the sonnavabitch." He grinned, a cold sadistic expression.

Kit watched him, shuddering involuntarily. He looked like a character out of bad B-movie.

"Impossible. You are no match for Mr. Coker. You lie. I do not know why, but I know what you say cannot be true. He will arrive soon, and I shall have him remove you from the premises." Ms. Evans' face was as ugly as her words.

"Then I turned Lapscott over to the sheriff," Ace added in the same tone as if Ms. Evans had not spoken.

"Why do you do this? Why do you torment me?" Ms. Evans voice rose toward hysteria. "Mr. Coker will be here. He will, he will—"

"How dare you upset *Grand-mère*," Matthew Thomas said. "This is simply too much. I will call the sheriff."

"Don't waste your time," Kit said. "You'll get to see him sooner than you'd like. I'm sure he'll have questions about Coker and Lapscott."

"*Grand-mère*, what does she mean? Why are they saying such things? Make them stop." Matthew Thomas' demeanor was crumbling into the spoiled brat that lay beneath his sophisticated outer layer.

Ms. Evans appeared to feed on his despair, her strength rallying. "Mr. Edwards," she said in a stronger voice. "Enough is enough. Just tell us why you are here. I have better things to do with my time than provide entertainment for the likes of you."

Ace hobbled to his feet as Kit scrambled to assist him. He nodded, and Kit returned the signal. She released him and stepped away, putting a few feet between them.

"Ms. Evans," Ace said, "your reign is over." He shifted his attention to Matthew Thomas. "Glad you're here. Saves me another trip to tell you you'll never sit on her throne."

Ace sat down heavily, and Kit moved to the other side of the room sandwiching the grandmother and grandson between Ace and her. She looked from one to the other. Cockiness and arrogance flowed from Ms. Evans and Matthew Thomas suddenly seemed more sure of himself. Kit sat in a wing back chair.

"Mr. Edwards, you have overstepped your bounds," Ms. Evans said. "I have no idea what you mean." She did not appear intimidated. "Finish your performance. You bore me."

Kit watched a smile flit around Ace's eyes. She had played enough poker with him to recognize it. It said he had a pat hand, a hand that could not lose.

"Yes, Mr. Edwards, *Grand-mère* is correct," Matthew Thomas echoed, appearing to gain strength. "You are grossly out of order." He turned to Kit. "Miss Levitt, move beside Mr. Edwards. I do not trust you at my back."

"Dream on, hot shot," Kit replied. "I'm comfortable where I am."

"Rest assured that *Grand-mère* will have your licenses revoked."

"Why don't you sit down and shut up," Ace said, a growl in his voice. "Pompous asses like you piss . . . me . . . off."

Kit took the nine-millimeter from her purse and lay it in her lap. "If I were you, I'd do what he says."

Both of them stared at the gun.

"Sit," Ace said.

They sat.

CHAPTER THIRTY-THREE

Ms. Evans gazed at the pistol laying in Kit's lap. "You two are despicable. How dare you bring a gun into my house. If Mr. Coker were here—" She reflected a moment. "Matthew Thomas. I have had enough. Call the sheriff."

"Up to you," Ace said. "Are you ready for his questions? Like, were Coker and Lapscott acting on your orders last night when they tried to kill Kit and me? Or, did you order them to kill Jade, Hugo, and Johnny? Maybe he'll even ask if you arranged my ambush. Then, while we're waiting for Bob to arrive, I'll call the Dallas news media." He paused, allowing his words to hang in the air. "Think carefully before you make your next move. I'll give you one minute." He shifted his attention to Kit. "I may need your cell phone. Please keep time for us."

"My pleasure." Kit held up her left wrist and made a show of watching it. Actually, she looked over the top of her watch, never taking her eyes off her two adversaries. The only sound in the room was the ticktock, ticktock of the Grandfather clock. "Time's up," Kit said.

Ace sighed noisily. "Good. You must have decided to listen. Now, here's what will happen. Ms. Evans, you will contribute fifty thousand dollars to the Dallas Police Benevolent Society— anonymously. Your dirty money will go to a worthy cause. I'll insure the money arrives."

"What makes you think—"

"Please be quiet, Ms. Evans. I'm not finished yet. You will notify your political cronies you are withdrawing from politics and will no longer contribute to them."

Matthew Thomas sprang to his feet. "Mr. Edwards. I cannot allow such disrespect to *Grand-mère*. I insist—"

"Oh, bullshit," Candi said, entering the room. "Sit down you little prick. Sorry I'm late. Hope I haven't missed the good stuff."

"No, the best is yet to come," Kit said, fingering the pistol. "I suggest you do what she says, Matt."

Candi closed the door behind her as Matthew Thomas settled into his chair, his eyes blazing.

"Hey, Spaceman, you're looking good," Candi said. "Kit, you look a lot better since you got your man back."

Kit grinned.

"I was explaining to Ms. Evans the changes she will make," Ace said. "There is only one more—the big one." He scowled. "You will not today, tomorrow, or any time in the future, promote your grandson for political office."

"What gives you the right? Mrs. Evans said, a snarl in her voice. "My Grandson's destiny is to carry on in the Adams tradition."

"What gives me the right, you ask?" Ace's voice rose. "The simple right of a man who loves his country." He hesitated, seeming to struggle for control.

"Hey, can I have a part of this?" Kit said.

"Sure," he replied, relief evident in his voice. "It's your ball."

"This is simply outrageous," Matthew Thomas exclaimed. "You cannot expect us to sit here and accept your ultimatums."

"Oh, but we can," Kit said. "Now, here's what you are *not* going to do. You will *not* run for public office, not even president of the local Lions Club. As of this moment, you are apolitical—not a Democrat, a Republican or an Independent. I don't even want to hear you identified with the Green Party."

His eyes flared at Kit, hatred pouring out. "I would have to be stupid to agree to that. I assure you I am not stupid."

"That's debatable," Kit said. "I've seen no evidence to support your argument." She gave Matthew Thomas a phony smile, then asked, "Is it time, Ace?"

"I'm ready." He shifted his gaze to Candi. "How 'bout you?"

"Unveiling time," she said.

He pointed at Kit. "You're doing a fine job. Continue."

"My pleasure." Kit took out her notebook. She had memorized its contents, but knew her remarks would carry more weight with the notebook documenting them. She pretended to study a page. "Remember the blackmail material that brought Ace here? We have it. Copies are safely stored in several locations. With it, we placed accounts of the execution of Jade and Hugo and Johnny's bogus suicide. If anything happens to any one of us, copies will go to the major news media. You can imagine the feeding frenzy that will precipitate." She looked at the notebook again. "That's the first thing on our list. Candi, you want the next?"

"You bet your bullshit ass I do." Candi stood and began to pace. "Ms. Evans, as you may know, we dug into your financial records. At first, it was difficult, but as we learned more about your techniques, they were a snap. All of us know Marston Coker embezzled from your household account. However, he covered his tracks well. One could conclude the funds were payoffs to him and Lapscott for services rendered. I have drawn up papers documenting the cash transfers. Believe me when I say they are properly witnessed, notarized, and airtight. Given a small push, the news media could decide you paid Coker and Lapscott for murdering Jade, Hugo, and Johnny. Also for shooting Ace. Those papers are secured with the blackmail material."

She stopped in front of Matthew Thomas who refused to meet her eyes. "But, that's not all we found in your grandmother's accounts. For years, she salted the field in preparation for your entering the fray." Candi resumed her pacing. "I found evidence of under-the-table payoffs to buy support for you. Results of those transactions are also documented and safeguarded with the others." She bent over and stared into Matthew Thomas' face. "How do you think those crooked politicians will react when confronted by the press?"

He shrank into his chair and looked toward Ms. Evans.

"We found other things. We found cash payoffs to politicians at times of votes on issues that affect Ms. Evans' business interests. A zoning ordinance changed, and one of her companies built a shopping mall. A protected area changed status allowing her to drill for oil. There are others." She wheeled with a flourish. "That's my report. Back to you, Spaceman." She sat.

Ace leaned forward. "I trust you now accept your fates." He stood, leaning on his cane. "Ms. Evans, I've chased criminals who stole from the handicapped. I've apprehended pedophiles. I've investigated Satan worship and the carnage it generates. Brutal rape cases, bloody molestations. Need I continue? Last night, I killed a man who took part in the murders of three people, one of them guilty only of being a weakling. You created an atmosphere that caused the deaths of those people and also," he pointed to the cane, "put me on this. You may as well have pulled the trigger." He paused. "If I thought there was any chance of justice, I'd call the sheriff. But I'm a realist and I know our justice system bends to money. So all I can do is take away what you covet the most— power. You can voluntarily give up that thirst or you can watch it wrested from you by a news media with no conscience—a news media built on inflammatory and not always accurate, reporting. Your precious Adams lineage will be the joke of Texas, perhaps the whole country." He gazed at Ms. Evans, loathing on his face, then at Matthew Thomas. "You two disgust me. You defile our wonderful state. Texas is simply too good for the likes of you." He turned his back on them. "Shall we go, ladies? The air is foul in here."

Kit was mesmerized by his speech. Never had she seen him so emotional, so deep into himself. Candi appeared to be in the same state.

"Ladies?"

Kit and Candi stood and fell in beside him as he limped from the room.

Kit twisted to close the library doors behind them. Matthew Thomas knelt beside Ms. Evans' huge chair, his head resting in her lap. She rubbed his back, cooing softly. the perfect picture of a woman comforting a small child.

CHAPTER THIRTY-FOUR

Kit awoke to Ace's tapping on the open doorway connecting their rooms. She sat up, holding the sheet up to her chin.

"Rise and shine," he said. "We're burning daylight. Coffee's up. For your morning pleasure, it's served in only the very finest Styrofoam." He placed a cup on the nightstand on Kit's side of the bed, leaned over and kissed her on the forehead. "I'd better hit the shower or Mother Temptation may win the day."

"Yeah and what makes you think I'm willing?" Kit threw a pillow at his disappearing back. She looked at the other side of the bed and saw the cats snuggled together. "When did you guys move up here?" She smiled, remembering Ace spooning her from where they now slept.

She stroked Sweeper and Striker, marveling that it all seemed so natural now, sharing her bed with them. But, at least they were educated enough to know when to leave the area. A frown creased her forehead. *When did they learn that?* "Forget it. I don't want to know the answer," she mumbled.

She lay with her fingers laced behind her head, reflecting on the last twenty-four hours. She wished things could be different. Watching Ace had only deepened her feelings for him and last night . . . She grinned as a flush of pleasure rippled her body. She heard the water in Ace's shower, dragging her from her recollections. "All right, you old tomcats, time to get up. Humans need breakfast."

Sweeper awakened and stared at her, then nudged Striker. Each selected an arm and gave her a few sandpaper-tongue licks. They stood, stretched and rubbed against her, purring loudly before jumping to the floor.

Striker raced into Ace's room with Sweeper right behind. Kit had begun to rise when Sweeper stuck his head back through the doorway. "Meow," he said, glaring at her.

She returned his gaze, wondering what he was up to.

He hunched his cat shoulders, tilted his head back and appeared to stare down his nose. On tiptoes, he walked back into the other room.

Kit gazed at his disappearing tail. Could he be impersonating Coker? No, no way. No matter how many times Ace opined about Sweeper, Kit refused to be convinced. He couldn't have ESP, could he? Yet, the ancient Egyptians had thought cats had mystical powers.

She shook her head and turned her thoughts to the last few days, ending with the licks the cats had given her a few minutes ago. Was it their way of offering congratulations for solving the case? Or did it show they'd adopted her? She hoped it was the former. The last thing she wanted was to break a relationship with them, too. The day was going to be tough enough without their soulful eyes staring at her.

She picked up her robe from the floor where Ace had tossed it last night, slipped it over her naked body and headed for the bathroom with coffee in hand. Thirty minutes later after a shower and quick blow-dry, she walked into Ace's room dressed in her usual jeans, T-shirt and boots. He was finishing his shave, his electric razor buzzing merrily. His cane rested against the vanity. She leaned against the doorframe. *Damn, he looks good.* Her eyes burned, and she vowed not to cry. Walking up behind him, she slipped her arms around his waist and rested her cheek against his bare back. "Are you always so slow, or are you showing off for me?"

"Almost finished. Showering with this leg and shoulder is still a challenge, but it's getting easier." He gave a cheek a last swipe and lay the razor down. Turning, he kissed her. "That's a better good morning," he said, his voice husky.

Ace's arms felt good as she snuggled into his chest. "Hmmmm, nice shaving lotion."

"Have I told you since last night you're the most beautiful PI I know?"

"Sure. I'm the only female PI you know—or, I'd better be." She leaned back and looked into his face. "I see it now. All you're interested in are my investigative skills."

"Not all." He brushed her eyebrows with his lips. You're gorgeous in the morning. I love that glow in your cheeks. Mind if I work to keep it there?"

Kit smiled. "You have to feed me first. I worked up an appetite."

Laughing, he said, "So did I. If we hustle, we might beat Candi to the restaurant."

* * *

When they had parted company in Ms. Evans' driveway the previous day, Ace, Kit and Candi had agreed to meet at the Sabine Café at nine-thirty for breakfast. They'd been both mentally and emotionally exhausted. No one was proud of what they'd done to Ms. Evans, but they concurred that it was right and necessary. But attacking a seventy-two year old woman had not made them feel holy. None of the three felt sorry about Matthew Thomas.

Ace had said, "Pompous ass deserved that and more."

Kit and Candi agreed, then Candi added, "Someday, I'll get him on the other side of the courtroom. It's going to be a real pleasure to decimate him in front of a judge and jury."

Kit and Ace arrived first, parked alongside the street and walked into the restaurant.

Mabel greeted them and called to the other patrons. "Show some respect, you deadbeats. Here's the two that blew the stink out of Grand Saline."

To Kit's utter surprise and from the look on Ace's face, his also, everyone in the restaurant stood and applauded. Soon they had shaken hands, been patted on the back and offered congratulations. Kit recognized most of the faces as people who'd averted their eyes a few days ago.

The men were especially interested in Ace's cane. One older gentleman tapped it and said, "Heard you cut that young scamp's arm right off. I could use one like that. My old legs are getting stiff."

Everyone guffawed.

"Outta my way," Mabel said. "I gotta seat these folks. Can't you see Ace's leg hurts?"

A path cleared as she escorted them to a table and poured two cups of coffee with a flourish. "I'll get your breakfast started. Today, you get the works, Ace, honey, I'll bring a bagel and cream cheese when I bring his eggs. How 'bout some fresh orange juice this morning? Yeah, that'll go great. I'll get it." She bounced away.

"You gotta love it," Ace said.

"Yeah, small towns," Kit replied.

"Great, hoped I'd find you here," Bob Galoway said walking in. "Come on, Dub."

Mabel was back at the table in a flash. "If you'd been on the ball, Sheriff, these two wouldn't have had to do your job." She giggled as Bob blushed. "I'll get you some coffee. Might wake you up enough to catch a speeder." She cackled again as she headed to the serving area.

"See what you've done," Bob said, chuckling. "My loyal constituents now doubt me." He paused. "Of course, I've never been sure where Mabel's politics lay."

"Don't you dare start without me," Candi said, shoving through the front door. She had a firm grip on a big man, tugging him behind her.

"Chip," Ace whispered. "Candi's betrothed."

"Yeah, I saw the ring—and the car," Kit said. "Looks like every woman's dream—the ring, not the man. You guys are interchangeable. Diamonds aren't." She laughed at the look of consternation on Ace's face.

Mabel spotted Candi and called out, "Here's the other in the Three Musketeers of Van Zandt." Again, the café erupted in applause and congratulatory remarks.

The older gentleman who had spoken earlier, said to Ace, "Wouldn't want to lend me that cane, would you?"

The grin on Chip's face grew larger with each compliment to Candi.

"What do you think?" Ace whispered to Kit, nodding toward Chip. "Is the Cheshire Cat in danger?"

Bob and Dub's faces glowed an embarrassed shade of red as they applauded with the others.

Chip grabbed Ace's hand and pumped it vigorously. "You did it again, you sonnavabitch. We called Jake last night. He sends his congratulations." Without missing a beat, his attention beamed on Kit. "Is this the little lady that pulled you through? Candi's been talking about you." He dropped Ace's hand and grabbed Kit's. "I told Jake about you. He's gonna send you some business."

While Chip molested Kit's hand, Candi engulfed Ace in a bear hug, and everyone else stood around grinning.

Kit wanted to respond with something cute, but before she could, Mabel pushed through the crowd. "All right, that's enough. Get back to your tables. I gotta feed these people. Ain't seen you in a while, Chip. You oughtta get up to the north end of the county more often. I'll bring the works for you, too. She stopped and stared at the group. "Hell, I'll bring the works for everybody. You earned it. Check's on Chip. He's loaded." She chortled and stepped away a couple of steps, but paused when the door opened again. "They're over here, Janie."

Janie Blackman, the reporter from the *Grand Saline Sun* walked to their table. "I've come for that exclusive you promised. She pulled up a chair beside Ace. "So, tell me about it, all the inside stuff. I can get a byline in the *Dallas Morning News* with this story." From her purse, she pulled a pad and pencil.

"Afraid you're looking at the wrong person," Ace said. "She's the one." He pointed toward Kit. "I just lay around in the lap of luxury with angels of mercy at my beck and call."

Janie spun on Kit.

"Oh no, you don't," Kit said. "It was really Candi who did it."

"I don't care who did what, I just want a story," Janie whined. "I'll listen to both of you—all three of you. I'll even listen to Chip if he can add anything."

"Leave me out of this," Chip said. "I'm just a simple rancher who's engaged to the most beautiful and brilliant woman in Van Zandt County. Excuse me, Kit, Janie, but it's true."

Janie and Kit grinned.

Candi beamed, her look one of pure affection.

Dub spoke up. "Janie, the sheriff and me was in this, too. Wanna hear my story?"

"I can make you heroes any day. This one is special."

For the next half-hour, Janie received an abbreviated version of what had transpired. The scene at Ms. Evans' house was skipped. Janie left happy, humming under her breath.

What a morning? The group talked, laughed, and promised to keep in touch. Mabel hovered like a mother hen, refilling coffee cups and orange juice glasses. Kit learned what she meant by the works—enough food to last the average person a week. Chip had no problem with his platter and helped Candi with hers. Ace and Kit were less aggressive. Bob and Dub had obviously grown up eating that way.

After an hour of satiation, Bob stood. "Guys, we gotta be moving on. We still have Mabel's speeder to catch. I appreciate what you did. It's a shame we won't have Coker in the courtroom, though. According to Lapscott, Coker planned everything. But with three murders and his fingerprints on Johnny's suicide notes, Lapscott will take his last walk in the state pen in Huntsville. Anyway, take care. Thanks for the breakfast, Chip. I owe you one." He put his hat on and moved toward the door.

"Ah, Bob," Ace said. "Aren't you forgetting something?"

Bob stopped and looked at him. "No, not that I know of. What?"

"Your hat. Remember? I have a big collection of hats from sheriffs I've helped with tough cases. I need to add yours."

Kit knew it wasn't exactly the truth, but not a complete lie. He had two others.

"The hell you say. This one's almost new." Bob's head swiveled. "Dub, give him your hat."

"It's all dirty and worn out. He don't want mine."

"Sure he does," Bob said. "That gives it character. Right Ace?" He swept it off Dub's head and tossed it.

Ace plucked it from the air. "A fine specimen. Thanks, Dub."

Bob took Dub's arm and guided him from the café.

Chip and Candi followed Ace and Kit back to the motel. "Now, you gotta promise to come to the wedding," Chip said. "No, I have a better idea." He looked at Candi who nodded. "Be my Best Man?"

"And I need a Maid of Honor," Candi said to Kit.

Ace and Kit looked at one another, grinning.

"Done," Kit said.

"Done deal," Ace said.

After another series of handshakes and hugs, Chip and Candi left. Ace and Kit went inside and packed for the trip to Dallas.

Kit looked around her room. It seemed as if she had spent a lifetime there. Every corner was familiar and every dust bunny seemed like part of her family. The cats ran back and forth between rooms, apparently psyching themselves for the trip. Kit loved it.

Ace walked in with his one overnight bag as Kit zipped her second suitcase. "Almost check-out time. Ready?"

Kit gave her zipper a last tug. "We have some time. We need to talk."

"Ah crap. That phrase sends spasms through every man in the world." He appeared nervous, shifting from one foot to the other. "What is it, dump time?"

"No, not that." Kit sat in the motel chair, took a deep breath and continued. "I love you, Arthur Conan Edwards. You're the strangest, stupidest, most wonderful man I've ever known. Your sense of humor is warped and your values are straight out of the nineteenth century. You're vain, egotistical and handsome—in an ugly way. You treat me like a princess yet make me feel like an equal. You're every inch a Texan."

Ace dropped onto the edge of the bed. "I see a but coming, and I don't want to hear it. I need you, Kit. You fill a hole in my being. You make me a complete man. Please, don't do this."

"You blew it," Kit said, her voice stronger. "I know you mean everything you said. But you left out the key words. You never said you love me."

His head drooped. "You know—"

"Yes, dammit, I know. It rips me apart every day. You're too damned honest to even lie to make me feel better." She was losing control, getting angry, but couldn't stop. "How would you like it if you had to share me with an old—" She stopped, took five deep breaths, then began again in a calmer voice. "You're still in love with Terri."

"Can't we handle it?" he asked quietly. "Marry me. I'll make you a good husband. I'll do anything to make you happy. You're so precious to my life. Next to Terri—" He froze. "So what happens now?"

"It's okay. It's because I love you that I understand." Kit breathed deeply again. "Marry you? Beautiful words. But not under these conditions. I only sleep two to the bed—excluding the cats, of course." She tried to smile, but it didn't happen. Tears came instead. She didn't want Ace to see her sniffling, but he did. She grabbed a tissue, blew her nose, and then angrily wiped tears from her eyes with the back of her hands. "I'm moving to Florida. A law firm offered me the job of lead investigator at a salary far more than I can ever make freelancing in Dallas. I accepted."

"Please change your mind." His voice was husky with emotion. "Stay in Dallas. We're a team. We belong together. Didn't we work great on this case? Maybe with time, Terri will go away."

"No, Ace. If I stay, I'll pressure you over Terri, and that's the worst thing for us. I can pass time in Florida as well as Texas. If it's meant to be, it will happen. Otherwise . . ."

"So, you've made up your mind."

"Yes." She leaned forward and kissed him, a long lingering kiss filled with her love and yearnings. She took two steps backwards. "That's what you could have. But I won't share you, and you can't give her up—not yet."

Ace reached toward her.

"No."

His hands dropped to his side. "Is it over? Are we history?"

"That's up to you and Terri. You know how I feel. When you can return those feelings, give me a call." She forced a smile, but inside, she was crying. "Otherwise, I'll see you at Candi's wedding."

He looked into her eyes and must have seen something that convinced him she was serious. "All right, at the wedding. When do you leave?"

"I drive out in two weeks."

CASE CLOSED

AUTHOR COMMENTS

Grand Saline is real, a small town in Texas. It is located in northeast Van Zandt County on US Route 80, 66 miles from downtown Dallas. The people are Texas-friendly and the countryside, lovely East Texas.

To the best of my knowledge, none of the people in my story has ever resided in Grand Saline—certainly no one with the bad manners of Ms. Evans or Matthew Thomas. That would be very un-Texan.

When I first considered Grand Saline as the setting for a mystery, the huge underground salt deposits were the attraction. *Whites* have exploited the salt dome, literally a mountain of underground salt, since 1845. Before that, Indians collected and evaporated the water from the salt marsh that penetrated the surface. Evaporation techniques continued until 1931 when the Morton Salt Company sunk the first mine. Estimates are the Grand Saline salt dome is extensive enough to supply the needs of the United States for many thousands of years.

In my mind's eye, I pictured a shoot-out between Ace and the villain in the salt mine caverns, so big that large earth-moving (make that salt-moving) vehicles roll freely. Then I learned about Clark's Ferry.

At the *Grand Saline Sun*, I obtained a copy of the November 11, 1999 edition. Pages 4A and 5A featured an article entitled *Students Investigate the Legend of Clark's Ferry*. It intrigued me so much it replaced the salt deposit and became an integral part of *JADE'S PHOTOS*. What made the article more interesting was high school students researched and wrote it for the school newspaper, *The Bloody Tomahawk*. The *Grand Saline Sun* republished it in toto. At the high school I met the authors, Josh Crain, Zack Ingrim, and Lindsay Stewart and their teacher, Ms. Shari Sauseda.

Several stories make up the legend. Each appears in the newspaper article. In the interest of brevity, I offer synopses of the two I used.

The Legend of Clark's Ferry

The Goat Lady

In the mid-1940's, a farm couple lived off Spider Lane near Clark's Ferry. The husband suspected his wife of infidelity and killed her, cutting her head off and throwing the body in the Sabine River. The mighty powers of the river revived her, and she crawled ashore. She needed a head so she took the head of a goat and put it on her shoulders. She stalked her husband, found him cutting wood in a field at the end of Spider Lane and killed him, burying parts of his body around Clark's Ferry.

Two episodes of haunting stem from this story. In the first, the woman walks the area seeking her lost head. The second has the husband roaming the field where she killed him. Some nights, he has his ax over his shoulder.

The Ku Klux Klan

From 1905 until 1935, or thereabouts, the Ku Klux Klan held regular meetings at Clark's Ferry. Estimates are that over one thousand people were tortured, raped or murdered. Often the heads were cut off and displayed on poles in the area now known as Pole Town. They served as a warning to anyone passing through the area.

It is said Clark's Ferry is haunted by the ghosts of those African-Americans tortured and killed. The newspaper article reports, ". . . I could hear literally hundreds of screams coming from every direction. It was tortured yells, people begging for their lives, the sound of whips tearing, slapping against skin and men yelling directions at each other . . ."

These reports have variations, but I attempted to capture the essence in this brief summary. The veracity of the legend is unknown, however I did visit Clark's Ferry. It is a thickly wooded, spooky place. Stories say screams, lights, and other strange phenomena occur.

When last I spoke to Ace and Kit, they were glad ghosts scream at midnight.

* * *

Writing and reading bring me great pleasure. I love to write for others' enjoyment and love to read for my own. I'd like to hear from you no matter what you think of my effort. Contact me at RandyRawls@att.net, and if you find typos—woe is me—let me know that, too. I'd much rather have the opportunity to correct them than live in ignorance.

If you should be inclined to post a review of my story, please send me a copy, whether it be good or bad.

Happy reading.

Randy

www.ingramcontent.com/pod-product-compliance
Lightning Source LLC
Chambersburg PA
CBHW030920120626
46554CB00001B/214